★

Returning from her all-night date, Glory found her grandmother seated in the comfortable armchair. Esther—may she rest in peace—was surrounded by baby-fine wool, and two knitting needles were poking out from her neck. A Weight Winners report card and goal certificate were practically buried in Esther's size-ten lap.

Glory instinctively raised one hand to her own throat. Nana looks like wet noodles covered with tomato sauce, thought Glory.

Then she screamed bloody murder.

★

"Denise Dietz proves that losing weight can be a killer!"

—Diane Mott Davidson, author of *Dying for Chocolate*

"Dietz is definitely someone to take notice of."

—Mystery Loves Company

Denise Dietz

Throw Darts at a Cheesecake

WORLDWIDE.

TORONTO • NEW YORK • LONDON
AMSTERDAM • PARIS • SYDNEY • HAMBURG
STOCKHOLM • ATHENS • TOKYO • MILAN
MADRID • WARSAW • BUDAPEST • AUCKLAND

THROW DARTS AT A CHEESECAKE

A Worldwide Mystery/December 1999

Published by arrangement with Walker Publishing
Company, Inc.

ISBN 0-373-26334-1

This book is dedicated to my mom, Bea Dietz,
who encouraged me to be creative.

I would be "insensitive" and "unsympathetic"
if I didn't mention my Rocky Mountain Fiction Writers
friends, especially fellow author and kindred spirit
Mary Ellen Johnson.

Thank you, Michael Seidman. I was fortunate to find
an editor who has good taste plus a sense of humor.

Thought: Why does man kill?
He kills for food. And not only food.
Frequently there must be a beverage.

—Woody Allen

ONE

SO MANY PEOPLE IN LINE, you'd believe they were giving it away.

With that thought, Ellie crept forward until she stood just above the buffet table's plastic sneeze-guard. An aroma of crisp bacon and melting chocolate overwhelmed her, and she heard the echo of a quotation by the late Gilda Radner: "Eating is self-punishment; punish the food instead. Strangle a loaf of Italian bread. Throw darts at a cheesecake. Chain a lamb chop to the bed. Beat up a cookie."

The tall man in front of Ellie looked familiar, the kind of familiar where you know you've seen him before without actually having been introduced. He wore an old-fashioned suit and sported a splendid mustache. His dark hair was parted in the middle. Tapping him on the shoulder, she said, "I'm Eleanor Bernstein. Have we met?"

"William Howard Taft," he replied. "Call me Bill."

Ellie stared at the gentleman, who weighed over three hundred pounds. "William How—holy cow! *President* Taft?"

"Harumpf! Never wanted to be prez, didn't enjoy playing head of state. Position I wanted was chief justice of the Supreme Court. Got that job in 1921. I'm the only person in history to be both president and chief justice. Big enough to do it, too," he added, patting his belly.

"But you died a long time ago, Mr. Pres—"

"Call me Bill." He reached for a chocolate croissant next to the eggs Benedict.

Ellie glanced longingly at the *foie gras roulade* studded with truffles; duck liver wasn't on her diet. She helped herself, instead, to a portion of smoked salmon.

After spooning *poularde au champagne* onto his plate, Taft reached for miniature cakes drenched in Kahlua.

Ellie's mouth watered. Reluctantly she shifted her gaze from Taft's food to his smiling face. "Didn't you die—aren't you dead, Mr. Pres—Mr. Chief Justice?"

"Of course, my dear. I died March 8, 1930, at the ripe old age of seventy-three. Wellll…guess nowadays you wouldn't consider seventy-three old. Just look at George Burns and Ronald Rea—"

"Ohmigod! Am I dead, too? Please tell me, sir, is there an afterlife? I mean, does heaven exist?"

Taft balanced his overflowing plate on the fingertips of one hand and stroked his mustache. His full lower lip twitched in a grin, and his small eyes sparkled like caramel chips sprinkled with sugar.

"Of course there's a heaven, my dear. Where do you think you are right now?"

With a happy sigh, Ellie reached for pretzels dipped in white chocolate…

…and heard the buzz of her egg timer.

Two eggs, boiling in a pot of water, looked like the eyes in the horror movie Ellie had watched on TV last night. Zombie eyes.

Which came first? The chicken or the egg?

The chicken, of course, she thought, removing the pot from her kitchen stove. God made birds and mammals, then he generated food. People ate his food, lost paradise, and gained weight.

At which point the diet club was created.

After losing fifty-five pounds, Ellie had become group leader for Weight Winners.

Which was why she consumed two boiled eggs for breakfast—along with a piece of wheat toast, a pat of low-cal margarine, a four-ounce glass of fresh-squeezed orange juice, and coffee.

Thank God for coffee. God (and the Turks) originated caffeine, and somehow that made everything else worthwhile.

So why did she still fantasize about heavenly buffets?

What the hell. As long as it was only a fantasy, she was safe.

THE RISING SUN SHIMMERED like a Day-Glo painted lemon.

Beneath a blue velour shirt, Ellie wore long-sleeved thermal underwear with an imprint of Mickey Mouse. Velour and Mickey were both tucked into black sweatpants. Ellie's cheeks were flushed from the cool morning's caress, and matched the color of her auburn ponytail. With a slow, steady jog, she crossed the small campus of Colorado College. At this early hour, the streets were nearly deserted, except for fellow exercise enthusiasts.

Leaving the campus behind, Ellie headed for downtown Colorado Springs. Pausing in front of a health club, she waved at two women, members of her Friday morning Weight Winners class.

Jeannie Dobson and Hannah Taylor—both clothed in gray sweatsuits—waved back, then walked at a fast pace down the cracked sidewalk. Jeannie, a half block ahead, waited for her friend at the curb, moving her feet like a mime performer faking forward motion. When Hannah caught up, the stoplight flashed the outline of a restraining hand. Jeannie's feet still moved, heel-toe, heel-toe, going nowhere; Hannah leaned against a bus-stop bench, panting.

"I'm getting too old for this," she said.

"Heck, Hannah, we're the same age. And fifty-three isn't old anymore; we're in our prime."

"Prime what?" Hannah sat on the bench, removed a sneaker, and rubbed her foot. "Prime number? Primeval? Primate? I wish I *were* a monkey swinging through the branches instead of running up and down hills."

Jeannie laughed and pointed toward the vast panorama of hazy mountains. Clouds were dripping like poofs of whipped cream from a can stuck inside an ice bucket too long.

"We could be backpacking up Pike's Peak," she said. "Anyway, we're not running, we're walking fast. I wouldn't want to be like them." Again Jeannie gestured, this time across the street.

"Who? Ellie?"

"No, not Ellie. *Them.*"

Hannah focused on a newly constructed building. Along the roofline hung a white banner that announced, in large red letters, the grand opening of a health club. Through plate-glass windows, Hannah could see the leotard-clad figures in an aerobics class writhing, bouncing, kicking their legs to the beat of a rock song. Strains of music wafted across the street like a thin, syncopated fog.

"Remember the old cartoons?" continued Jeannie. "They used to put them on the screen at picture shows between double features. For fifty cents there were even guest stars. Gosh, I remember when that clown from Howdy Doody paid us a call...uh...Clarabelle?"

"What's your point?" grumbled Hannah.

"Some of the black-and-white cartoons didn't have words, just music. There was one where farm animals

joined in a square dance until the barn expanded and
expanded, then exploded.''

"I see what you mean," said Hannah, again glancing
toward the health club's window. "Wasn't there a character in those old cartoons named Farmer Gray? Skinny,
with a long beard, looking like Moses, or maybe God?
As though God had joined Weight Winners and lost a
hundred pounds.''

"Did God sign up for Weight Winners when I wasn't
looking?'' asked Ellie, having finally crossed the street.

"I believe God *invented* Weight Winners," said Jeannie.

"Holy cow! I had that very same thought while eating
breakfast.''

"Holy cow?'' Jeannie laughed. So did Hannah.

Ellie's cheeks turned a shade pinker. "When I was in
high school, the nuns wouldn't let us cuss, but it was
okay to desecrate a cow. Little did I know that beef
would some day be limited on my diet. I used to love
cutting into a sixteen-ounce sirloin. Rare. Marbled with
juicy fat.''

"You know what I think?'' Hannah scowled. "Diets
and exercise just help people gain weight slower.''

"If that were true, I wouldn't have dropped fifty-five
pounds of 'weight pollution,' '' said Ellie, "and if I can
do it, so can you or God or even Santa Claus. I promise,
Hannah. Just look how well Jeannie's done.''

"I've lost thirty-five pounds and have five to go,''
Jeannie bragged. "Maybe today the darn scale will eat
my last five. Do inanimate objects get hungry, too?''

"My old car used to drink gas like I used to drink
chocolate malts,'' replied Ellie, "but I traded it in for a
Honda Civic, which proves you *can* change things. Will
I see you both later at the meeting?''

Hannah and Jeannie nodded yes, then watched their leader jog down the cracked sidewalk.

"Why do I always get that funny feeling when I think about weighing in?" Hannah asked. "Kind of like when a policeman motions me over to the side of the road."

Jeannie's lips twitched at the corners. "That goes away. Honest Hannah, I look forward to stepping on the scale."

"But *you're* almost at goal weight."

THE CLOCK ON THE FIREPLACE mantel read 8:30 a.m., as Jeannie Dobson, fresh from her walk with Hannah, a soothing shower, and a satisfying "Good Morning America" weather report, made sure her weight-loss report card was nestled neatly inside her purse.

She was preparing to leave for her usual Friday morning breakfast at Village Inn, where she always ate breakfast before attending Weight Winners meetings, so she wouldn't become hungry during the nonsense questions about forbidden food. *Could I substitute a Twinkie for a piece of fruit?* About to turn on her telephone answering machine, she heard a knock, followed by the insistent ring of her doorbell.

"Hello, what are you doing here?" Jeannie surveyed the stout form whose feet were planted on the welcome mat. "Of course I'm happy to see you," she added, knowing it was a fib. With an effort she kept her eyes from straying toward the mantel clock.

"Maybe it's too early?"

"Oh, that's all right. Come in, come in." She opened the door wider.

"Nice house. Two bedrooms?"

"Yes. I live alone, but one bedroom's for guests. You

know…if somebody's in trouble and they need a place to stay. Why don't you take off your jacket and gloves?''

''No, that's okay.''

''I was about to leave for breakfast, but I could make some coffee if you want to talk.''

''Thanks.''

Jeannie filled two mugs with water, placed them inside a small microwave whose digital clock numbers read 8:41, and pointed toward a chair at her kitchen table.

The visitor sat, reached into a basket-weave centerpiece, pulled out a stuffed banana with cross-stitched eyes and smile, then tossed the happy fruit into the air a few times while singing, ''Yes, we have no bananas…we have no ban-nan-nas today.''

Jeannie laughed nervously and rescued her banana, adding it to a cloth carrot, red apple, and purple beet. ''Bananas are fattening,'' she said. ''I mean, well, they're not low in calories like, well, oranges for instance.''

''Understand you're at goal weight,'' said the visitor in a hoarse voice, coughing a few times to clear phlegm.

''Not yet. I have five more pounds to go. I think the last few pounds are the hardest, don't you?'' Jeannie realized she had opened mouth, inserted foot, because this visitor had a lot more than a few pounds to lose. ''Sweet'n Low?'' she asked quickly, reaching into a cookie jar for the pink packets.

''I drink it black. Say, you wouldn't have an aspirin handy, would you?''

''Oh, you poor thing. Do you have a headache? The flu is going around, and you do sound wheezy. Look, I have some homemade chicken broth stored inside my freezer. You could bring back the container—''

''Aspirin would be better.''

"Oh, okay. It's in the bathroom. Will you excuse me?"

"Sure."

Jeannie walked into her bedroom, its tidy symmetry interrupted by a conspicuous scale under a large wall poster that read: TODAY IS THE FIRST DAY OF THE REST OF YOUR LIFE.

She looked at herself in the sink mirror, pleased with her short dark hair, recently frosted blond at the tips, two spit curls framing her ears. Blue shadow creased into the lines radiating from her brown eyes. Unfortunately, no makeup could hide the grooves running from her nose to a mouth covered with tangerine lipstick.

Today she wore a white blouse tucked into a straight, nubby-tweed skirt. Her matching jacket, with Joan Crawford shoulder pads, fit her slimmed-down body just right. A scarf, stenciled like an American flag, wound about her neck, although its frivolity clashed with her support pantyhose and sensibly laced shoes.

She had never felt so attractive in her life and—to tell the truth, the whole truth, and nothing but the truth—her life had never felt so attractive to her.

Since she had lost thirty-five pounds on the program, she was always ready for new activities. Daily she walked around her residential neighborhood and the Colorado College campus with her friend Hannah. Every other day she jogged to the post office to mail her multiple coupon contest entries. If she filled out enough forms, she might win a car like Ellie's that didn't drink gas.

Humming happily, Jeannie reached for a bottle of Chanel No. 5 and removed the glass stopper. As she dabbed drops behind her ears and at her throat above the scarf, she remembered the beginning of a quotation from *Macbeth*: "All the perfumes of Arabia will..."

Will what? Maybe Hannah was right about aging. Jeannie would have to look the quote up later at the library. The library was across the street from the bank, not a savings and loan like Silverado.

Fridays Jeanie attended Ellie's lecture and ran errands. Post office, bank, library, supermarket. Then she cooked a spectacular, calorically legal meal for herself and Al, an insurance salesman from Allstate, who had courted her for ten years but never popped the question. After an evening of "Dallas" reruns (she'd had a crush on Larry Hagman ever since "I dream of Jeannie") followed by a game or two of Scrabble, Al would suggest they "scrabble to the bedroom." Al thought he was making a big joke, but Jeannie had once found the word in her dictionary and discovered that scrabble meant to grope about frantically.

The image of her guest suddenly filled the mirror.

"Sorry, I was daydreaming," she started to say.

Before Jeannie could turn around, she felt a gloveless hand cover her nose and mouth. Gasping for breath she struggled as the words on her poster blurred into TO-DAY...YOUR LIFE. Desperately scrabbling, she closed her eyes.

When she opened them, she sat on the bathroom floor, leaning against the tiled wall. Overhead, a striped green and peach towel hung damply from its rack. On the floor beneath the sink lay her purse.

Jeannie had the feeling that, if she gazed into the mirror again, she'd look like Clarabelle the clown. Her makeup was smeared...and why the heck was she worried about her appearance, anyway? Her flag scarf was knotted about her wrists, tied tightly behind her back, and support pantyhose bound her ankles. Her mouth was covered with different shaped Band-Aids. An open Johnson and Johnson tin perched on the edge of the sink, the last Band-Aid looking like a stuck-out tongue.

And…oh, dear God…her visitor ran water in the tub. Jeannie could see steam rising. She recalled the repairman's words when he fixed her water heater: "Be very careful, Miss Dobson, or you could scald yourself."

Why are you doing this? What did I ever do to you, she thought, and actually formed the words behind the sticky bandages. Still dizzy, sick to her stomach, she tried to escape her bonds.

The figure bent down and ran fat thumbs over her body, laughing as she cringed. "In a week you'll be at your goal weight. In a few months you won't weigh nothin' at all."

Jeannie felt her body being dragged across the floor. She smelled pine disinfectant and gagged. *Help,* she tried to scream. *Hell-puh-puh-puh!*

Grunting, the attacker rolled her over the white porcelain, until she splashed into the overflowing tub, landing on her back. Her skin turned lobster red. Writhing like the figures in the morning aerobics class, screaming silently, Jeannie watched through steam as the blurry figure emptied her purse of its contents. She felt pudgy fingers push her head under the water and tried to think of a last prayer. But she could only recall the missing words of Shakespeare's quote: *All the perfume of Arabia will not sweeten this little hand.*

The visitor walked into Jeannie's kitchen, washed the coffee mugs, reentered the bathroom, and placed the tin of Band-Aids in the medicine cabinet.

Then the killer retied Jeannie's scarf about her dead throat. Stripped the soggy bandages from her slack mouth, pocketed them, and carefully draped Jeannie's pantyhose over the shower rod.

The front door opened. The door closed. Opened again.

"Stupid doody-face; almost lost the game," muttered the killer, retrieving a pair of gloves that slouched over the stuffed fruit, then stomping through kitchen and bathroom, cleansing all surfaces with a comet-saturated sponge.

"Good night ladies, good night ladies, good-bye ladies, we're gonna leave you now. Merr-a-lee we…yes, we have no bananas, we have no ban-nan-nas to-day."

The microwave's digital numbers read 9:07.

TWO

WHEN JEANNIE DOBSON DIDN'T show up for the meeting—10:00 a.m. at the Good Shepherd Church of Colorado Springs—Hannah Taylor wasn't unduly alarmed. Jeannie had probably received a last-minute phone call seeking help for the Special Olympics or Planned Parenthood or the League of Woman Voters, whatever.

No, Hannah wasn't apprehensive, but she did feel somewhat annoyed when George Bubbles took her friend's seat at the long table. Georgie Porgie (as Hannah and Jeannie gigglingly called him) looked like he had once been the runt in a litter of beagle puppies. Always searching for attention, he had grown into an adult, overweight Snoopy.

Georgie Porgie kissed the girls and made them cry, thought Hannah. It was mean, she knew, but she couldn't erase the image.

"Hiya' babe." George perspired profusely, even though it was September and cool inside the open-windowed room. He wore an orange blazer, open, showing off a white T-shirt whose red letters spelled out: *WORLD'S GREATEST LOVER*. His black, wool-blend pants had the tiny fuzz balls that accumulate when heavy thighs are rubbed together.

"Hello, George," Hannah said primly. She reached inside her purse and retrieved a Ziploc bag full of fresh carrot sticks and celery stalks. These she munched noisily, although the crunch dissipated amid all the chatter.

Ellie entered the church classroom, walked around the

table, and greeted members. Hooping her thumb and first finger into a circle of satisfaction, she gave silent approval to Hannah's midmorning snack choice, then watched the woman's thin lips rotate as she chewed.

Hannah's facial features were the only thin part of her. A recent Weight Winners "before" picture had indicated small brownish eyes, like two M&M's candies. Gerbil-hued hair, unsprayed, unmoussed, valiantly cascaded to her earlobes, and colorless plastic-framed glasses pinched the bridge of her narrow nose. Hannah's neck was short, circled by a black bead necklace. She had changed from her gray sweatsuit into navy blue stretch pants and pink overblouse.

Hannah didn't need makeup or a flattering hairdo; her face displayed...integrity?...sincerity?...yes, but also honest-to-goodness *goodness*. When she lost her excess pounds, she'd be lovely, and healthy. Jeannie Dobson had once confided that her friend had high blood pressure, and the dangerous food addiction had been caused by depression over a deceased husband. Ellie watched Hannah extend her plastic bag toward the world's greatest lover.

"Would you care to share my veggies, George?"

"Never touch the stuff. Rabbit food. Yuck." He shifted in his seat, and both Ellie and Hannah noticed the pink and white Dunkin' Donuts sack peeking from his trouser pocket.

Ellie shook her head, then hid a sigh. She'd have to work harder with this particular member.

"You ate doughnuts," Hannah whispered.

"I skipped breakfast and I have a bad cold. I'm counting it as a bread portion."

"Bread? You can substitute cereal, melba toast, pita—" The word stuck in Hannah's throat as she pictured jelly doughnuts parading to "Seventy-six Trombones." Her stomach growled. Defiantly she bit into a carrot stick.

"I lost three and a half pounds," George whispered. "How'd you do, babe?"

Ellie made a mental note to prepare a lecture on the fallacy of food substitution as she walked toward the front of the room. Too bad George had lost weight this week, but he'd gain it back and more if he continued cheating.

"How'd you do, babe?" George repeated.

Snoopy! Hannah pretended she hadn't heard the question. How'd she do? She had registered a quarter-pound loss, and truly felt that the young girl at the ugly white medical scale was being kind to give her that minus on her report card. "Plateau" was the magic word that Wanda, the friendly weigher, had announced sympathetically.

That tiny minus made Hannah's total loss seven pounds—four the first week and three over the next five. Good grief! Snoopy and his damn doughnuts! It wasn't fair! She wished Jeannie had been instrumental in getting Hannah to join. "You'll feel like a new person," she had said.

A new person. That's what Hannah wanted to be. She was lonely. Her daughter, Earline, lived in California and son, Jack, in Houston. Earl's sudden death had occurred three years ago. They'd been so happy. Hannah had always fought her weight problem, but Earl had teased that she was "pleasantly plump." *He* could eat anything and never show it; metabolized by pushing his chair away from the dinner table. Then he died of a heart attack. God's practical joke. One moment Earl had been splashing Old Spice after-shave across his chin while singing,

"Fifteen men on The Dead Man's chest…Yo-ho-ho and a bottle of rum. Drink and the devil had done for the rest…Yo-ho…*Oh!*" The next moment he lay dead on their sterile bathroom floor. Their pink and white bathroom—the same color as the doughnut bag in Georgie Porgie's back pocket.

Hannah switched her attention to Ellie, who was writing on a chalkboard at the front of the room. Dressed in a straight turquoise skirt and white sweater, the group leader resembled Hot Lips on "M*A*S*H." Wavy auburn hair flirted with Ellie's shoulder blades, and her eyes matched the color of her skirt. A small nose, well-defined mouth, and square, determined chin made Ellie appear younger than her actual age, which Hannah knew was forty-three.

Brushing chalk dust from her fingers, Ellie stood back to survey the message?

A GREAT INVENTION FOR DIETERS IS A REFRIGERATOR
THAT WEIGHS YOU EVERY TIME YOU OPEN THE
DOOR AND REACH FOR THE WRONG FOOD.

"I think last week's message was more emphatic," said Ellie, turning toward Wanda. "'What you don't eat can kill you.' I was trying to get across the dangers of fasting, then bingeing."

"*Kill* seems a bit much, Ellie."

"Losing weight is a war, sweet pea."

"Aye, aye, Captain," Wanda said, saluting.

"There are some casualties and lots of victories. Speaking of winners, I saw Jeannie Dobson earlier this morning. She looked great."

"I'm so happy for her," said Wanda sincerely.

"Me, too. She finally licked her problem with water

retention. Get ready, Wanda, here comes Darlene and the Benedicts.''

Ellie watched what she privately called The Smoke Eaters enter. Good Shepherd didn't allow lit cigarettes inside the premises, so a group of nicotine addicts always gathered outside the church door, inhaling and coughing until the last possible moment.

One young married couple, Brian and Kelly Benedict, appeared every week, rain or shine. Together they ran their own decorating business, working from a customized van. Brian had lost fifteen pounds and was eleven over goal; Kelly needed to shed fourteen more to reach her designated amount. That Brian had pulled slightly ahead wasn't unusual, males frequently did.

Next to them stood Darlene who had once been a professional Las Vegas stripper. Darlene had dropped seventy pounds. Due to receive her goal certificate this very day, she would graduate to a modified, extracalorie food plan. Ellie admired the young woman, who was tall and sported a Julia Roberts mane of reddish brown hair. When Darlene wasn't smoking, she popped sticks of sugarless gum into a mouth that also resembled the actress's.

Ellie watched Darlene chew, the busy pink tongue darting out, like a blunted arrow, to capture droplets of saliva at her mouth's bowed corners. Then Ellie called the meeting to order and introduced herself.

''I would guess one of the most important ingredients of a weight loss plan is humor,'' she said. ''but when you go on a diet, the first thing you're apt to *lose* is your sense of humor. It was a long time before I could produce this snapshot in public,'' she added, then passed around one of her fat-pictures, showing fifty-five supplementary pounds. In the photo, Ellie's determined chin was doubled. A bulging midriff hid her breasts, and her arms and legs had several layers of cottage cheese cellulite.

"Were you, uh, pregnant in that picture?" asked a new member who was desperately attempting to hide a stack of introductory pamphlets.

"No, that was all me. Every pound. It took W.W. Two for my appearance and life-style to change."

"W.W. Two?"

"Weight Winners Two. The first time I joined, I was skeptical and didn't really believe it. Even when I started dropping pounds I thought it was a mistake. Water loss. The first party I attended...well, I just pigged out. Then I continued to binge for weeks. I was always planning to start back on the program *tomorrow*. How many members here are rejoins?"

A dozen people tentatively raised their hands.

"One thing you can be sure of," continued Ellie, letting her eyes sweep the room and smiling at each individual member, "there will always be more people going on a diet *tomorrow* than those on a diet today. When I rejoined Weight Winners, I decided it was my very last chance. After all, I had tried every other diet under the sun. The rice and mineral oil diet, the sunflower seed diet..." Pausing, she watched a few members nod their heads in agreement. "Anyway, I rejoined the club, followed the program, exercised, and convinced myself that I was a wonderful person. I *deserved* to be thin and attractive. I can't really determine where my fifty-five pounds went; I call it weight pollution. Then I decided to help others to do the same thing, and here I am."

While the members applauded, a man shuffled into the classroom. He seemed embarrassed, as if he had suddenly found himself onstage by mistake, just in time for the rousing curtain call. Tossing Ellie an apologetic glance, he shook his wrist a few times to explain, wordlessly, that his watch was broken. Then he sneezed and fumbled inside his pocket for a handkerchief.

As he stumbled across the room, Ellie searched for a name. Something ethnic. German? Swedish? Jenson? Jenkins? She gave up and, instead, watched him lean against a side wall, as though he considered his body too bulky for a chair.

That was me a couple years ago, she thought sympathetically. At least Jenson or Jenkins didn't flee from the room when he found himself momentarily the center of attention. I would have. Two years ago, I would have spread my layered wings and flown. Good for him!

"You *all* deserve that wonderful ovation you just gave me," she announced, making sure she caught Jenson-Jenkins's eye. "This morning I told two ladies that Santa Claus could shed his belly with the right food and exercise."

So could William Howard Taft, thought Ellie, picturing the twenty-seventh president and the brunch table filled with forbidden goodies. When Taft was running things, fat bullies kicked sand at skinny guys. You couldn't be too rich or too heavy.

Darlene accepted her goal certificate. Ellie remembered when Darlene had first joined them, her body hidden by a sweatshirt three sizes too large, trying to scrunch down on a chair so she wouldn't be noticed. Now Darlene's sweater molded her breasts.

Peripherally, Ellie saw George's mouth drop open while beads of sweat gathered across his balding forehead.

She gave Darlene a congratulatory hug, then greeted new members—including a coterie of well-fed, serene-faced nuns from the Catholic novitiate—and asked them all to stay after the meeting for a detailed description of the food program.

"Probably nothing in the world arouses more false hopes than the first six hours of a diet," Ellie warned. "I want to see you all here, hopeful and thinner, six *weeks* from now, okay?"

Enthusiastically, she gave a short prepared lecture explaining how to use spare time for other activities besides eating. Specific weight loss amounts were read aloud. A chorus of *oooh*s and *ahhh*s greeted every forfeited ounce. George Bubbles beamed and nudged Hannah in the side as his three and a half pounds generated applause.

"It'll catch up with you, George," she said irritably. "Next week you'll gain it all back.

At the conclusion of the meeting Ellie offered to snap Polaroid "before" pictures so that beginners could eventually view their successes. The woman who had timidly asked earlier if Ellie had been pregnant volunteered to pose, standing in front of the scale. She had a beautiful round face with a flawless complexion and looked like an advertisement for queen-size pantyhose. Ellie snapped one picture. Then, backing up to refocus her camera, she bumped into a figure clothed in dark pants whose cuffs were tucked into mud-encrusted, thick-soled shoes. A blue workman's shirt escaped from the waistband of his belted trousers.

"Hi, Henry."

"Ellie. Howya' doing?"

"I'm fine. You?"

"Took a break from the building on eighth. Thought I'd treat Wanda to lunch. There's a new pizza joint with a buffet spread." Henry smacked his lips, creating little sucking sounds of enjoyment. His eyes blazed with excitement and mischief. He lit a cigarette, inhaled, then blew the smoke toward Ellie.

She coughed. "Put that out, Henry. They don't allow smoking in the church."

"Right. Don't want to break no rules." Dropping the cigarette, he crushed it beneath his heel.

Joseph "Henry" Henry, Wanda's husband, was a leading character in Ellie's favorite lecture—negative influences from family and friends. The overweight construction worker always put the program down, then offered Wanda food bribes to make her break her diet. Ellie had seen Henry arrive after a meeting, toting heart-shaped boxes of candy. Ellie didn't know how Wanda resisted, but her young friend had maintained a sixty-pound loss and was employed by the Weight Winners organization as a record keeper and weigher.

Without taking time to focus, Ellie snapped a picture of Henry and handed him the result.

"Why don't you join us for a couple of meetings? Just to see if you like the program. We have several male members—"

"No way!" Henry slowly and methodically ripped the Polaroid snapshot in half, then quarters, and dropped the scraps into a wastepaper basket. "I ain't fat like him." Henry's pudgy finger indicated Jenson-Jenkins. "I can lose any time I want. 'Fact, I was thinking 'bout joining that new health club to lift weights. Used to play football, y'know? I'm a bit soft in my muscles is all." Thrusting his armpit toward Ellie's nose, he flexed his biceps, and she was almost overwhelmed by a sour body odor unsuccessfully masked by an overlay of cologne.

Win some, lose some, she thought, grinning at her choice of phrase. Cary Grant once said, "We should all just smell well and enjoy ourselves more." But I'm sure good ol' Cary never had a weight problem in his life.

Distastefully, Ellie waited until Henry unflexed. Then she bent forward, pinched his unfiltered butt between her thumb and first finger, and dumped it into the trash next to pieces of the photo.

"If you ever change your mind, Henry—"

"I ain't fat," he repeated, sucking in his gut. "Hey Wanda, let's go."

Wanda waved good-bye to Ellie and Hannah.

Hannah returned the farewell salute, then dug through her purse for a coin to call Jeannie Dobson from one of the church's two pay phones. Maybe they could meet for lunch at a seafood restaurant or salad bar.

Nobody answered Jeannie's phone, not even the stupid machine, and Hannah changed her plans. She would walk a few blocks to the golden arches and order a McFish sandwich—or whatever the damn thing was called. She would count the seasoned coating as a bread. Surely that was better than eating doughnuts like Georgie Porgie Bubbles. Hannah's stomach growled ominously. Trying to ignore her hunger pangs, she sang, "If I knew you were coming I'd have baked a cake, hired a band, *goodness sake. If I knew..."*

SEVEN HOURS LATER, the insurance agent, Al, left his Sears cubicle, drove carefully through the potholes on interstate 25, and parked his black Volvo behind his lady friend's station wagon.

He entered the house and rushed past the kitchen.

"Gotta take a leak, Jeannie."

Not waiting for an answer, he burst into the bathroom to find his sweetheart in the wide, white tub. Her eyes

stared sightlessly at the ceiling, and her frosted hair
looked like what's-his-name? Oh yeah, Don King.

Al just stood there, fly open, grasping his penis as if
he held a water pistol. Then he turned, ran from the bathroom, and scrabbled for the phone.

One hour later, a soggy report card (smeared ink in-
dicating a total weight loss of thirty-five pounds was discovered stuck to the fabric of Jeannie Dobson's Joan
Crawford shoulder pads.

THREE

INSIDE JEANNIE DOBSON'S KITCHEN, Lieutenant Peter Miller tried to calm the hysterical insurance agent, but the poor slob kept hollering, "Don King. Yeah. Don King."

"Okay, okay, buddy," Miller said. "Does this King person have anything to do with Ms. Dobson's, uh, accident?"

"Jesus, D-D-Don King is a fa-fa-fight promoter. You know, the one with all that stupid heh-heh-hair."

"Right." Miller asked a few more questions, then said, "Uh, you might want to, uh, zip up your fly."

The insurance agent nodded eagerly but didn't move. "It's almost time for 'Dallas' reruns," he said. "Jeannie loves La-La-Larry Hagman."

Well, at least Miller knew who La-La-Larry Hagman was. *Who killed J.R.? Who killed J. Dobson?*

"You really think it's murder, Pete?" asked Detective William McCoy after Miller had entered the bathroom.

"Did you find anything missing?" Miller ushered McCoy into the living room. Dobson's bathroom wasn't all that big to begin with, and it now resembled a scrubbing bubbles commercial. Only the bubbles were full-grown photographers, technicians, and, bracketing the door, a pair of lounging paramedics."

"Nothing out of place; no sigh of a robbery," said McCoy, sinking into an armchair. "But why murder, Pete? Couldn't she have filled her tub, blacked out or something, and drowned?"

"Nope. She didn't intend to take a bath. She was fully clothed for going out. Spiffy."

"Okay, she was about to empty the tub, reached for the drain plug, and—"

"Christ! How'd you ever pass your homicide exam, Will? Didn't you see her face? Legs? Hands? She was practically scalded."

"So?"

"Are you suggesting that she filled the tub while she got all gussied up, then decided to empty it?"

"Gussied up?" Freckles merged when McCoy grinned. "Shit, Lieutenant, you're—"

"An anachronism?"

"I was gonna say barking up the wrong tree," mumbled McCoy, rising, stretching, weaving fingers through his all-American haircut, then caressing his diamond-studded earlobe. "Okay, motive. A neighbor saw her vamoose early this morning, clothed in sweats. Maybe the robber broke in, then was interrupted during—"

"There was no forced entry and her door has a sturdy dead bolt."

"Maybe she left the door unlocked."

"Sure, our perpetrator hides, waits for his victim to change clothes, then drowns her, then panics, leaving behind a TV, silver tea service…jewelry?" Miller waited for McCoy's nod. "Plus all other hockables."

"C'mon, Pete, there might have been money lying around. A coin collection. Stamp collection."

"The boyfriend swears she didn't own any coins, stamps, or letters signed by Abe Lincoln. The purse in the tub included seventeen soaking-wet bucks. Her kitchen was neat as a pin, but I found an instant coffee jar and a checkbook on the counter, both almost hidden behind the microwave. There was a signed withdrawal slip inside the checkbook, as though she planned to hit the bank sometime during the day. If she had money lying around—''

''What about the boyfriend?''

''You mean jealous or something? Ummm…that's a possibility. The lady was in love with J.R.''

''Who?''

''Larry Hagman.''

''Shit, Pete, no need to get—''

''Defensive?''

''Sarcastic.''

''Sorry. In any case, I don't think the boyfriend could kill a fly. Zip one, either.''

''Then what's the motive?''

''I don't know. Our perpetrator's not too bright; tried to make it look like an accident, but didn't even bother to undress the lady before he drowned her. Dumb! De, dum, dum. Just the facts, so I guess I'll wait for the forensic results, autopsy, etcetera. But I've got a gut feeling he's an impulsive wacko.''

''How'd you ever pass *your* exam, Lieutenant?''

''What do you mean?''

McCoy's freckles merged again. ''How do you know our perp is a he?''

''Because *he* had the strength to dump her in the tub. *He* held her head underwater.''

''Shit, Pete, you're so—''

''Positive.''

''Chauvinistic. My girlfriend works out, hefts weights. *She* could hold my head underwater with one hand and shave her legs with the other.''

THE CLOCK RADIO SCREAMED. Silence. It screamed again. Silence. The third scream was longer, more insistent:

Hey, wake up. C'mon. We're all in our places with sun-shiny faces, you asshole.

George Bubbles finally heard the alarm and awoke from a bad dream. *Shit!* He was going to be late for work again. Oh, it was early enough, but he had things to do first and it was double-damn Monday. George hated Mondays. He liked Fridays. Friday was his day off.

"Every other day of the week is fi-yine," he sang, adjusting the faucets in his shower, waiting for the water to turn hot. "Monday, Mon-day, can't trust that day."

Grabbing a Diet Coke from the refrigerator, George surveyed the empty bed in his studio apartment. Rumpled, lonely bed. Rumpled, lonely George. He had spent a lot of dough-ray-me on That Girl last night. He had approached The Girl in the supermarket veggie department and treated her to supper at the Olive Garden restaurant (not just soup and salad, either), then she had refused to come home with him. She'd even giggled when he explained how he was being considered for the lead in a new television series.

"Remember that show about what's his name? That overweight detective? Not Raymond Burr, the other one. Well, a friend of mine is writing a script about a fat sheriff in the old West. People *trust* heavy men."

She'd merely giggled.

Women were all a bunch of teasing sluts. Like vegetables. Celery, carrots, and tofu (stupid bean curd) looked great but tasted lousy. George preferred the taste of cheesecake. Cheesecake tasted fi-yine.

WHILE LIEUTENANT MILLER WAITED impatiently for results from Jeannie Dobson's autopsy report, and George Bubbles waited for his shower water to heat, Eleanor Bernstein turned up the volume on her radio. The Beatles sang about Eleanor Rigby and the lonely people...*where do they all come from, where do they all belong?*

Swishing her sponge across the butcher-block kitchen counter, Ellie jostled the postage scale used to weigh her food portions. The tiny plastic dish, perched atop the scale, bounced once on the counter, then fell—like an erratic, miniature Frisbee—to the no-wax tile floor.

Ellie's huge black Persian cat, Jackie Robinson, investigated the fallen object, sniffing for a possible speck of neglected food.

"Forget it," said Ellie. "You've already had your morning Kal Kan portion. Kitty stew: beef and veggies and by-products. My God, if they offered a Weight Winners class for cats, I'd sign you up."

Mournfully, Jackie Robinson maneuvered his thick bristly tail into the air and sauntered off toward his litter box, distended belly swaying from side to side, whiskers aquiver: *Meow, you'll be sorr-ee. Ain't gonna rub 'gainst Ellie-woman's legs. Ain't gonna purr. Mee-ow.*

The fat feline lived a life of deprivation, thought Ellie, especially since Jackie Robinson was addicted to Oreo cookies and they had been absent from her pantry shelves for over two years. Like an alcoholic who pours liquid down a sink drain, Ellie had collected all the tempting illegal foods in her home and donated the filled sacks to a local charity drive.

She followed the cat out of the kitchen, turned right, and entered a bedroom. Shrugging her body from its bathrobe, she stepped into a pair of purple sweatpants and a yellow velour shirt. Ribbed socks and tightly laced jogging sneakers completed her outfit. Next, Ellie ran a comb through her auburn hair, then pulled it away from her face with a rubber band.

Seven a.m. She trotted through the streets, past dorms,

fraternity houses, and the empty halls and classrooms that made up the small campus of Colorado College. She waved toward a couple of other Monday-morning joggers, whose earphone wires extended down toward their pockets like the outline of an elephant's trunk, then watched three bike riders circle the corner, their bulging calf muscles flashing in rhythmic symmetry.

Seven blocks south. Two blocks east. Ellie approached Acacia Park and slowed to a fast walk. Her mind veered in all directions...in what her son Michael called "middle-age meditation."

Seated on a park bench, feeling the cold wooden slats through her shirt, Ellie shut her eyes and saw herself leading the Colorado Springs Symphony Orchestra from atop the picturesque Victorian bandstand. Opening her eyes, she watched squirrels scamper through September-hued foliage. Although it was too early in the morning, Ellie sniffed and could swear she smelled the hot-dog vendor's warm sauerkraut.

Food. Her thoughts always returned to food. Hooray for Weight Winners. In addition to her Friday class at the Good Shepherd Church, Ellie was involved with several other groups, and was usually available for last-minute lecturing substitutions. She loved her group leader duties. It provided income, kept her busy, and made her feel good. *All the lonely people...thank God for Weight Winners.*

Her life had been such a cliché. An overweight adolescence. High school prom with an improvised and reluctant cousin, an inch shorter and thirty pounds lighter than she; Mutt and Jeff dancing to the soporific strains of "Theme from a Summer Place"; Ellie desperately wishing she could metamorphose into Sandra Dee, with bee-stung lips and a cute curvy body.

Ellie's Troy Donahue had been a boy who won a five dollar bet by giving Ellie-Belly Bernstein her first sloppy kiss, while, at the same time, trying to unsnap her bra. She'd dented his crotch with her pointy-toed shoes.

A scholarship and diet pills, dispensed freely by an ancient family physician, made college years more fun, more satisfying, and led directly to pregnancy and marriage, do not pass Go, do not collect two hundred dollars.

Tony. Half Italian Mafia; half Jewish prince. His mother shoveled eggplant Parmesan and homemade chicken soup (along with fresh-baked garlic bread and buttered matzo squares) down Ellie's throat. Tony said he liked a woman with meat on her bones, and Ellie happily complied.

Tall, lean Tony—blond hair, dark eyes, and Semitic nose adding as much to his success in real estate as his buy-and-sell expertise. Tony—Kirk Douglas with a mop of Robert Redford hair—who took his women in the bedrooms and finished basements of his listed homes.

Like the speeding clock hands in an old B-grade movie, her married years passed quickly. Tony listed more houses and screwed more clients, while baby Michael grew from adorable toddler into reclusive hard-rock advocate.

Michael, who insisted on being called Mick after his Rolling Stone idol, began to have interests that ran to *Playboy* centerfolds ("Jesus, Mom, the short stories are cerebral masterpieces. They must be 'cause I don't understand 'em!") and Volkswagens with oversize black tires. His patched jeans and rock-tour T-shirts never left his body long enough for laundering, and he traded earrings with a big-breasted high school cheerleader named Lisa. Which meant, decided Ellie, that her son was going steady ("*Steady?* Jesus, Mom!"), or getting laid ("Of course I use protection, Mom, whadaya think I am, stupid?''), or maybe he just liked Lisa's earring better.

Ironically, Tony found his own cheerleader, an ex-Dallas Cowgirl who swiveled her hips and jiggled her boobs into Tony's Italian-Jewish heart. He became faithful at last—to his chirruping, short-shorts, vociferous, pom-pom lady. Sexually devoted to 110 pounds of unfettered titties, minuscule waist, and liberated buttocks.

It was a friendly divorce. Tony signed over their house and provided a large alimony settlement. He admitted guilt, but, unable to relinquish his delicious noncaloric morsel, he moved from Colorado Springs to Denver and actually married his young cheering-squad centerfold.

For a while Ellie and an unexpectedly supportive Michael drew closer. Then her son journeyed to Boulder, Colorado, to spend his college years majoring in music and skiing. Ellie was alone for the first time in her life.

She spent her days filling in crossword puzzles and reading mystery novels. She even began creating a short story about a cheerleader who murders members of a football team and is exposed by an average housewife fan. The cheerful fiction sat inside a file cabinet, incomplete.

Ellie became obsessed by Orson Welles movies. Fat is beautiful, she decided. And, after all, the luscious Marilyn Monroe had a *zaftig* tushy.

In order to keep busy, Ellie devoted volunteer hours to the main library. There she met Laurie, who carried Tupperware-filled grocery sacks to work, and slid from a size sixteen-plus to a slender size eight. Ellie wondered if the miraculous change had occurred due to voodoo, hypnosis, or a wasting-away illness. Laurie launched into a diatribe against all fad diets, followed by a twenty-minute tribute to Weight Winners. Ellie was hooked.

She joined, lost ten pounds, then attended a party to raise money for proenvironmental, prochoice political candidates. It was more social than political since few such candidates existed in Colorado, but several people told Ellie she was "lookin' good." Tony and his young wife were at the same affair, and Ellie had sucked up the refreshments like a recently repaired Hoover. Embarrassed by her regression, she dropped out of the diet club.

Then Laurie—still munching turkey breast and sprouts—became even more persistent. Ellie rejoined the group. This time she stuck to the food program, reached her goal, and jokingly referred to her experience as W.W. Two.

Ellie smiled. She felt happy, healthy, and, despite her old jogging outfit, definitely sexy.

During the last year of marriage, Tony had become an indifferent bedmate and lover. In retrospect, Ellie realized that if she had only dropped her poundage sooner and learned to do splits and shout rah-rah, her relationship with Tony might have turned out differently.

Yet, even toward the end of their wedded bliss, Tony had offered her a few crumbs of sexual attention, like the remains in the bottom of a Chips Ahoy cookie box.

Ellie had been celibate since her divorce.

I'm like a piece of overripe fruit ready to drop from the tree, she thought. I wish some incredible Prince Charming would come along and take a bite out of me. The program did include a variety of fruit portions.

"Tout est pour le mieux dans le meilleur des mondes possibles," Ellie said aloud.

"What?" Wanda plopped her rounded behind on the bench.

"'All is for the best in the best of possible worlds,'" Ellie translated. "It's a quote from *Candide*."

"Do you always daydream in French?"

"No, sometimes Latin. I learned both in Catholic school."

"All is for the best..." began Wanda, then sighed.

"Problems?"

"Just Henry. Ellie, what made you decide to take the final step and get your divorce?"

"I didn't, sweet pea. Tony walked out on me."

"I wish I had the nerve."

"Has Henry been abusive?"

"Oh no! Well, not physically. He hurts with words, then tries to make up with food gifts. He wants me to get pregnant again. That way I'll have to put weight on. I told Henry the twins are like three or four children, instead of two."

"Where are the twins? Is Henry watching them?"

"Are you kidding? They spent the night with my mother, so I thought I'd take advantage of a guest pass to that new health club." Wanda brightened. "It's neat, Ellie. Aerobics on a special floor. Swimming pool. Sauna."

"Do you plan to join?"

"Henry wouldn't let me. I had to fight to work for Weight Winners, and I can only do that when Joseph Jr. and Becky are in school. Sorry, didn't mean to bitch about my life. I was on my way to pick up the twins at my mom's and saw you sitting in the park."

"Wish I could be more help."

"Well, I'll keep repeating that best of all possible worlds thing, although I must admit it's hard, especially when I think about Jeannie Dobson?"

"Jeannie?"

"Oh dear, I thought you knew. Last Friday...probably

before our meeting…it was in the newspapers and on TV."

"After the lecture, I drove to Boulder for the weekend. No paper, no TV. What happened? Please tell me."

Wanda took a deep breath. "In this best of all possible worlds, Jeannie drowned in her bathtub."

"What? No!"

"Yes. The poor, dear woman apparently fell into the tub, thunked her head or something."

"God! How unfair. Damn!" Ellie fisted one hand and pounded at the wooden slats of the park bench. "Damn, damn, damn! I feel like I've just lost a relative."

"That's why you have such success with the group, Ellie. We know how much you care."

"Don't make me into a saint, Wanda." She sighed, then pointed. "Do you believe in instant reincarnation? Jeannie could be one of those feathery critters chirping away on that tree branch. If she is, she'll build a nest with a guest bedroom for troubled robins or humming-birds."

"You're right." Wanda's mouth trembled with the semblance of a smile. "Good healthy worm soup. You always make me feel better, Ellie."

"Guess I'll jog home and have a good cry; that'll make *me* feel better."

"Jeannie wouldn't approve of tears, but I don't blame you. That's why I left the twins with my mother last night; I cried and cried. Speaking of my kids, I'd better scoot and pick them up."

After watching Wanda cross the park toward her car, Ellie bent down to retire a shoelace. Tears plopped, stain-ing her sneakers. Knuckling teardrops away, she stood and stretched, using a bench like a ballerina's barre.

From the corner of her eye, Ellie saw a figure half

hidden behind a gnarly tree trunk. She couldn't make out the face clearly, but she had an uncomfortable feeling that the stranger's glare was directed straight toward her. She lifted a hand to wave, thinking maybe the tree-shaded person was someone she knew, but whoever it was turned abruptly and stumbled away in the opposite direction. The person's head was covered by a stocking cap. A gray-green pea jacket, worn over jeans, rendered the body sexless.

Ellie changed the wave into a salute, then had the definite sensation of being followed as she again crossed the college campus, now peopled by early-morning students on their way to study. Glancing several times over her shoulder, Ellie saw nothing threatening.

FRIDAY MORNING. The chalkboard read:

WELCOME TO WEIGHT WINNERS. LOSE TO WIN.
A DIET IS LIKE A BALL GAME—YOU'RE THE
UMPIRE BEHIND HOME PLATE.

Hannah clutched her report card in dismay. She felt very much as she had forty years ago. Unable to propel her chubby body up the knotted ropes or complete three laps around a running track, she had flunked physical education.

Five pounds! She had gained five pounds over the last week. Ever since learning about Jeannie Dobson's death, Hannah hadn't been able to stop eating. Cheesecake and cookies and ice cream. An entire jar of peanut butter. Food to soothe her sorrow. Food to compensate for the guilt that she was alive, while Earl and Jeannie slept forever.

"Hiya' babe."

"Hel-hello, George."

"What's the matter?"

"Haven't you heard about Jeannie Dobson?"

"Lost so much weight she melted away?"

"That's not funny! Jeannie's dead." Tears dripped from Hannah's eyes and fell onto her jutting overblouse. She was so hungry, she felt physically ill. Although no telltale pink and white doughnut bag peaked from George's pocket, a light sugary residue outlined his lips.

"I gained this week," he muttered, awkwardly patting Hannah's shoulder. "You were right. I gained back the weight from last week, and more."

Further down the table, Brian Benedict turned his face toward his wife.

"Good for you, Kell," he said proudly. "Four and a half pounds. Do you realize you have less than ten to lose before you reach goal weight?"

"It's not the program," she replied sadly. "After I read in the paper about Jeannie Dobson, I couldn't eat a thing. Didn't you notice! I just choked up. Jeannie was so nice. It's different when somebody you've met and talked to every week is murdered."

"Hey, you don't know she was murdered. Accidents happen in the home all the time, especially the bathroom. That's why we recommend slip-proof tubs when we decorate."

"But the newspaper said the police are investigating."

"The police always investigate. Take it from me, darling. She was reading her report card—"

"In the bathtub, Brian? Fully dressed?"

"Reading her card, totaling her loss, and not thinking about what she was doing. She probably slipped and clunked herself on the head. It happens all the time."

"Not to people I know, Bri." Kelly sighed. Deciding

to change the subject, she asked, "How much did you lose this week?"

"One pound, but I feel great. And horny."

"Brian!"

"Wouldn't it be fun to make love inside the Good Shepherd? Such a religious experience. Ahhh, woman. Ahhh-men."

"If the church doesn't allow cigarettes on their premises, I doubt they'd condone, well, what you're thinking about," said Kelly with a grin. She ruffled Brian's dark brown hair, growing like weeds in a thatch. Sensitive gray eyes were slightly magnified behind glasses. With weight loss and exercise, his body had become firm and taut. Kelly felt her own body tingle. Ah-men.

Brian smiled tenderly. "I like your hair that way, honey," he said, bending sideways and hugging her.

Another positive result of Weight Winners, thought Kelly. They had both become more aware of each other, sprinkling their conversations with compliments. Instinctively, Kelly patted her long sienna strands. She had weaved two plaits away from her forehead, then brought them together into one heavy braid. Her brows arched, like birds in flight, over deep Technicolor blue eyes.

"I'd probably be at goal weight if I cut my hair short," she said mischievously.

"You'd lose a hundred eighty pounds," replied Brian. "You'd lose me. Look, here comes Laurel and Hardy."

"More like Hardy and Hardy," mumbled Kelly.

The doorway was literally filled with a popular couple, longtime members of the Friday group. Tubby and Little Lulu Evergreen resembled the appointed Grant Wood farm couple, expanded by over a hundred pounds each, minus pitchfork and silo. Lulu had once been called Lydia but had changed her name when she married

Tubby—whose real name everybody, including Tubby, had forgotten long ago.

Tubby had wispy brown hair, combed across a balding skull, and wore granny glasses. Denim coveralls encased his body, the straps crisscrossed over an extra large undershirt.

During one meeting, Tubby had confided that he liked his name. "You know how kids are always called something else? In our gang, the kid with the big ears was called Dumbo, and the boy with the long nose, well, we called him Nokeo for Pinocchio. On the other hand, we also nicknamed kids the opposite of what they looked like. I remember one guy had so much hair that we called him Baldy. I was skinny then, and didn't look at all like that comic strip character, Tubby. That's why they named me for him, instead of Slim or something. You see, the others gave me that name and, when they did, well, I really belonged to the gang, y'know?"

Little Lulu, like *her* cartoon namesake, had black ringlets permed into short corkscrew curls. Her button eyes were nearly lost between a low forehead and puffy cheeks. She wore a shapeless muumuu with purple and yellow polka dots on a white background.

Tubby and Lulu were greeted with enthusiasm by the roomful of dieters. The couple was always good for a laugh, contributing stories of their various food cheats. News about Jeannie Dobson had cast a gloomy shadow over the group; the Evergreens were a welcome diversion. Only Wanda, Hannah, and Kelly refused to smile as the couple posed, trading quips with fellow members.

"We're back," shouted Tubby. "We missed last week's meeting, but we're back."

"Where were y'all?" drawled a tiny woman, who, when she lost her weight, would resemble Sally Field.

Tubby motioned drawing an imaginary gun from a holster. "Bang! Bang! Gotcha', Texas." He winked. "Lulu and me—no, better not tell. Ellie'd kill us."

Ellie stood at the doorway, greeting her members as they entered. She grinned when the three nuns from last week crossed themselves before stepping on the scale.

When somebody says he diets religiously, he probably means he doesn't eat anything in church, thought Ellie. Her eyes moistened. Again. Despite her adorable nuns, she found it difficult to be her usual up-self, still devastated by Jeannie's death. As the pounds melted away, Jeannie had become a valuable member of Friday's Good Shepherd Group, always ready to listen, soothe a troubled conscience. "I cheated, Jeannie, ate some nuts." "Nuts don't have many calories." "They do when they're surrounded by chocolate."

Ellie saw the Evergreens sit and regale their cohorts with a story about a recent journey through a smorgasbord, describing (in detail) the New York cheesecake.

The flamboyant couple irritated her—like two buzzing flies at a windowpane. Tubby and Lulu could use their influence in a positive manner; tell a funny story about *refusing* cheesecake at a smorgasbord. There she went judging again.

Sandra Connors, Ellie's favorite protégée, blew her a fingertip kiss, then swept into the room. Usually clothed in jeans or cutoffs, today Sandra wore a fuzzy pink angora skirt and matching sweater. Her long, wheat-colored hair was drawn through a couple of rubber bands and floated down her back over a red headband. She looked like a healthy bunny with droopy ears. Sandra was below goal weight and faithfully attended at least one meeting a month to maintain her loss. But Ellie saw her more often, since Sandra was "madly in love" with Michael aka Mick.

The meeting went smoothly. Ex-stripper Darlene announced that she had lost another pound. The group planned a Halloween party, and Darlene promised to entertain with a self-censored version of her Las Vegas act.

A sweet grandmother type named Esther Abramowitz—whose fingers constantly clicked knitting needles as background music to Ellie's lectures—had reached goal weight after losing twenty-seven pounds. Ellie saved her for last, hoping to end the meeting on an upbeat note.

But usually shy Esther talked at length about the program and how she had stayed "legal and kosher." Then she announced that she had sent a donation for a tree in Israel in Jeannie Dobson's name.

Subdued again, the members filed out of the church.

"Wouldja' like to go for a drink, Hannah?" asked George.

"A cup of coffee?"

"Nope, a real drink."

"Mercy! It's not even noon!"

"So?"

"Besides, we're not allowed to drink spirits, George."

"You can have a glass of wine, Hannah, that's allowed. Hey, why don't we ask Darlene if she wants to join us," he said, eyeing the tall figure hungrily.

Darlene declined.

George watched the ex-stripper walk away then turned to Hannah. "Aw, c'mon, babe, I know a place that has a piano player. It's called the Dew Drop Inn and the bartender, Charley, is a friend of mine."

George Bubbles isn't Snoopy; he's just an overgrown puppy eager to be loved, thought Hannah, and she found herself promising to meet him later for happy hour.

Inside the lecture room, Ellie handed Wanda the membership file. "Join me for lunch?"

"I'm meeting Harry."

"How do you manage to stay legal?"

"He takes me for pizza, and I raid the salad bar. I sometimes feel like I've been sent out to graze, but it fills me up."

"Good for you. Did you see the nuns cross themselves before stepping on the scale?"

"One said her rosary. They're so darling, Ellie."

"Sister…Maria?…reminds me of my cat. Her habit practically bristled when I told her that no Oreos were permitted, and she looked so mournful."

A member approached Wanda, phrasing a question. A few more people patiently waited their turn, chatting amicably.

Wanda just might take Jeannie's place as consultant and confidante, thought Ellie with satisfaction. She collected her purse and a cash box containing the weekly fees, then walked briskly through the open doorway and almost collided with a tall man eating an apple.

No weight problem there, she decided, appraising the slender, suited figure. A few drops of juice from his half-eaten fruit had accumulated on the edges of his black-and-silver-streaked mustache.

"Ms. Bernstein?" he asked between apple bites.

"That's right. How may I help you?"

He didn't wander into Good Shepherd by mistake, thought Ellie. Could he be a Weight Winners graduate? *No way!* This man had never been overweight in his life.

"I'm Lieutenant Peter Miller. Homicide Division." Miller held out the apple, chuckled, and juggled it to his other hand.

Ellie returned his firm shake. "Lieutenant?"

"Do you need to see a badge?"

She realized that Miller was still grasping her hand. Releasing his grip, clutching the cash box with all ten fingers, she said, "Did I do something wrong, Lieutenant? Unpaid parking ticket? Spitting on the sidewalk?"

Miller raised his dark eyebrows. "Do you spit, Ms. Bernstein?"

"All the time. The best way to cook a gourmet meal and taste to see if it's done without gaining weight is to put the food in your mouth, then spit it out before you swallow."

Miller took a big bite, chewed, hesitated, swallowed, then searched through his pockets. "I have another apple here someplace. Granny—"

"Smith?"

"No, Miller. Granny used to say, 'The best thing to put into an apple pie is your teeth.'"

"Please stop mangling your pocket seams, Lieutenant. I really don't want an ap—"

"Can't eat fruit on that diet of yours?"

"Of course I can. Fruit is healthy and has natural sugar." Ellie inexplicably blushed. "How may I help you?"

"I have a few questions—"

"About Jeannie Dobson?"

"Correct."

"Let's get away from the door, or I'll be inundated with last-minute conversation."

Ellie walked briskly around the corridor and over to a window, peered through the panes of glass, and grinned at a tandem bike. A couple of elderly members rode the double-pedaled vehicle to every meeting. Ellie privately called them Daisy and Beau.

Henry Henry was striding through the parking lot, an anticipatory pizza-induced grin on his face. Poor Wanda.

Brian and Kelly Benedict stood close together, hugging and kissing.

Tubby and Lulu appeared to be arguing.

A cigarette dangled from Darlene's pouty lips. She cupped her hands and flicked her Bic.

Sandra Connors was singing. A small crowd gathered to listen. George Bubbles waved one of Hannah's celery stalks like a conductor's baton.

Turning away from the window, Ellie watched with fascination as Peter Miller carved an umbrella above and below the apple's seeded middle, then carefully discarded the remains in a nearby trash receptacle.

"Wait a minute, Lieutenant, why are you asking questions about Jeannie? Didn't she drown accidentally?"

"It sure looks that way, Ms. Bernstein."

"What do you mean *looks* that way?"

"We're investigating every possibility."

"That's ridiculous! Who would kill Jeannie?"

"Well now, that's what I was going to ask you."

"The answer is nobody. Jeannie didn't have any enemies; quite the opposite. Every person she met confided in her and asked for her advice. She is…was the nicest, sweetest woman in the world."

"Okay, calm down."

"What makes you think she was murdered?"

"We're investigating every—"

"Why, Lieutenant?"

"Ms. Dobson was fully clothed."

"So? I'll run a tub while I'm still clothed. It's almost automatic. Turn on the taps and get undressed while the water's running. Look, I met Jeannie jogging last Friday, so she'd want to bathe before—"

"Ms. Dobson wore a skirt, blouse, and jacket, not exercise garments, as if she were planning to go somewhere."

"My meeting. But couldn't she have already taken her bath, leaned over to drain the tub, and hit her head?"

Miller searched through his pockets again and pulled out a heavy pocket knife, the kind with a corkscrew and nail file, then a lint-infested Tootsie Pop. No apple. Finally, he said, "I didn't mean to upset you, Ms. Bernstein."

Ellie had the feeling that he'd been about to refute her theory. What fact was he keeping from her? "Jeannie didn't have any family. She owned an old car and a small house, so she wouldn't be the prey of robbers. Besides, what burglar would take the time to drown a woman in a bathtub? Jeannie did have a boyfriend."

"The insurance agent? He was at work. Plenty of witnesses. I appreciate your answering my questions, Ms. Bernstein. You see, we have to investigate every—"

"Possibility. Yes, I know. Sorry I couldn't help, but you're way off base with that murder theory."

First base, second base, third base, home run. Ellie suddenly recalled the sexual jargon of her childhood. First base...an open-mouth kiss. Second base—touching a breast. Third base...fondling beneath the skirt? Panties? Yes, panties. Home run...all the way.

Ellie pictured a baseball bat striking an apple. Juice squirted and the peel shredded, like strips of bloody skin.

Blood. Jeannie Dobson.

"Did Jeannie bleed a lot when she thunked her head, Lieutenant?"

"She didn't hit her head."

"You weren't there. How do you know?"

"The autopsy. I believe it was murder, Ms. Bernstein."

"For goodness sake, call me Ellie. You're so—"

"Polite?"

"Wrong."

FOUR

"LOLLIPOP, LOLLIPOP, oh lolli, lollipop," sang Sandra Connors. George Bubbles waved his celery stalk and tried to picture himself as Leonard Bernstein (any relation to Ellie?), but the only image he could conjure up was Elmer Fudd. Eyes downcast, George headed toward his car.

Brian and Kelly embraced again.

Tubby Evergreen nudged his wife. "Look Lulu, we're gettin' a free show, an X-rated movie."

"That's sick, Tubby. I think it's nice to hug and kiss. The priest says—"

"What does your priest say, Lu? Seems to me you ain't seen him in months."

"I can't go to confession, Tubby. I'd have to tell Father about…about…"

"Tell him what?"

"You know." Her face tightened. "Father O'Sullivan says a good Catholic should make lots of kids, Tubby. Maybe when I lose weight we can have a baby."

"Dream on, Lulu. I had my piss checked and it ain't my fault. I want a son more than anything else in the world. Hell, you're the one who can't conceive."

"Maybe when I lose weight I'll change inside."

NOON.

Most people were eating lunch. Some restaurants added cottage cheese to a greasy hamburger and called it a diet plate. Some restaurants smothered tuna in gobs of mayonnaise and called it salad. Some restaurants touted all-natural ingredients and, naturally, charged a fortune. Brian and Kelly decided to postpone the midday meal.

Instead, they parked their van on a dirt-surfaced circle designated for sightseers, tourists, and shutterbugs. They were halfway between Cripple Creek and Colorado Springs above an incline that dipped into a tree-trimmed valley of jutting rocks and boulders. The aspen leaves were a panorama of bright orange-gold, and the mountains glowed with a lavender tint. The view was truly spectacular—had Brian and Kelly chosen to speculate. But they were in the back of the van culminating desires teasingly built at the Weight Winners meeting.

Discarding the butt of her cigarette in an ashtray on the side of the van, Kelly straddled Brian's supine body. Her hips and thighs were large, but her rib cage was toned beneath small breasts whose nipples blossomed like the flowers that dotted the mountainside.

"I'm ready again," she whispered.

"Why are you whispering? There's nobody within hearing distance for miles."

"I'm ready again," Kelly shouted.

"Sorry darling, twice is my limit." Stretched out flat on the van floor, Brian's stomach was taut.

"Are you sure?" Kelly lowered her face and nibbled at the hairs on Brian's chest, then kissed his belly button, an insie. Finally raising her chin, she said, "Okay, I give up. Funny how losing a few pounds makes one so superbly sexy. I could do this all day."

"The resident W.W. Two nymphomaniac," said Brian fondly, his eyes dreamy and unfocused without the thick-lensed glasses. Even though the Benedicts weren't rejoins, they had picked up Ellie's nickname for the class.

"I'd rather make love than eat, wouldn't you?" asked Kelly happily.

"It used to be the other way around."

"Good ol' Weight Winners. How to keep busy in your spare time."

"That was last week. This week we're supposed to control our emotions without using food. I thought that was appropriate after Jeannie Dobson's accident."

Kelly shuddered at the mention of Jeannie's death... *murder* she amended silently, even if her husband didn't agree. Cuddling her body close to Brian's, she placed her head on his chest and listened to his heartbeat.

"I have only two emotions," she said, blue eyes sparkling. "My love for you and being oversexed. Is wanting to make love to you all the time an emotion?"

"I guess so," replied Brian, reaching around her body for his pack of cigarettes. "What the hell—?" The van had rocked back and forth twice, then stopped.

"Damn Colorado breezes," said Kelly, lighting two cigarettes and handing Brian one. "Should we start back soon, honey? I hate to drive through the mountains when it's windy. The van sways."

"I want to check that antique shop in Cripple Creek for the Trasks. Honestly, those people have given new meaning to the words art deco. Then we have an appointment with Esther Abramowitz's granddaughter."

"Oh boy, a nursery. I love to design nurseries. Didn't Esther look great today? She's such a love. Bri, the van's moving again."

"It must be the wind."

"But we're going forward, not side to side."

"Did you pull up the emergency brake, hon? It sticks."

"Yes. I swear."

"Did you lock the cab?"

"No. Yes. I think so. Brian, let's get out of here."

Crawling to the back of the van, he grasped the door handle. "It's locked from the outside."

"It can't be. I have the key." Helplessly, Kelly jangled her key ring like discordant castanets."

Brian pushed against the double door with all his strength. "It's jammed, Kell. Somebody's put something through the handles."

The van dipped forward again, and they skidded to the front, finally halted by a hand-built wall that separated the van's body from the cab. Material swatches, carpet samples, and miniature Venetian blinds tumbled off their neat pegs and fell on top of Brian and Kelly's nude bodies.

On his hands and knees, Brian pulled a hammer from a box of tools and started pounding frantically on all sides of the truck.

Metal reverberated—background music composed for an avant-garde symphony, Leonard Bernstein conducting Frank Zappa.

The van dipped lower.

"Brian…"

"Kelly, I love you."

The van's back tires lost traction, and the vehicle plunged forward into space, turned over several times, rebounded off a jutting boulder, then exploded into flames at the bottom of the mountain.

GEORGE BUBBLES AWOKE from a late-afternoon nap, his dream still vivid.

He had been buried in one of his mother's casseroles—mashed potatoes, frankfurters, and peas—digging his way to the top with his hands and mouth.

Spuds, hot dog, veggie, ugh! As a kid, George used to imagine that a monster lived inside the casserole dish. A monster with a puffy white face, sausage-stuffed penis, and lots of round, squishy green eyes. But Christal claimed it was a super-duper supper; Georgie-grub when Mommy couldn't stay home; special chow for Mom's Night Out.

George's mother had been petite. Ninety pounds dripping wet. George believed that when God molded Christal Bubbles, he had reserved the additional putty for the young woman's first and only issue. Dad had died the day after George's birth, leaving as an inheritance a yellowing photograph and a pair of cowboy boots. The photo showed a small wisp of a man with a bow tie and bowlegs. George had outgrown his father's size seven boots by the age of ten.

As an infant, George was dimpled. As a toddler, he was chubby. The adolescent became hulky, the adult rotund.

His name didn't help. Christal had worked as an exotic dancer and legally changed her last name to Bubbles. George would have changed his own name, but he kept it as a memorial after Mom died on a skiing trip. She fell off a mountain, and, buried by snow, she suffocated. No wonder he dreamed about mashed potatoes.

And monsters. And sex.

George had heard that sex used up calories. That was why Christal remained so skinny until the day she tried to eat her way through the snow. George wished he could join one of those sex clinics. This Weight Winners thing wasn't working. A sex clinic sounded like a much better way to lose weight. And he was tired of picking up girls at the supermarket. They spent his money and never paid him back.

Glancing at his watch, George realized he was due to meet Hannah for happy hour.

She's a good egg, he thought. Older. A widow. Experienced. She wouldn't spend his money then laugh in his face.

He recalled the Benedicts standing near their van in the church parking lot. They had hugged and kissed. Brian Benedict wasn't that great looking. Why did some people have all the luck?

I'm forty-nine and still a virgin, he cried silently to his image in the bathroom mirror. *Ain't that a double-damn joke?* Even his bow-tied, bowlegged father had stuck it into Christal.

After a quick shower, George shaved and splashed his face with cologne. Then he kissed the life-size, painted portrait of Mom, hanging on the wall near the door.

He was ready for Georgie's Night Out.

HAPPY HOUR at the Dew Drop Inn Tavern.

Hannah was miserable. The round wooden top of the barstool was inadequate for her rump, and her legs were too short to reach the floor. She sat there, feeling like a lump of clay, while the Friday night revelers celebrated early rites of weekend. The Bible should have included a chapter called TGIF, she thought. Sodom's Palestinians could worship Chivas and Moosehead.

Close to the bar stood a table laden with free food— ground beef swimming in grease, shredded cheddar cheese, lettuce, and tomatoes. The gringo version of taco à la indigestion. An odor of corn tortilla shells overpowered perfume, popcorn, and beer. A portable TV, mounted above the bar, played a silent rerun of ''L.A. Law'' on cable's Lifetime channel. Hannah thought how about auburn-haired Susan Ruttan had lost weight and now kind of resembled Ellie Bernstein.

Ellie would not approve of the tacos. She had once handed out a typewritten list with the caloric amounts of fast-food goodies. While Kentucky-Fried Chicken headed the list, Taco Bell wasn't far behind.

Hannah watched George refill his plate for the third time. Red salsa dripped onto his chin as he sampled, not content to wait until he had returned to his space at the bar. Finally, he set a paper plate between her elbows, then pressed his perspiring form close to her seated one.

"I can't eat that."

"Why not? Beef and salad. You can count the shell as a bread." George signaled the Dew Drop's owner-bartender. "Bring my pretty lady a schnapps, Charley."

Charley placed two overflowing happy hour shot glasses in front of Hannah. "No, George, really," she wailed, trying to read the numbers on her Timex, holding the watch up to the glow from a neon Jack Daniel's sign. Six-oh-five. Five! Oh! The same number as the pounds she had gained last week from bingeing.

She spied a young girl at the buffet table, scooping mounds of lettuce onto her taco. The girl was skinny, dressed in a white jersey miniskirt and shirred halter top. Hannah watched with fascination as the young woman leaned over the table toward the napkins.

"Look at that *tush*," said Charley.

No underwear! My God, what if she was in an accident...a car crash, thought Hannah. *How indecent!* Hannah defiantly downed the schnapps. It tasted like peppermint mouthwash. She bit into a taco, savoring the crispy corn shell and tangy filling. Assailed by sudden thirst, she lifted the second shot glass. "Here's mud in your eye, George."

"Atta' girl," he said, again signaling Charley.

Another set of glasses sloshed on the bar's surface.

A couple of hours later Hannah tried to focus on George's face. She saw extras of everything. Four faded blue eyes, two heads of brown hair, parted in the middle, and a double set of double chins.

"I know why you're doin' this; to ease your con... consh...conscience. If you're gonna cheat, you want company. I know." She took another sip from her schnapps, which now tasted like an after-dinner mint, and hiccuped behind her hand. The free tacos had disappeared and the end of happy hour, but the thirst remained. "Down the hatch, Georgie."

"Atta' girl." George seemed to have run out of vocabulary, and he said the same thing every time she downed her drink.

"I'm gettin' drunk as skunk as drunk as skunk," chanted Hannah. She couldn't recall ever in her entire life being inebriated. Giddy, maybe, from the bubbly champagne served at her daughter Earline's wedding. "Drunk as skunk as...I...I'm..." She thought the word inebriated clearly in her head, but couldn't get the word out. "I'm detoxicated," she finally shouted triumphantly. Two strolling revelers burst out laughing. "Are you drunk, Georgie Porgie?"

"Nope."

"Don't believe you. Say something."

"What do you want me to say?"

"Susie shifted she-shells at the she-shore while shy-lent Sammy smiled."

"Don't know that one."

"Everybody knows 'Susie She-shells.'"

"I'm not drunk, Hannah. Listen. Peter Piper pricked a

peck of pickled peckers. How many pecks of pickled peckers did Peter Pipe prick?''

"Okay, you're not drunk Georgie."

"I'm large-boned like you, Hannah. We can drink more than ordinary people."

"Ordinary people," she repeated, wincing and watching George slurp the last of his beer, then the glass of whiskey next to it. "Boil-er-makers," he called them. She and Jeannie had once played Scrabble and looked up the word boil. It meant "to generate bubbles of vapor when heated." *Boil down*... "to undergo reduction in bulk by boiling." *Boiling*... "intensely agitated."

Funny how she could remember that when she couldn't even say "Susie She-shells" or "Peter Pecker."

"Bottoms up, Georgie."

"Atta' girl."

Another glass of slosh schnapped. How many had she drunk? Not, not drunk...toxic...toxicated.

"I'm not large-boned. Earl used to say I was peasant, uh, pleasantly pumped."

"I'll pump ya', Hannah. Want one for the road?"

"No! Please. Can't drive. Glasses don't work. Fuzzy. Fuzzy Wuzzy was a beer. I mean, bear."

"I'll drive ya' home." George helped her off the stool. "The Dew Drop should buy from my discount furniture outlet. Better stuff, and I'd get Charley a good price."

"You own a furn...furn'ture store?"

"Not exactly own, but I got stock. C'mon, babe, we need to work off those taco calories."

Guiding Hannah toward the exit, George furtively studied her. If Hannah cut and fluffed her hair, lost about seventy-five pounds, and removed her glasses, she'd look a lot like Christal. The double-damn spittin' image.

"BRING ME SOME PINEAPPLE slices, Lulu," ordered Tubby Evergreen, settling onto the couch in front of the console television.

"You already had three fruits. The plan says you can only eat three."

Tubby rose from his ass-dented cushion, then walked toward his wife, who was washing dinner dishes. He spun her around and slapped her hard across the face.

"Don't tell me what I can or cannot eat. Don't tell me what to do."

"But Tubby, you said to count your food portions…" Lulu hesitated when her husband again raised his hand in a threatening gesture. "There's no more fruit," she cried in alarm as Tubby pulled open the refrigerator door. "I always go shopping on Saturday after Friday's meeting. I make lists of all the right foods and…what are you doing?"

"What does it look like I'm doing, you dumb bitch?"

"You found a can of beer. You can't drink beer on Weight Winners."

Tubby threw the Coors can toward Lulu's head. She ducked just in time. The can hit tiles above the sink and burst; foam sprayed the freshly washed dishes and Lulu's black ringlets.

"There's no more Coors," Tubby whined, his head buried inside the refrigerator.

"You said I shouldn't buy beer. You said to keep the wrong foods out of the house."

Tubby brushed past his wife and yanked open the door to a utility room. He rummaged through a wicker hamper of dirty laundry, tossing soiled clothing in every direction.

"Lulu, dammit, I hid a package of chocolate-covered graham crackers in here."

"I know. I found them. I threw them away."

"*What?*"

"You said to throw out all the wrong food."

"When did you dump the cookies?"

"Yesterday."

"The Fig Newtons in the bathroom cabinet?"

"Yes-yes-yesterday."

"You dumb bitch!"

"I was only doing what you told me to do."

"Tubby weaved his fingers through his wife's damp curls and pulled her across the kitchen, into the living room. Roughly, he pushed her unresisting body on top of a sturdy piano bench.

"Play something," he ordered.

"What do you want me to play?"

"I don't care. Sing about the mule. That's what you remind me of, Lulu. A mule's sterile, can't have babies."

"Do you mean the Erie Canal song?"

"Yeah. Keep playing until I tell you to stop."

Lulu hit a few introductory notes. Tremulously she warbled, "'I've got a mule, her name is Sal—'"

"Her name is Lulu," sang Tubby.

"'Fifteen miles on the Erie Canal. She's a good old worker and a good old pal... Fifteen miles on the Erie Canal.'" Lulu hesitated, her hands poised above the keyboard. "Where're you going, Tubby?"

"Out. Can't get no food in this damn house. Keep playing."

"'We've hauled some barges in our day,'" she sang. "Tubby, please don't go out. 'Filled with lumber, coal, and hay.' Tubby, you'll be mad if you don't lose weight this week. 'And we know every inch of the way.' Tubby, I'll make you a shake with skim milk and vanilla extract.

'From Albany to Buff-a-low-oh'—*oh, Tubby,*'' she wailed as she heard the front door slam.

'' 'Low bridge, everybody down. Low bridge, for we're going through a town. And you'll always know your neighbors, you'll always know your pal....''' Lulu slammed her fists across the black and white keys. Suddenly she desperately wanted a Dairy Queen hot-fudge sundae.

I could go to church, she thought, tears streaming down her face. I could go to confession, but then I'd have to tell Father about Tubby, about me, about us.

Why did Tubby act that way? So mean all the time. Because she, Lulu, was overweight, that's why. She'd seen the admiring glances her husband bestowed on Ellie, Wanda, Kelly, and Darlene. Lulu knew she'd never look like Darlene—not even if she lost a trillion pounds.

Walking into the kitchen, she retrieved the Coors can, entered the foyer, and hurled the can at a wall mirror, hard as she could. The mirror shattered. But it didn't help. Because now she could see herself slivered into a trillion Lulus. And they all looked the same. As if they'd lost hope rather than weight.

THEY GOT LOST once or twice on the way home, with George trying to follow Hannah's incoherent directions. Finally, they pulled into a driveway only a few blocks from the recently deceased Jeannie Dobson's house.

"Thank you, Mr. Boilermaker," said Hannah politely, swaying at the doorstep. She extended her hand, but George brushed past.

"Nice," he announced, surveying the entrance hall and hanging chandelier. From the back of the house came a series of sharp high-pitched barks that trailed off into a wheeze. "What's that?"

"My dog...my Doberman. His name is Killer, and I have to keep him chained because he bites. He's a watch dog." The cool breeze had cleared her head a little. Had she really said pump for plump? Beer for Bear? Toxic for intoxicated?

George looked momentarily disconcerted. Then he placed his arm around Hannah's shoulders. "Where's the bedroom?"

"Upstairs. But, Georgie, you mustn't stay."

"C'mon, babe, I can't find my way out of this neighborhood in the dark."

"Well, all right. There's a sleeper couch in the den."

"Let me help you upstairs first."

"Thank you, but I really feel fine."

"Every other step of the week is fi-yine," sang George. "Which room?" he asked after they'd ascended.

"Turn right. Here. This one. Thank you. Good night."

"You gotta be kiddin'." Swiftly George pulled off his blazer, wool trousers, and slip-on loafers, leaving thin-ribbed socks, the WORLD'S GREATEST LOVER T-shirt, and a pair of oversize shorts.

He was at the waistband of his shorts when Hannah said, "Go home, George."

"I didn't figure you for a tease, babe."

"I wasn't teasing. I said you could sleep in the den. I didn't invite you up here."

"Aw, c'mon," pleaded George, using his weight to nudge Hannah backwards until her legs pressed against the side of the bed.

"If you don't get out of here, I'm going to unchain Slayer—"

"Killer."

"Yes, and I'm going to sic him on you," yelled Han-

nah angrily, remembering the shade of fear he had shown
in the front hallway.

"I don't believe you have a dog." George laughed
unpleasantly.

"I do have a dog!"

George slid his fingers beneath the black beaded necklace around Hannah's throat and twisted it into a small
knot at her pulse throb.

She gasped for breath.

"I spent a lot of dough-ray-me on you tonight. Now
deliver." Pushing her onto the bed, he jumped on top.

The phone rang.

"George, my telephone—"

"Let it ring."

"No." With all her strength, Hannah shifted her body.
Susie sifts seashells by the seashore, she thought clearly.

George rolled away until he reached the edge of the
bed, fell over, and landed in a sprawled position on the
floor.

Hannah staggered into a guest room, closed and locked
the door, then picked up the extension. Earline calling
collect from California.

She was full of complaints.

The baby had the earache again and they were thinking
about taking out his tonsils. Her car needed repairs and
you couldn't live in California without a car. There was
this new diet doctor who counted many famous movie
stars among his clientele. He charged fifty bucks a visit,
but guaranteed the results, and Earline would send Hannah the formula, so it was really like paying only twenty-
five dollars. And why did all the women in the family
get the fat genes because Daddy and Jack were so
skinny? Her whine indicated Hannah's fault.

Feeling fuzzy (but no longer fuzzy-wuzzy) Hannah

tried to total the amount of the check she'd have to send her daughter. Another "gift."

The hallway grandfather clock chimed nine times as she reluctantly returned to her bedroom. Georgie Porgie boilermaker Bubbles had disappeared.

Hannah walked over to the window. The night was dark as a sheet of semisweet chocolate, but she could see that George's car had vanished, too.

THE SMELL OF FRESH-BAKED challah still permeated the kitchen. Esther Abramowitz finished rinsing the last dinner dish and wiped her hands on the terry-cloth towel she wore as an apron. Then she patted her neat silver bun of hair.

It had been a nice Sabbath meal. Judith, six months pregnant, with her husband, Manny, beaming at her side. They had tried so hard to conceive—five years—and just when they had given up, and Judith was calling her third-grade elementary school class her "children," God had answered Esther's prayers.

"If it's a boy, we're going to name him for Papa Sam," said Judith. Esther had felt such a rush of love for her eldest granddaughter, and sorrow that her husband, Samuel—may he rest in peace—had died of cancer before he could witness this happy event.

Esther's youngest granddaughter had picked at the roast chicken, then excused herself for a date. Twice-divorced Glory—whose real name was Gertrude—looked skinny to the point of being anemic. Or what did they call it now? *Anorexic.* To Esther, anorexic sounded like a soap opera star on TV.

And what kind of name was Glory? "A model's name," said her youngest granddaughter, looking even thinner next to Judith's blooming pregnancy. Gertrude…Glory was trying a modeling career in New York City, but had flown into the Springs to attend her high school reunion.

"You look like a model yourself, Nana," Judith had said, before leaving with Manny for the short drive home. Judith and her husband complimented Esther's weight loss, admiring the report card and goal certificate. Gertrude had originally greeted her grandmother at the airport with a skeptical glance. "You look skinny as a wet noodle, Nana," she announced in disapproving tones.

Esther removed her towel-apron. She straightened her size-ten black dress, decorated by a string of pearls around her neck. Real pearls. A 1987 Chanukah gift from Samuel, may he rest in peace.

I used to be fat as a loaf of my challah, thought Esther, but now I'm skinny as a wet noodle, and proud of it.

Padding in floppy slippers to the living room, she settled into a comfortable armchair and pulled her knitting needles from a carpetbag satchel. She was making a sweater for Samuel—may he rest…no, no baby Samuel ("Or Samantha," said Judith) and had already completed a blanket and booties.

The doorbell chimed.

"Who's there?"

"Ellie Bernstein."

"Come in, come in, darling," said Esther, removing the chain lock. "Good Shabbas. You just missed my Judith and her husband. A piece of fresh fruit or a small glass of Manischewitz?"

"No, thank you. I hope you don't mind, Esther, but I was driving, thinking about Jeannie Dobson, and I passed your house. The lights were on…"

"Sit, darling, you look sad."

Ellie smiled. "Don't be polite, Esther. I look awful...lonely."

"Sad, lonely, the same thing. My son's in Israel, but my granddaughter is a delight and lives close. Your little boy is away at school, isn't he?"

"Yes, only he's not so little anymore. Don't let me interrupt what you planned—"

"I planned to knit and watch that good-looking reporter announce the news on my color television. What's his name? Ron? Sit, relax, and maybe we'll have some good news for a change." Esther pressed her remote-control button.

The screen showed a sincere man with thickly sprayed and sculpted hair. Ron was talking about an accident on the mountain where a van had plunged off the top and burned one of its occupants. The other victim was in critical condition at the hospital.

Frowning, Esther reached for what Samuel, may he rest in peace, had always called the "clicker." "We don't want bad news, do we Ellie?" About to switch the channel, Esther heard Ron announce names. Brian Benedict, dead, and Kelly Benedict, hovering between life and death.

That nice young couple from her Weight Winners class.

"Oh dear, Judith complained that Mrs. Benedict didn't show up for an estimate on a new baby nursery. Ellie? Ellie dear, are you all right?"

"I have to leave, Esther. I'm sorry. I'll drive to the hospital and see if there's anything I can do for Kelly. First Jeannie, now Brian and...and...what the hell is happening to my friends?"

"You shouldn't drive alone. You're too upset. I could telephone Judith's husband, Manny—"

"I'm okay Esther. Thank you."

After closing and bolting the door, Esther returned to her armchair and switched the TV to another channel. Johnny Carson, only it wasn't Johnny because Johnny was never on his own show. And it wasn't the funny Jewish lady, something Rivers. She'd left the show before Samuel died. Samuel, may he rest in peace, had loved watching Rivers.

Esther picked up her needles. Knit one, purl one, knit two, purl two.

How awful, she thought, people dying. Not old people either, although Jeannie Dobson, may she rest in peace, was no spring chicken.

Well, death is a part of life, thought Esther philosophically. She glanced at the framed photos gracing the mantel of her fireplace. Would she be so accepting if it had been her beloved Judith inside that van? Or her son who lived near that filthy demon, Arafat.

Tomorrow she would attend Saturday morning services and say Kaddish for both Jeannie and Brian. Should she send another donation for a tree in Brian's name?

The chime of the front doorbell interrupted her thoughts. She smiled. Ellie had changed her mind and decided to return. Good. Unalarmed, Esther padded to the door, her backless slippers flapping. The glow from the Sabbath candles created a soft heavenly aureole.

"Who's there?" she called before releasing the bolt.

SIX-THIRTY a.m.

Esther's television flickered into colorful animation with its first Saturday morning kiddie-cartoon. "The Bugs Bunny and Tweety Show."

Returning from her all-night date, Glory found her grandmother seated in the comfortable armchair. Esther—may she rest in peace—was surrounded by baby-fine wool, and two knitting needles were poking out from her neck. A Weight Winners report card and goal certificate were practically buried in Esther's size-ten lap.

Glory instinctively raised one hand to her own throat. *Why did Nana change her necklace from pearls to garnets?*

"I t'ought I taw a puddy tat," chirped the yellow bird in delighted fright.

Nana looks like wet noodles covered with tomato sauce, thought Glory.

Then she screamed bloody murder.

FIVE

GLORY EDEN (née Gertrude Edith Abramowitz) bolted from the house.

"No, not noodles, worms. Tweety eats worms! Tweety eats worms!" she shouted over and over.

A few curious neighbors appeared. Men in bathrobes. Women holding spatulas. Several children formed a circle and sang: "The worms crawl in, the worms crawl out..."

Finally one woman walked up to Glory. "What's the matter, dear? Did something happen to your grandmother?"

"And one little worm who was very shy crawled in her ear and out her eye...."

APPROXIMATELY SEVEN MILES away, Ellie jogged toward Colorado College. The sun gleamed faintly, like a Brach's butterscotch candy packaged in cellophane.

I should have worn gloves, she thought, shivering. Ellie had once been told that Colorado had two seasons—winter and July.

The month of September was fickle. Like a woman with a full closet of clothes and nothing to wear, Ms. September could never decide if she wanted to continue with sleeveless blouses or break out the heavy sweaters. And the weather was about as easy to predict as the state's lotto game.

Today's sun made a valiant effort to shine through. Gazing up at the cloudy sky, Ellie estimated that it might be tomorrow, or next July, before heat successfully permeated. Already the distant mountains wore snowcaps. Hadn't George Bubbles once confessed that his mother was buried in an avalanche? Poor George. How could he endure living in Colorado after that terrible mishap?

Ellie wore her Mickey Mouse thermals, blue velour, and black sweatpants. Around her wrist was an orange change purse with a Denver Bronco logo. Thick socks were tucked into tightly laced sneakers, keeping her feet toasty. Only her fingers and knuckles felt the bite of impending winter. A few more blocks of jogging, then Ellie could warm her hands on a steaming mug of hot coffee.

She was meeting Sandra Connors for breakfast and looking forward to the break in routine. Sandra, with her exciting review of a personal life fraught with important trivia, would sweep away Ellie's depression over the deaths of Jeannie Dobson and Brian Benedict. Kelly, comatose, still clung to the barest thread of life. Although Ellie had dozed in the hospital's waiting room most of the night, she hadn't been allowed to enter ICU. Finally she'd given up and returned home.

Two accidents in two weeks. Could number three be waiting around the corner? Ellie could recall her mother reading the Milestones section of *Time* magazine and enumerating the deaths of famous personalities. Business tycoons or obscure authors and statesmen didn't count; only superstar quality need apply. And they always arrived in increments of three. Rationally, Ellie supposed that if you waited long enough and gruesomely kept close track, a third demise would have to come along. Crossing her fingers, she prayed that Kelly would recover.

She thought about her brief interview with the police detective, Peter Miller, and his insinuations that Jeannie's death had been a homicide. He had paused when Ellie expounded her sensible conclusion.

Why? She pictured the scene. Jeannie had bathed, dressed, then returned to the bathroom for last-minute ministrations to face or hair. The tub had not been emptied. Leaning over, bending forward, Jeannie reached for the drain release or rubber stopper.

Then what? Jeannie lost her balance and tumbled over the edge. How big was the bathtub? Why didn't she just haul herself out again, dripping wet and wearing a blue streak? Because…because she'd bumped her head.

But the detective insisted she hadn't hit her head. Furthermore, Jeannie had a terrific sense of balance. Even overweight, she'd displayed a ballerina's grace.

Ellie snapped her cold fingers. *Of course!* Lots of times her members fasted before meetings in a last-minute effort to lose a final pound or two. Instead of sticking to the food program, they would follow a liquid diet to drain a few ounces before stepping on the intimidating medical scale. Jeannie had been so close to goal weight. ("Maybe today the scale will eat my last five," she'd said that very morning.) Perhaps Jeannie wanted to reach her magic goal number and denied herself sustenance, and become dizzy from lack of food…that made sense, didn't it? Dizzy and weak, Jeannie blacked out, fell into the tub, and drowned.

Ellie had always told her members that if they averaged one pound a week, they'd finish the year losing fifty-two pounds. Did she fail to get her point across? Was Jeannie's death partly her fault?

Mentally, Ellie began composing another lecture warning against the extreme deprivation technique of fasting. *What you don't eat can kill you.* Two meetings ago,

Wanda had complained that the message was a bit much. Ellie had to disagree.

Arriving at the restaurant, she ducked inside, grateful for immediate warmth. She was exactly on time, since Sandra had promised to meet her at seven. A few people sat reading Saturday morning newspapers. Ellie released her auburn waves from the restrictive rubber band, and the freed hair tumbled about her shoulders. Sighing in comfort, she signaled for a mug of coffee.

A long-skirted, Greek-sandaled waitress handed Ellie the steaming brew. "You must be the diet-club lady."

"That's right." Ellie studied the *zaftig* young woman. If *I* looked like that, I wouldn't worry about a few excess pounds, she thought. Dark hair and eyes sparkled with healthy vitality, and the colorfully patterned skirt emphasized comfortable curves. *She* probably thinks she's overweight. Was the positive identification an invitation to discuss Weight Winners? Ahhh...fame!

"The girl described you perfectly; Roxanne on 'L.A. Law.'" The waitress placed tiny cups of cream in the middle of the table. "You're wanted on the phone."

Sandra's voice sounded tired as she canceled the breakfast appointment. Her college dorm-mate, Natalie, had the flu. Ellie wanted Sandra to be careful and not catch Natalie's bug. (After all, Jeannie wasn't around with her plastic containers of frozen chicken broth.)

Returning to her little round table, Ellie brushed against an open newspaper and some pages fell to the floor.

"Oh, I'm sorry." Bending forward to retrieve the entertainment section, she looked up into blue-gray eyes. "Good morning, Lieutenant Miller."

"Good morning, Ms. Bernstein."

"For goodness' sake, call me Ellie."

"Still spitting?"

"Not in public." She handed him the newspaper pages. "Still investigating homicides?"

"Yup. In fact, I planned to call you."

"Why?"

"I need a list of your diet-club members."

"All of them?"

"Yes, ma'am."

"I can get you the list by next Friday's meeting. Wanda Henry has that information."

"Why will it take six days—?"

"Because I can't just hand over the original file. All the information is confidential. Some of my members are really heavy, and they wouldn't want their weight broadcast to the public, or the damn-fool police department for that matter."

"Now wait a minute—"

"And I want to talk to an attorney; find out what my legal rights are. Maybe you need a subpoena or something."

"A subpoena?"

"I told you Jeannie had no family, but apparently there's a nephew. Does he inherit her station wagon?"

"Yes, but he was in Boston."

"Good Lord, you guys are serious. Don't the police have enough work to do solving real crimes?"

"Why are you so angry?"

"Because I consider myself a pretty good detective and I can't think of one single motive for killing Jeannie."

"Some murders have no obvious motives, Ms. Bernstein. Why do you consider yourself a good detective?"

"I'm not even tolerable at math or science, and computers scare the hell out of me. But my mind stores in-

formation like the proverbial sponge. I've never seen a
TV show where I haven't figured out the killer and motive by the second commercial. That's not bragging. It's
just something I'm good at. By the way, what information were you keeping from me about Jeannie's accident?''

Miller chuckled. "You sound like Peter what's-his-
name, that movie detective."

"Peter Ustinov? Peter Sellers?"

"No, Peter Falk, Columbo."

"How would Peter *Miller* respond to my question?"

"Ms. Bernstein, has it ever occurred to you that the
police withhold information until they're sure they've
captured the real killer? To keep all the nuts and dolts
from confessing."

"Am I a suspect, Lieutenant?"

"Everybody's a suspect in an investigation. That's
why I'd appreciate a list of your diet clubbers ASAP."
Miller softened his voice. "Did you hear about the Benedicts? Weren't they memb—"

"Are you suggesting that the accidents of Jeannie
Dobson and the Benedicts are connected?"

"We're investigating every—"

"Possibility. Yes, you've told me."

"You're getting huffy again."

"Huffy? The big bad wolf huffs. I'm furious."

"Why?"

"Because I don't like your insinuations about my diet-
club members. They all admired Jeannie. Kelly and
Brian, too. What would be the motive? Jealousy of
weight loss?"

"Wouldn't you consider that a motive?"

"Not at all. Weight Winners is a *support* group, Lieutenant. We all cheer one another on, applaud successes.

And why pick on my group? There are dozens of weight reduction programs in the city.''

"I don't know the answer right now. If there is a connection, that's what I have to discover.''

"Would you care to join me for a cup of coffee?'' Ellie found herself asking.

"Yes, but I have to find a phone. My Roadrunner-beeper interrupted breakfast. Maybe another time.''

If Miller had been wearing a hat, he would have tipped it as an exit gesture, thought Ellie, returning to her table and cold coffee. Mr. Polite. Sipping a fresh cup of brew, she watched the waitress clear Miller's table. He had consumed a hearty meal; all that remained were pits and peels from a fruit plate. His beeper *interrupted* breakfast? Had he meant to order more food? Holy cow!

A couple of weeks ago, I compared myself to an overripe piece of fruit ready for the picking, Ellie mused. Yesterday Miller sculpted his apple like Michelangelo carving a miniature statue. Investigate every possibility, indeed! Miller had ended that interview politely, too, and Prince Charming rode off into the horizon behind the steering wheel of a Plymouth Scamp. Not even a real police car. Scamp. The name fit.

Why have I been dwelling on that Scamp? Wasn't he part of the reason I drove around aimlessly last night before I imposed on Esther? Why? Because I'm attracted to the man, that's why.

Do I believe in love at first sight? No. Lust at first sight? You bet! The next time I see Peter Miller, I'll get myself some of those swishy pom-poms and wear my tennis outfit with the ruffled panties. Rah-rah!

Maybe I've been thinking about him because of his stupid murder theory. Killing Jeannie doesn't make any sense. What would be the motive? Weight loss envy?

Jeannie went out of her way to help fellow members. She'd be the last person a killer would choose. If a deranged psychotic was stalking a loser, why not pick on me?

Abstractedly, Ellie noted her *zaftig* waitress spraying blue-hued cleaner across wide windows that fronted the street. As the pane of glass became clearer, an outline of a face appeared—indistinct features under a stocking cap pulled low. The streaky windows blurred the image, but it had to be the same person who had spied on Ellie from behind the gnarly tree in Acacia Park.

Throwing five quarters on the tabletop, Ellie abandoned her cup of coffee and swiftly scurried through the open door of the restaurant.

"I'm going to find out who the hell you are," she muttered, jogging around the block, trying to discover denim pants and pea jacket.

The sidewalks were bare, the shops closed, and only the enticing odors from a bakery on the southeast corner invaded the eerie stillness. The bulky figure who had just lurked at the restaurant's window had either ducked into one of the parked cars that dotted the street, or else had disappeared into thin air. *Thin* air. There, that proved it. Why didn't the stalker pull Ellie into the recesses of a doorway, shout "I'm jealous of your successful weight loss," and clunk her over the head or something.

Startled, she watched a Plymouth Scamp skid up the curb. Peter Miller unfolded his long legs to the street, then walked toward her.

"Did you change your mind about that cup of coffee?"

"Would you come with me, please?"

"Have you decided that I'm your number one suspect? Wait a minute, you're serious. What's happened?"

"I'm on my way to the home of another diet-club member."

"Who?"

"Please get in the car."

"Who, Lieutenant?"

"Stubborn! Are you always so stubborn?"

"Who's been hurt now?"

"Mrs. Abramowitz. I wanted to tell you before you heard about it on the news."

"Esther? I saw her last night. She was fine. What the hell happened? Why are you looking so…so strange? Esther's dead, isn't she. Number three, dammit."

Ellie felt Miller's arms circle her shoulders.

"Ms. Bernstein, are you okay? Ooops." Swiftly, he pulled open his car door. "Here, sit on the seat. Bend your head between your knees and take a deep breath. That's a good girl."

"I'm all right. Go away, Lieutenant."

"It's my car," said Miller softly.

She took another deep breath. "Was it an accident?"

"No, ma'am, this time it was definitely murder."

BEING ON A DIET REQUIRES GREAT
WON'T POWER.

Hannah saluted the chalkboard, stepped off the scale, and tossed her report card inside her purse. She had lost the five-pound gain from last week.

After hearing about Esther's murder, Brian Benedict's death, and Kelly's lingering coma, she had again felt like gorging herself, but Ellie's lecture about not letting emotional problems result in an eating binge had stuck. Besides, all she had to do was think about last week's debacle with Georgie Bubbles and her desire for the wrong food would evaporate.

Was that stupid evening her fault?

She pictured George sprawled on the floor. He'd turned from menacing to pathetic, his lips quivering like a little boy's, and had subsequently flown the coop.

The very next morning, with the first hangover of her entire life, Hannah had made a mental pledge to reach her goal weight. Maybe she could set an example for George. So she had stuck precisely to the food program for the rest of the week, and Wanda had been ever so complimentary.

Smiling at the young woman, Hannah thought how Wanda Henry had lost sixty pounds in spite of a husband who poked fun at the diet, plus overweight parents who were always telling her that she "looked sickly."

If Wanda could do it, so could she.

Standing beside the medical scale, Wanda—who would celebrate her thirtieth birthday on Thanksgiving day—knew she had never felt healthier or looked prettier. Her ginger-colored hair, once extremely short, had grown to shoulder length, and she wore it in a soft curly perm. Kelly green eyes were subtly enhanced by light makeup, which she had learned to apply at a free seminar provided by the Weight Winners organization. Her trim body was clothed in a plaid pleated skirt with a wide belt cinched over a crocheted sweater; secretly, she thought that her waist looked almost as tiny as Vivian Leigh's in the opening scenes of *Gone With the Wind.*

Wanda shifted Hannah's card to the back of the index file. For the last few weeks she had been trying to organize the cards in her spare time. There were graduates, dropouts, transfers, and, of course, the deceased.

Jeannie Dobson, Brian Benedict, and sweet Esther

Abramowitz, whom Wanda adored. Esther had even promised that, after the birth of her first great-grandchild, she was going to knit Wanda a muffler. Wanda dabbed at tears with the back of her hand, tears that had begun when the homicide detective questioned her earlier. He was now talking to Ellie in one of the church's Bible classrooms.

After weighing in another member Wanda placed his index card behind Hannah's. There was an additional reason for categorizing the list. Wanda planned to make attractive parchment scrolls for Christmas presents. Even though the holidays were two months away, the intricately designed parchment, like diplomas, took hours to create, and she still had to cater to Henry and her ten-year-old twins.

The scrolls, which were headlined LOSE TO WIN, included the member's name, plus a witticism: THE IDEAL DIET IS EXPRESSED IN FOUR WORDS: ''NO MORE, THANK YOU.''

Wanda noticed Tubby and Lulu Evergreen enter the room, and she winced because she believed that Tubby's humor was hurtful rather than amusing, even when directed at himself and Lulu. His sarcastic barbs enlivened the meeting, but Wanda thought they were negative rather than positive. Tubby Evergreen worked for the Department of Motor Vehicles and bragged about scaring the hell out of first-time applicants before they took their written exams. Sometimes Lulu appeared at the meetings with bruises and joked about being so clumsy, she'd trip over her own shadow. (''Don't know how I can trip over my own shadow, Wanda, since it's big as me.'') Today Lulu wore a duplicate of her husband's denim overalls and a frilly yellow blouse.

Tubby approached the scale, then mimed removing all

his clothes, including his diamond pinkie ring and rimless glasses. Wanda thought his antics grotesque, but the rest of the group laughed. He did register a two-pound loss. Dropping to his knees, Tubby pretended to kiss Wanda's feet.

Lulu repeated, with less success, the imaginary action of removing her garments.

Darlene was right behind them. "I can do that, too," she announced with a smile. The ex-stripper started a short, sensual dance, discarding imaginary long gloves. Turning her back, she pretended to unzip a dress and release her bra. The class applauded; Tubby leered; Lulu scowled.

Aha, so Lulu *can* react, thought Wanda. Maybe she's not Tubby's doormat. I wonder what would happen if Lulu really lost her temper and fought back. She looks strong.

Before weighing Darlene, Wanda slipped Tubby's and Lulu's cards to the back of her file.

COLORING-BOOK PAGES of Christ were mounted on the classroom walls. One benevolent Jesus, in green robes and with purple-tinted skin, gazed down at the man and woman squeezed into miniature chairs with attached arm-desks.

Ellie surreptitiously glanced at her watch and realized that it was almost time to start her lecture. But Lieutenant Miller continued asking questions about her late-night visit to Esther. Today he wore a charcoal wool-blend suit, a white shirt that smelled of bleach, and a knotted tie, slightly askew.

He fingered his mustache where silver strands mingled with black. A long nose, once obviously broken, had been incorrectly reset, and angled in the same direction as his tie. His dark hair was too long and curled untidily at the neckline. Ellie stared into his blue-gray eyes.

"How old are you?" she blurted.

"Forty-five. Is that too old?"

"For what?"

"For anything."

It's the nose, decided Ellie. That's why I've been thinking about him so often. The broken nose. Her ex-husband Tony had movie-star-quality features, but Peter Miller's nose had character.

"I don't believe I really thanked you for telling me about Esther last Saturday, for letting me know in person."

"How are you feeling now?"

"Better. After the sorrow comes blind anger. You hear the crime statistics and watch clever murders on television, but you're not really prepared for it in real life. By the way, you guys did a good job of keeping the photographers away. Esther wouldn't have appreciated having her picture splashed all over the newspapers."

"I guess the 'damn-fool police department' has a few redeeming qualities."

"I'm sorry I said that. And I did try to get your list ASAP. The Weight Winners headquarters is located in Denver. I called and they promised to send me a duplicate list. But ever since the postage rates went up, it takes a millennium to receive mail. Wanda spent the week with her parents. Unlisted phone and I don't know the address. Her husband…well, he gets a tad belligerent about Weight Winners, so I didn't think he'd give me—"

"Why does he get belligerent?"

"Henry's like an alcoholic who ridicules AA."

"Would he be jealous over somebody losing weight?"

"Oh no, quite the opposite. You see, Henry doesn't

believe he *has* a weight problem. When Henry looks in the mirror, he sees Don what's-his-name?"

"Don King?"

"No. Don Knotts...Andy Griffith's deputy. Speaking of deputies and police procedures, was the motive robbery? Esther had some really expensive stuff."

"She wasn't robbed. Valuable silver candlesticks and a pearl necklace were untouched. That wacko didn't even try to make it look like an accident this time."

"This time?"

"Ms. Bernstein, we now have an MO. Do you know what that means?"

"Of course. I watch TV."

Although his eyes remained troubled, the detective responded with a lazy grin. It's the mustache, thought Ellie. The mustache gives his mouth character.

"We could write off the van as an accident," said Miller, "but the ladies with their Weight Winners cards...well, that's too much of a coincidence. And I would venture to bet that the Benedicts were among the victims."

"Victims," Ellie repeated.

"They were all members of your group who had either reached or were close to their goal weights. Remember when we discussed motive?"

"Have you really concluded that the killer is an unhappy member who hasn't lost weight?" she asked incredulously. "His or her motive is murdering thin people because they're thin?"

"That would be an obvious conclusion. Or else it's somebody who was jealous of the weight others had lost, which I suppose is the same thing. In any case, I really do need that list of members today, especially recent dropouts and people who have been unsuccessful—"

"Holy cow! Lots of men and women lose very slowly or plateau for a few weeks."

Miller grinned again. "One of my detectives thinks I'm a first-class anachronism, but I've never used cows to express my feelings. Bulls, maybe."

"It's a long story," Ellie mumbled.

"I need you to enumerate the names of those who don't lose at all, or have a certain attitude," said Miller, serious again. "You'd know the difference, wouldn't you?"

"Yes, but—"

"And I want the names of those who are close to...graduating?"

"Well, it's more complicated than that. There's the maintenance program and lifetime membership. How far back do you want me to go?"

"Let's start with six months."

"All the Weight Winners groups or just Good Shepherd?"

"The church."

"Okay, my only recent graduate is Darlene. Darlene...uh...I'll have to look up her last name. Anyway, she's on her maintenance program and has been very successful. To my knowledge, Jeannie and the Benedicts were the only others close to goal weight. And Esther, of course. I still can't believe she's gone." Ellie swallowed a sob.

Miller patted her shoulder with the hand that had once juggled an apple. "I need your membership file today," he repeated softly.

"Of course." Ellie hesitated, then asked, "Why did you wait so long to question me about Esther?"

"Truthfully, we were eliminating other possibilities. Despite what you've read about investigations, there's lots of paperwork, and we've been contacting other states to see if a similar MO is in progress.''

"I thought you just punched a few buttons on a computer."

"I thought computers scared the hell out of you. How about dinner tonight?"

"What?"

"The meal following lunch, before a midnight snack."

Ellie squeezed out a strained smile. "I don't snack late at night," she replied emphatically.

"It's in the line of duty, and you're not wearing a wedding band."

"How perceptive, detective. I'm divorced. Are you married? What do you mean by line of duty?"

"If the killer is permanently removing weight losers...or winners...you would be an obvious victim...choice," Miller revised as Ellie winced. "You've not only reached your goal, but you're helping others to do the same thing. It's logical to get you out of the picture instead of eliminating members of your group one by one. I'm assigning myself to keep an eye on you. That's what I meant by line of duty. No, I'm not married."

"The person in the cap."

"What man in the cap?"

"Not man. Person. Lately, when I jog, I have the feeling I'm being watched, followed. Somebody wearing a stocking cap, jeans, and a bulky gray-green pea jacket."

"Well, I'm not too hot to trot—I mean, jogging's not exactly my thing—but I guess I can partner you."

"Don't be ridiculous. There are always other people around. And I like to jog alone. I use my exercise time as thinking time, Lieutenant."

"What hour in the morning do you do this lope?"

"Actually, I had almost finished when we ran into each other at the restaurant. I start around six-thirty."

"Christ!" Miller exploded, and both faces instinctively glanced up at the pictures thumbtacked on the wall.

"Could you assign somebody to watch out for Wanda? If I'm scheduled to be a…a victim, she would be too."

"I'll make the arrangements, Ms. Bernstein."

"If we dine tougher, you should call me Ellie."

"Okay, Ellie, what's your favorite food?"

"I'm a chocoholic. But I'll settle for seafood."

"I'm a barbecue ribs man myself. We'll have to find a restaurant with a varied menu. Do you mind if I sit in on the meeting?"

"Holy cow, the meeting! It was supposed to start ten minutes ago."

As Ellie entered the lecture room, she gazed fondly at individual members. Including a cold-blooded murderer? That's impossible, she thought. I would sense it. I'd *know*. Yet she studied the group carefully as she read the cards and announced successful losses.

"Our beautiful Hannah Taylor dropped five pounds of weight pollution," Ellie announced with pride.

Hannah, who had purposely chosen a seat between Darlene and Lulu in order to avoid George Bubbles, noticed with a combination of relief and dismay that the World's Greatest Lover had decided not to attend.

SIX

"ARE YOU TELLING ME that members are being killed by a jealous classmate?" Darlene cradled the phone's receiver on one naked shoulder. "That's crazy, Ellie."

"I agree, but, according to the police, diet-club report cards were found near Jeannie and Esther."

"I suppose Brian and Kelly's cards burned in the van."

"Well, yes, I imagine that's true, especially if the accident occurred right after Friday's meeting."

"There! You see, Ellie, you said *accident*."

"Lieutenant Miller admitted that Brian's death could be fluky, but not Esther's or—"

"How's Kelly?"

"Alive. Unconscious. Look Darlene, I'm only suggesting you stay inside and lock your door. I don't mean to frighten you, but if there's any truth at all to that jealous classmate theory, you could be a…well, a victim."

"Ellie, I've been a victim my whole life, at least until you and Weight Winners came along."

"Would you like me to drive over and keep you company? I have a dinner date, but I'd be glad to cancel and—"

"Don't be silly."

"It's no problem, Darlene. I'm a bit nervous—"

"Afraid you'll cheat and eat the wrong thing?"

"Something like that."

"Don't worry, Ellie. Enjoy your date. I'm a big girl and I've learned how to protect myself."

"You're a waitress, aren't you?"

"That's right. You have no idea how many men hit on waitresses. Especially if they're tall and have breasts."

Ellie laughed. "Especially if they're gorgeous. I'm so proud of you, Darlene. Have you ever thought about joining the organization as a group leader?"

"*Me?* Me lecture instead of waiting tables or taking my clothes off? You must be kidding."

"You're an inspiration, sweetie. I mean, well, you could appear on Oprah. If you did, we'd have to switch our meetings from Good Shepherd to the Air Force Academy. Everybody would want to join. Meanwhile, keep your eyes open for anything or anybody out of the ordinary, okay?"

"Sure. Thanks. Bye-bye, Ellie."

Smiling, Darlene hung up the receiver and sat at her dressing table. She applied makeup, adjusted her curly wig, hooked her bra, then checked the stocking seams beneath her short skirt, and the knife hidden inside her purse.

THE HUNGRY FARMER RESTAURANT had a varied menu, but all entrees included homemade oatmeal muffins, cinnamon rolls, and a bottomless bucket of soup.

Ellie refused the soup.

"Have another cinnamon roll," urged Peter.

"I shouldn't."

"But you don't have to lose any more weight."

"Maintaining weight loss is a continuous battle."

"I don't see any battle scars."

"Except for the report cards, what proof do you have that Jeannie's and Esther's death are related?"

"Finish your cognac, Ellie."

"You can't really believe the Benedicts are involved in this murder plot of yours. It was windy that day. I know, because I battled chinook breezes all the way to Boulder in my little Honda Civic. Kelly and Brian's van would have been affected by a strong wind."

"Who were you visiting in Boulder?"

"My son Mick."

"When did you get divorced?"

"Two years ago. My god, do you always eat like that?"

"Like what?"

"When you chewed your apple, the first morning we met, you left nothing but seeds and stem." Ellie smiled and pointed toward Pete's plate. "An archaeologist could reconstruct an animal's body from those rib bones."

"I don't like waste."

"Neither do I. Jeannie, Brian, Esther——"

"Is Mick your only child?"

"Yes. How long have you been a detective?"

"How long were you married?"

"What is this, Platonic dialogue?"

"Finish up your shrimp, Ellie."

"Do you want a taste, Peter?"

"Let's trade. I'll give you one of my ribs."

"Eve supposedly evolved from a rib."

Peter reached for her watermelon garnish. "And paradise was supposedly lost because of a piece of fruit."

TEN-FORTY-FIVE.

The only light shone from a bedroom TV. "Jeopardy."

In the German Version of Monopoly, it's called "Goethestrasse"; in the British, it's "Piccadilly"; and in the French, "Rue Lafayette." The American version's property is called...

"Marvin Gardens," murmured Ellie.

"What is Marvin Gardens?" asked a contestant, winning eight hundred dollars.

"It's been a long time," purred Ellie. She stretched like a contented cat, disturbing the resident contented cat, who usually shared her waterbed. He had refused to be dislodged when she and Peter had urgently melted together onto the clean, bleach-scented sheets.

"A long time?" Peter grinned. "Could have fooled me."

"Do you think I do this with just anybody on the first dinner date?" asked Ellie indignantly, nudging the condom wrapper with her big toe.

"No sweetheart, I don't. But I was attracted to you the moment I saw your lovely fanny swivel into Good Shepherd's hallway. Do you think I offer to share my apples with just anybody?" he mimicked gently.

The name of the prince who woke up Sleeping Beauty with a kiss in Walt Disney's version of the popular fairy tale.

"Prince Peter," murmured Ellie.

"Who is Prince Charming?" asked a contestant.

"Sorry, that's wrong," said Alex Trebec. "The prince was called Philip. Sleeping Beauty's given name was Princess Aurora."

"Trebec is so damn pompous; the question—answer—didn't mention *Beauty's* given name." Turning toward Peter, Ellie added, "Tonight wasn't in the line of duty?"

"Hardly." Peter stroked Ellie's chin, then kissed her slight cleft. Jackie Robinson crept up, over, and around the two bodies for his share of attention. "The last lady I had to protect was eighty years young, and brave enough to identify the perpetrator of a gangland killing. She might have been fun in bed, but I resisted temptation."

The eighty-years-young lady would have responded eagerly to Peter, thought Ellie. My instincts were right on target.

During their dinner, after the opening repartee, Peter had entertained her with anecdotes about a politician and mixed-up parking tickets. She had doubled over with laughter when he described a citizen's arrest of a dog walker by a man the whole precinct called "the pooper-scooper-stalker." Then, while savoring her broiled shrimp in garlic sauce, Ellie had found herself outlining her divorce from Tony. But Peter had been reticent about his own background. He wasn't married, divorced, or widowed, and Ellie wondered why. Of course, she'd read about the statistics of failed marriages among police officers. Maybe Peter was scared to take a chance on a lasting relationship. In any case, he avoided her personal queries the same way he avoided her questions about murder clues—by adroitly changing the subject.

In bed he created an atmosphere of tenderness and consideration. Despite her instant arousal, Ellie had felt awkward and shy, her technique rusty from disuse, her ego crushed after learning about Tony's affairs.

Despite *his* arousal, Peter had curbed his own desires, patiently bringing Ellie to a peak of sexual satisfaction she'd never experienced before.

"Rah-rah," she said.

"What does that mean?"

Ellie felt her cheeks burn. "My ex-husband married a

cheerleader, and I guess I was cheering your performance.''

''It wasn't a 'performance,'''

''Don't you wish you had been assigned to watch over Darlene?'' asked Ellie lightly, disconcerted by the exchange and her emotions.

''Darlene who? I call the assignments. Are you digging for compliments or are you really that insecure?''

''Yes.'' Ellie sat up, turned on a bedside lamp, and ran fingers through her tangled hair. ''Peter, I'm a good amateur detective, and I realize that every time I mention Jeannie, Brian, or Esther, you change the subject. I assume it's because you're 'going by the book,' or whatever, and I'm a suspect. At least tell me about your other cases.''

''*Now?*''

''Please? I love a good mystery.''

''I prefer to work with all the mysterious parts of your lovely body.''

''You must be very good at what you do.''

''I haven't heard any complaints.''

''I meant police work, Peter.''

''Ellie, relax. Forget about police work for a while.''

''I can't. Take me, for instance.''

''I thought I just did.''

''Holy cow, that's a typically chauvinistic remark; we took each other.''

''I stand corrected. Apology rendered.''

''Apology accepted. I was referring to your protect Ms. Bernstein bit. You can't be serious. I mean, this whole thing was an excuse to get together because we're…well, attracted to each other, right?''

''Wrong.''

''You really believe I'm in danger?''

"Why won't you believe it?"

"Because I can't accept your premise. My Weight Winners members are like a family, Peter. They support each other, not kill—"

"Stubborn! You're so damn stubborn. Ellie, there have been three deaths. Do you want to become number four?"

"Wait a minute. You haven't convinced me that Jeannie's death wasn't an accident. Even you admit Brian's van could have accidentally rolled off the precipice."

"What about Mrs. Abramowitz?"

"I agree that's murder, but surely it could be unconnected to Weight Winners. A robber interrupted before he could rob. I once saw a TV show where—"

"Shit, Ellie, don't compare real life to television."

They both instinctively glanced toward the TV, which showed a marathon of commercials before Final Jeopardy.

"Your big deal is report cards, Peter. I saw Esther the night she was killed. She had the card right next to her, and she kept looking at it. She was so proud of the weight she had lost. And Jeannie always kept her card in her purse, so when her purse fell into the tub—"

"How do you know that?" interrupted Peter, startled.

"A TV reporter mentioned it; speculated that Jeannie leaned over the tub to drain—"

"Okay, okay. But do you believe it's mere coincidence? Three diet-club members getting murdered?"

"*One* murdered. The other deaths could be accidental, and yes, it's a weird coincidence, but it doesn't mean—"

"Dammit Ellie, there are always things the police keep under wraps."

"Aha! What things?"

"I don't want to discuss this. Family or not, your diet-club members are high on my list of suspects and I wish you'd trust me enough to develop a sense of imperativeness or at least self-preservation.'' Peter paused for breath, yawned, then asked, ''Do you have any objection to me spending the night?''

Final Jeopardy's theme music sounded. The category was television, and the printed answer superimposed across the screen read: THREE EPISODES DREW THE LARGEST AUDIENCES IN SERIES HISTORY. NAME TWO.

'''M*A*S*H,''' guessed Ellie. ''The very last show.''

'''Dallas,''' said Peter. ''Who shot J.R.''

They were both right. Number three was the final episode of ''The Fugitive'' in which the one-armed killer was finally caught.

''May I spend the night?'' Peter repeated.

''How will you protect me if you fall asleep?''

''I'm a light sleeper.''

''Who will protect me from you?'' Ellie aimed her remote control toward the TV.

As the room darkened, leaving only the lamp's glow, Peter bent his head and gave her a deep kiss.

''You taste like garlic, Princess Aurora.''

''Shrimp scampi strikes again, Prince Philip.'' Ellie reached over and turned out the light. ''But you! I've never seen a person eat barbecued ribs so lovingly, sir. I knew right away that I wanted to go to bed with you.''

''I adore ribs…and breasts, and legs, and thighs.''

Again, she thought happily, I want to make love again. But I can't, he can't, yes, he can. *Holy cow!*

Ellie closed her eyes, allowing sensations to overtake sensibilities.

Jackie Robinson gave a plaintive meow and leaped from the bed to find more comfortable resting quarters.

The cat's abundant fur bristled as he hissed at the shadowy figure outside the bedroom window.

DARLENE STOOD NEAR a downtown corner and shifted from one stacked heel to the other. A scoop-neck sweater defined her breasts. Earlier, she had spent twenty minutes parked on a dark side street with a three-piece suit who smelled of expensive tweeds and pipe tobacco. At the conclusion, Mr. Meerschaum-Pipe had tucked a twenty-dollar bill inside her bra. A dollar a minute, not bad!

She hadn't even mussed her heavy makeup or the curly blond wig that covered her reddish brown mane. Checking her gartered nylons for runs, she straightened her skin-tight, red-leather skirt. From the corner of her eye she could see a male figure pretending to study the contents displayed inside a pawnshop window. The store was closed, so it had to be a cop. She could always tell, could practically smell pigs from a distance.

Darlene recalled Ellie's warning about anything or anybody unusual. A cop lurking nearby wasn't unusual, not in her line of work. Waitress? Not on your life!

After losing seventy pounds, Darlene had taken to the streets. It was part financial and part, she had to admit, just plain ego. Overhead was low—wig, garter belt, prophylactics. Her going rate included a "discount" of one hundred dollars for two hours, and she was doing very well.

She wished her husband, Ken, could see her now. As her manager, he had stuck like glue while she headlined the leggy chorus at Caesar's Palace. She wanted to quit and have a baby. Instead, Ken fed Darlene booze and munches before and after each show. Her weight climbed until she eventually ended up at a dive off the strip, collecting sweaty George Washingtons in her G-string. Darlene the dumb victim! Ken had disappeared with all her money, even the change she'd kept in an empty peanut-butter jar. Broke and fat, she had hitchhiked to Colorado.

Weight Winners had slimmed her; waitressing had sent her to the streets in search of easier income. Although prostitution was, admittedly, a low-esteem occupation, Darlene received a certain satisfaction from using her body to accumulate the necessary funds for a new career. Her nest egg was growing, and soon she'd have enough to return to Vegas. This time she didn't intend to strip; she'd take a course on running the roulette wheel or dealing cards. Suddenly she recalled one of Ellie's chalkboard quotes: "Fashions fade, style is eternal."

I have style when I'm hooking, yes indeedy.

She strolled another block. The figure followed. *So obvious,* thought Darlene, grinning. She was tempted to flirt with the cop, play her role, then back out with feigned indignation at the last moment. ("What kind of a girl do you think I am? I have style.") But it was late, there were 120 tax-free dollars tucked neatly inside her shoulder-strap purse, her tummy growled with hunger, and it was beginning to turn cold.

Darlene considered covering her body with the fake fur jacket she carried over one arm, then heading for her favorite coffee shop. The manager, a friend, kept fresh fruit and skim milk available just for her. Darlene yawned. First she'd shed Dick Fuckin' Tracy.

Abruptly she turned and ran down several streets, finally ducking behind a parked car. She stayed there until positive the cop hadn't followed. Then she stood and pushed her arms through the sleeves of the fake fur.

Jeeze, she felt so healthy and so optimistic. This morning's horoscope had read:

Be ready for new experience, meeting with fascinating member of opposite sex. Be practical, seek counsel from one with experience.

Darlene believed in horoscopes.

DETECTIVE WILLIAM MCCOY HIT his open palm with the closed fist of his other hand. *Damn!* He had lost her. Why hadn't Miller informed the girl that she was being followed for her own protection? *Shit!* McCoy had waited for two hours outside a garish motel while Darlene took her own sweet time inside. He had been tempted to break into the motel room—after all, her partner could have been what his precinct now called the Diet-Desecrator—but Will had stayed outdoors, straining to hear anything other than yelps of pleasure.

It certainly wasn't easy following a hooker. Miller said he didn't want to "scare" the lady. McCoy wondered if the lieutenant knew what this *lady* did for recreation.

Now he had definitely lost her. Oh well, he had her home address and would stake out there until she returned.

DARLENE WALKED QUICKLY, her stacked heels clicking on the sidewalk, thoughts of the warm shop and coffee adding momentum to her stride. She added another stick of sugarless gum to the wad in her mouth, and her left cheek pouched like a lopsided chipmunk.

A block away from the restaurant, she was hailed by a large figure whose face was hidden by shadows. *Dammit*, thought Darlene, *I'm too tired.* The man stepped onto the sidewalk, blocking her path.

"Forget it, mister, I've closed up shop for the night,"

she said, shifting the gum to her right cheek and simulating a yawn.

Absurdly, the man was waving a ten-dollar bill in her face.

"Ten bucks?" Darlene laughed. "Ten bucks won't even get you a hand-job. What kind of girl do you think I am?"

"Pretty girl," said the man, sounding as if he had to clear his throat of phlegm. "Pretty whore. I want you to make me happy…um…you know."

"My minimum price for that is twen—fifty dollars, but I'm really exhausted. Another time, okay?"

"Pretty whore. We can do it against the wall."

Grasping her arm, the man pulled her toward an alley. A street lamp briefly illuminated his face, partially covered by a stocking cap.

He sure looked familiar, thought Darlene, but she always had trouble remembering a male's face and name. It was dark, he was wearing a bulky pea jacket, and his knit cap had been pulled low, hiding his features. His pants were black or navy. She couldn't see his feet at all.

"Do I know you?" she asked, lighting a cigarette with her Bic, hoping to get a better look at his face.

The man stepped away from the flash of flame.

"You've seen me plenty," he said, "and I sure noticed you, Darlene."

"Where?"

"You remind me of others who give it away. Only you're bigger, Darlene, with the prettiest bazooms—"

"Give it away? What are you talking about? I don't give it away free for nothin'."

"That makes it better. You should stop losing so much weight. I don't like skinny women. Will you make me feel good?"

"Do you have fifty bucks?"

"I'll owe you. This is a down payment," he replied huskily, waving the ten in her face.

"Fuck off, mister, I don't do charity work."

Wrenching her arms free, Darlene felt instant pain. Unbelieving, she looked down at her arm where blood seeped through her sliced fur jacket and the fleshy part above her elbow. Even without illumination, she could see the wicked blade in the man's hand. Her mouth opened in surprise, and her gum fell to the pavement.

"Wait a m-m-minute—I remember—I d-do know you," stuttered Darlene, thoroughly frightened. "That changes things. I'll do anything you want for t-ten bucks. For free," she pleaded, dropping her cigarette and reaching into her purse for her knife.

"Sing me a song."

"What?" *Where was the fuckin' knife?*

The man slapped Darlene's face. At the same time, he tugged at her purse with such force that the strap snapped and the purse fell to the ground near her wad of gum.

"Sing me a song, bitch," he growled.

"Okay. Sure. You bet. Which one?"

"The sheep song."

"I d-don't think I know—"

"The one about lost sheep, Darlene. We've lost our way. What do sheep say, girlie?"

She tried to smiled. "Oh, I know the song you mean. Baaa…Baaa…Baaa."

"That's right. Go on. Sing the second line."

"We're little lost lambs who have gone astray."

"Take off your clothes."

"Sure. Anything you say."

Where was a cop when you really needed one?

THE POLICE DISCOVERED Darlene's body in the alley behind the Loaf 'N Jug at approximately 3:00 a.m. Her throat had been cut.

During the autopsy, the coroner noted that, along with knife slashes on Darlene's arm and throat, the killer had carefully carved out the numbers 7 and 0 around her navel. The Coroner thought the numbers had something to do with gambling, but the police force knew 7-0 meant seventy pounds. Their Diet-Desecrator had struck again.

Awakened by his beeper, summoned to the Loaf 'N Jug, Peter Miller didn't spend the whole night with Ellie at all. Or the following night, either, when he joined a guilt-ridden William McCoy inside Murphy's Bar, then drove the drunk detective home.

"She was so pretty," sobbed McCoy.

"You did the best you could under the circumstances."

"When Irish eyes are smilin'," sang McCoy, tears streaming down his cheeks. "Happy Saint Pat's day, Pete."

"It's October," said Miller softly.

"You know wha', Pete? You're such a—"

"Friend?"

"Smart-ass." McCoy belched. "I can't sing Irish eyes in October." He belched again.

"You can sing anything you want, pal." Peter guided McCoy up the front steps.

"Can't carry a fuckin' tune." McCoy halted, sank to one step, and hung his head between his rubbery legs. "I'm not Robert what's-his-name."

"De Niro?"

"No! Robert Goo-fuckin'-lay." He belched for the

third time, said, "Jesus, Pete, gonna puke," and did. All over his shoes, the pavement, and yesterday's newspaper—which carried a story about Darlene's murder, right next to an ad for discount furniture.

SEVEN

OUTSIDE, LARGE RAINDROPS looked like colorless jelly beans. Ellie glanced toward her window. "Wasn't it Ronald Reagan who munched jelly beans all the time?"

"Right," said Peter. "Carter had a thing for peanuts, and Bush won't eat broccoli. Why?"

"I don't know. A month ago, I had this dumb daydream about President Taft. I guess I was wishing it was a month ago...before all this started."

Ellie tried to smile. She and Peter sat facing each other on the beige carpeted floor of Ellie's family room. The walls were filled with reproductions of Chagall paintings, plus a framed poster of Roger Rabbit.

A plush-cushioned couch faced a fireplace. An entire wall of shelves held books, mostly mystery novels and mainstream historicals. A rocker-recliner fronted the TV/VCR/stereo, and a refinished Chippendale table held a Tiffany-shaded lamp whose scripted Coca-Cola logo blended into red-green-gold leaded glass.

Instead of shades or drapes, two recessed windows were curtained with healthy plants. One overgrown ivy auditioned for the lead in *Jack and the Beanstalk.* Through the giant leaves and panes of glass, falling rain obscured Ellie's magnificent mountain view. And, although it was only midmorning, a three-globed ceiling fixture shed subdued light.

On the floor between Ellie and Peter were the index cards from Wanda Henry's file container. Ellie's face scrunched up thoughtfully as she tried verbally to paint a biographical sketch of each member.

"This is impossible!" she finally exclaimed. "Peter, we have people who join and quit after two weeks. Visitors drop in from other groups. There are lifetimers who come once a month. It could be anybody...or none of them."

"We have to start someplace. Police detectiving isn't all shoot-outs and car chases. There's lots of boring paperwork; information that leads nowhere."

"I realize that...aha!"

"Aha, what?"

"Robbie Janssen. *J-A-N-S-S-E-N*. That's the name I was trying to remember when Robbie came in late. I knew it had to be Scandinavian."

"Tell me about him."

"Wait. Let me think. It was the day Jeannie Dobson died. I had already started my lecture when Janssen arrived. He kind of hinted that his watch was broken."

"What sort of a man is he?"

"Very quiet. Joined last year just before the holidays. Made it through Christmas and New Year's, then dropped out. Rejoined last summer." Ellie studied the card. "He loses steadily. Some members give their life stories during meetings, but Robbie never opens his mouth. Yet he did come in late that morning."

"How did he seem? Agitated? Stimulated? Do you understand what—"

"Yes, if you...well, drown a woman, I suppose you'd have some sort of emotional reaction, right?"

"And Janssen?" Peter prompted.

"The same as usual."

"Think, Ellie."

"I am thinking. I can't create a suspect just because

we're at a dead end. Janssen was quiet and shy and apologetic. He arrived while other members were applauding some remark I made, and I admired his poise under a barrage of attention. My God, you can tell what sort of person he is by his name. For instance, take your average Hollywood star, like, well, Robert what's-his-name?''

"Goulet?"

"No, De Niro, *Robert* De Niro. Janssen calls himself Robbie. Not Rob or Bob. Even Ronnie Howard became Ron after he reached puberty. Janssen's a big ol' teddy bear.''

"You're getting defensive again. Janssen could be a grizzly bear. I assumed he's elderly.''

"Right. Around our age, Lieutenant.''

"The name could indicate immaturity. Immaturity could mean spur-of-the-moment rage, wacko jealousy.''

"You can't condemn a person because he goes around with a nickname. My son calls himself Mick instead of Michael. My ex-husband was christened Anton, and he's always been called Tony. Even Ellie is short for—''

"Okay, okay, you win. I was grasping at straws. Do you recall wet clothing?''

"What do you mean?''

"Janssen's clothes. There might have been splashes or stains from water, especially if Jeannie Dobson struggled.''

Ellie shuddered as Peter's voice conjured up unpleasant images. The detective shifted to her side and put his arms across her shoulders.

"You know what, Peter? It's so different when it happens for real. I'm always pleased with myself if I solve the mystery before the book's final chapter. All the horror films...you scream when the dead body swings out from the closet. Then you look for the name of the actress in the credits. It's not the same—''

"I know, sweetheart."

She took a deep breath. "Robbie Janssen wore a blue shirt, cheap cotton, the kind of material that shrinks in a hot-water wash. Dark pants. A leather belt; the first three holes were scuffed, as if he'd lost inches in his waist. His shoes were blue suede, shabby. His shirt was wet from perspiration, but in the usual pattern...under the arms and at the neckline. It was food-spotted rather than water-stained, and his sleeves were rolled up."

"Good Lord," said Peter admiringly. "What a marvelous police-person you'd make. What an eye for detail!"

Ellie's cheeks flushed. "I used to read tons of detective stories. It was something to do when Tony worked late. Newspapers, too. I'd read about a crime in the paper and try to solve the case. I still stand in a supermarket line, memorizing some unsuspecting suspect. It hurts to be wrong, Peter. I was angry when we met because I couldn't believe Jeannie had been murdered. No obvious motive. The picture pieces didn't seem to fit. Holy cow!"

"What's the matter?"

"Picture pieces! Peter, I have photographs. I take Polaroid snapshots of new members so that they can visually compute their progress. But it's strictly volunteer, and some people don't want to pose."

Ellie left the room, heading for the kitchen, and Peter heard a drawer opening and closing. When she returned, she carried a weighty manila envelope and a bowl filled with popcorn. She almost spilled both, but managed to capture the popcorn while the envelope poured its contents into his lap.

"Holy bull, they all look alike."

"Lieutenant! That's a chauvinistically skinny remark if I ever heard one. Just because a person is heavy, it doesn't mean he or she isn't beautiful. I try to emphasize the health aspects of my Weight Winners program. It's really balanced nutritionally, you know. But we tend to put so much emphasis on being skinny—''

"Sorry, I didn't mean to imply that your photos were ugly. It's just that all your participants are trying to hide from the camera.'' Peter glanced down at his lap. "Except this young man. I love his middle-finger gesture.''

Ellie smiled, hitched up her jeans, and sat with her knees on the carpet, her rump on her heels. "That's a 'before' picture of John Russell.''

"The entertainer?''

"Yup. That slim gorgeous hunk who plays piano at the Dew Drop Inn. I took the picture before he grew his beard. By the way, a friend of mine, Sandra Connors, sings with John occasionally.''

"Where's Janssen?''

Ellie sifted through the photos. "Here he is. Damn, it's not very clear. I think he moved as I pushed the button. Actually I was surprised he agreed to pose because he's so shy.''

Peter studied the blurry picture. Janssen had his right arm raised as though to ward off a blow or as if he had decided at the last minute that he'd made a mistake and wanted to wave Ellie away.

Collecting all the snapshots, Peter flipped through them. "Not much help here,'' he said with a frown. "Nobody looks mean or murderish, just embarrassed. Wait a minute. This guy looks happy, or at least smirky. Why is the picture Scotch-taped?''

"That's Wanda's husband, Henry. I snapped my camera rather impulsively.''

"I thought you said he wasn't a member and made fun of the club."

"He's not. He does. That's why the damn thing's taped. He wasn't posing, and tore up the photo when I suggested he join our meetings. I fished it out of the trash."

"How come?"

"I don't know. Artistic ego? It's not a bad photo considering I didn't take time to focus, and I suppose I hope he'll change his mind. For Wanda's sake. He couldn't be our perp," added Ellie, watching Peter grin at her slang. "Since he's not a member, he wouldn't be aware of goal-weight winners, and he's definitely not jealous of losers. Honest, Peter, he couldn't care less."

"Okay. Grasping at straws again."

A long unhappy silence ensued, intensified by the gloomy weather outside the window. It had stopped raining, but the sky, glimpsed between spiraling plant leaves, looked slate gray.

"What time was Jeannie killed?" Ellie finally asked.

"It's hard to determine the exact time."

"Why? I thought modern forensic chemistry—"

"We figure the water in the tub started out very hot. Her body had, well, scalded."

"So?"

"Ellie, you don't want to hear—"

"Yes I do, Peter. Hot water..."

"I've told you that the police keep some things under wraps and—"

"Not for publication. Yes, I know. But if you want me to be helpful, you've got to share secrets. I'm taking you very seriously since Darlene's murder."

"Are you crying, sweetheart?"

"I don't have any tears left. Darlene's death was partly

my fault. I phoned to warn her, but there was no—what's your word? Imperativeness? Urgency? I was overly defensive about my 'family members' and didn't concentrate on victims. Dumb, dumb, *dumb!*''

"It doesn't help to assume blame. Detective McCoy is doing the same thing because he messed up his assignment, and he's a professional. I intend to keep close to you, sweetheart, very, very close.''

"That's nice. However, I doubt the killer is after me, Peter. He's had too many opportunities—''

"Knock it off, Ellie, I really don't like your attitude. You said you're taking me seriously.''

"I am. I'll be careful, but you can't hide me under wraps, I'll suffocate. Speaking of keeping evidence under wraps, tell me about Jeannie's bathwater. You started to say that the time of death was hard to determined because of hot water.''

"That's right.''

"Why?''

"Stubborn!''

"Why?"

"Shit! All right! The hot water kept the body from decomposing quickly. Made it harder to pinpoint the exact time of death. We've estimated between eight and ten a.m. We know it wasn't much earlier because Jeannie was out walking with Hannah Taylor, but it could be later.''

"Holy c-Christ, Peter, no wonder you hesitated that first day at the church when I proposed my idea about Jeannie falling in while draining her tub. If she took the time to get dressed, the water would have cooled. Why didn't you refute my stupid theory?''

"At that point you were a suspect, sweetheart. You

could have tripped yourself up by mentioning the hot water.''

''Was it only the scalding water that made you think homicide instead of accident? Was there anything else?''

''The contents from her purse had been dumped into the tub. There was no sign of a struggle outside the tub, no crumpled bath mat or knocked-over trash basket, so your friend was probably bound. No blood,'' he added softly. ''We saw pantyhose hanging from the shower rod, but that didn't prove anything. However, if Jeannie had been holding her purse and fallen into the tub, it wouldn't have opened.''

''Jeannie's purse had a strong clasp,'' said Ellie, ''not Velcro or something cheap.''

''Right. The killer went to great pains to make her death look accidental. Then, somewhere along the way, he lost his cool...had to have the report card as part of the scene. My suspicions were confirmed with Esther's card.''

''If we...if you don't know the exact time of death, the murderer might be somebody who came to the meeting early or didn't come at all. We're back to step one. Forget straws. It's like looking for a needle in a haystack.''

''It's not all that bad,'' soothed Peter. ''The killer has a pattern. So far, he's only attacked your class members. That narrows the field considerably—''

''That's the second time you've said *he*. How do you know the killer's a male?''

''We just do.''

''How?''

''Ellie, why don't you put the pictures away and—''

''How, Lieutenant?''

''Dammit, Darlene was raped.''

"Raped? Wait a minute, you said Darlene was, uh, hooking that night."

"Her panties were ripped apart, and the semen was, well, recent. It had to be a man, unless there are two people working together. And we know something else."

"Yes?"

"It had to be somebody familiar. There was no forced entry at either the Dobson or Abramowitz residences."

"And Weight Winners is the only connection, right?"

"I'm sorry, sweetheart."

"Peter, how is Kelly Benedict? They give me the same information every time I call the hospital. Critical condition. She's still in ICU. Am I a member of the family? It sounds like a prerecorded message."

"Kelly's in a coma," said Peter shortly. He seemed agitated, as though his terse comment conjured up unpleasant memories. "Wish I could question her. She's our only witness, especially if the murderer followed the Benedicts' van from Good Shepherd's parking lot."

"I saw the lot that day. We were standing by the window after the meeting."

"What did you see?"

"You. I saw you eating a damn apple. I wasn't concentrating on the parking lot."

"Think, sweetheart."

"I am. It's no good, Peter. It was just after the meeting, and all the members were leaving." Ellie slanted her blue-green eyes thoughtfully. "Daisy and Beau's tandem bike...my senior citizens. Tubby and Lulu Evergreen were arguing. Wanda's husband was picking her up for lunch. Darlene lit a cigarette. Sandra was singing. George Bubbles waved a celery stalk. Hannah—"

"Was Janssen in the parking lot?"

"Don't interrupt, I'm getting a picture in my head. Yes, Robbie was there. He was talking…"

"To who—whom?"

"He was talking…"

"To the Benedicts?"

"To a few nuns."

"Nuns?"

"Weight Winners members."

"Nuns?"

"Yup." Ellie auditioned a tiny grin. "Sisters want to feel healthy, look beautiful. Remember Sister—"

"Teresa?"

"No, honey, Sister Luc-Gabrielle. She became an overnight sensation with a song called 'Dominique.'"

"The Singing Nun!"

"Right. Anyway, she wanted to look good on TV, Ed Sullivan I think, so she—"

"Anybody else in the parking lot?"

For a moment Ellie was confused; she'd been pondering a simpler time. Then she said, "Everybody else, Peter, except for a few members who remained in the lecture room. Look, maybe the van thing really was an accident. It doesn't quite follow your MO, except Brian and Kelly were close to goal weight. But they only reached within ten pounds of goal that day. How could the killer react so quickly?"

"We're not even sure what the Benedicts did immediately following your meeting. We found an appointment book in their apartment. It indicated a shopping expedition to Cripple Creek for antiques, but they stopped along the way to, well, make love maybe."

"Holy cow! What makes you think—"

"They were both nude. Anyway, later that afternoon they planned to give Esther Abramowitz's granddaughter an estimate on a nursery. And you're right, Ellie, the van plunging over the cliff could have been accidental. That's why I hope Kelly recovers soon. By the way, has anyone shown any extraordinary interest in Kelly's progress?''

"Well sure, just about everybody. Since I'm their leader, they figure I must know anything new, and it's their first question."

"Which members show the most interest?"

"They all ask. Hannah, of course; she's very warm-hearted. And Lulu Evergreen. Kelly was nice to Lulu, and I don't think that lady has many friends. She's so overshadowed by her husband."

"Janssen?"

Ellie shook her head. "I understand what you're getting at, honey, but I honestly believe I would recognize an interest in Kelly different from the norm."

"Ms. Amateur Sleuth," he said tenderly.

"Peter, what if I volunteered to play decoy?"

"Absolutely not!"

"Why?"

"You've been watching too much TV or reading too many books. It's not that easy and it's very, very dangerous, even for trained personnel."

"You could wire me—"

"*No!*"

"Would our relationship have anything to do with that vehement no?"

"I wouldn't want the woman I'm falling in love with to expose herself to danger. But the answer would be no in any case, so forget it."

"The woman you're falling in love with?"

"Did you have doubts? I take back what I said before about being perceptive."

Peter gave her a kiss and Ellie snuggled closer within the circle of his arm.

"Have you ever been in love?" she murmured.

"Of course," he replied lightly. "Marilyn Monroe, Bardot, Stevie Nix, Loretta—"

"Young?"

"No, Swit. The 'M*A*S*H' lady."

"Blonds."

"Ingrid Bergman. She wasn't blond."

"Anyone real? I mean, in real life?"

Peter was silent for a long time, and Ellie wished she hadn't posed the question. "Sorry, I have no right to pry."

"You have every right," he said, tightening his arm around her shoulder. "Besides, it's what you like to do."

"Fall in love or pry?"

"I'd call it probe. Discover. And you're good at it. You have a fine mind. I just wish you weren't involved—"

"But I am involved, Peter. Why can't I help?"

"No, not if it places you in danger. And I promise I'll relate my mysterious past, tell you about Cathy some other time. Right now I've got to grab something to eat and head for the precinct."

"I'll make you lunch," Ellie said, startled by the sadness she saw in Peter's eyes. Grabbing the manila envelope, jumping to her feet, she headed for the kitchen, then tripped over Jackie Robinson, who had been sitting in the hallway. The envelope opened again, spewing photos.

But Peter caught her just in time, turning the mishap into a long embrace. His lips traveled from the sensitive skin around her eyelids to the tip of her nose, and traced the contour of her jawline from ear to chin.

Ellie caught his errant lips with her own and almost bit his tongue in an effort to keep his mouth imprisoned against hers.

"Forget lunch," he whispered. "I have other appetites to satisfy."

"Yes...time is so fleeting, Peter. Life is so brief. Making love is reality, isn't it? Sex and chocolate are true realities. I don't want to think about death anymore. I need to celebrate life."

Together they backed up through the hall and into the bedroom. Ellie managed to shed her sweater and bra before their two bodies tumbled onto the waterbed. Her mind subconsciously registered the different textures of her lover. Peter's soft lips and a mustache that was both silky and bristly. The scratchy material of his laundered shirt smelled like popcorn, and spray starch.

The links of Peter's watchband caught a few strands of her auburn hair, but instead of pulling away, Ellie leaned over and kissed the pulse at his wrist where it throbbed beneath the band.

Then she threw her head back, ignoring the pain from her sheared strands, concentrating on the exquisite pleasure Peter brought to her body and senses.

Other men might look ridiculous, thought Ellie, clothed only in shirt and socks. But the well-defined muscles in Peter's legs bunched and flowed as—afterward—he fought to sit up on the undulating bed while reaching for his crumpled jeans.

He caught the look of renewed desire on Ellie's face and grinned. "No time," he said, carefully removing the hair trapped beneath his watchband.

"Next time take that damn thing off," she murmured, rubbing her scalp.

"Sorry. Does your head hurt, sweetheart?"

"No, my head's fine," she grumbled. "I just don't like watches or clocks because they tell you when to leave."

"Watches and clocks are reality, too."

Ellie donned her jeans but didn't bother replacing her top as she walked with Peter toward the front door. She had the nagging sensation that she'd missed some clue about the identity of the killer, then the thought blurred.

Peter leaned over and gave her a loving kiss.

"Wish you didn't have to go."

"Wish I could stay."

"When will you be back?" She almost said *back home*.

"I'm not sure. Late. Do you have a class to lecture tonight or this afternoon?"

"No. I plan to curl up with a good detective...novel."

"Make sure everything is locked up tight after I leave. There'll be a police car parked across the street."

"For heaven's sake, the killer's not after me, Peter."

"Sweetheart, you and Wanda Henry are the only ones left alive at goal weight."

"That's not true! There are several successful graduates—"

"Our killer seems to be concentrating on recent members. Thank God. We could never protect every single Weight Winner who's graduated over the years. That's why the murderer himself has to be a recent member. He *knows*...never mind. It's my job to find him. Just relax and—"

"Get it out of my pretty head?" asked Ellie.

"Something like that. I was going to say forget about this decoy nonsense. I'm not kidding, okay?"

"Okay," she agreed reluctantly. "What about lunch?"

"I'll try and pick up something on the way to the

precinct," he replied, giving Ellie a final quick kiss before walking outside into the gloom.

She doubted he'd eat anything but caffeine and vowed silently to prepare a hot healthy meal that evening. It would be hard to time with Peter's uncertain schedule. Again a nagging thought crept into her brain, then retreated before she could focus on a clear image.

Peter halted and turned around. She thought he mouthed the word "later," then pointed to his watch and shrugged his shoulders. All of a sudden, Ellie realized she was nude from the waist up, standing framed by this open entrance. Across the street was the police cruiser.

She slammed the front door, hesitated for one small moment of rebellion, then secured the lock.

Advancing into the hallway, she knelt and began gathering spilled photos. Jackie Robinson's sharp claws and teeth had perforated three snapshots. From the remaining scraps, Ellie could determine that the cat had chewed up John Russell, Henry Henry, and Lulu Evergreen.

"Bad puss," she admonished.

Tail waving, whiskers aquiver, he seemed to reply: *Meow, what do you expect? No Oreo cookies, no melted ice cream, no cheesecake crumbs. Garfield wouldn't put up with this nonsense. Mee—ow.*

EIGHT

ELLIE TRIED TO AVOID the shower head's spray as she massaged shampoo into her scalp. Her own head throbbed where Peter's watch links had pulled at her hair. Then she accidently rubbed hard.

"Ouch! Holy cow!" Perhaps that tiny spot led directly to her cerebral hemisphere, because the nagging idea finally crystallized and remained in place.

Time.

No time.

Next time take the damn thing off.

Watches and clocks are reality, too.

Ellie pictured Peter pointing to his watch and shrugging. Where had she seen that identical gesture before?

Robbie Janssen!

When? The morning of Jeannie's murder. Robbie had pointed to his forearm, indicting a broken wristwatch. What would cause a watch to become inoperative suddenly? Any number of things, including loss of warranty, Ellie thought wryly.

But what if Robbie's watch weren't waterproof? A soak in the bathtub would render it useless. How long did it take to hold a defenseless woman's head under hot water? How much time?

Ellie hurried to wash the shampoo from her hair and get out of the shower.

Maybe the discoloration from perspiration on Robbie's blue shirt *had* been water stains, she thought, toweling her body.

What other evidence implicated Robbie?

None. Because there *was* no evidence.

No fingerprints.

No weapon in the case of Jeannie. Or Brian. Esther had been found with knitting needles poking out of her neck, but she'd been strangled first, thank God, and gloved thumb marks indicated a man or a large woman. The knife used on Darlene had been ordinary, the kind of blade sold in any K Mart.

Blood spatterings found at the murder scenes had belonged to the victims, not the perp.

Ellie composed a mental checklist:

First, the scene of the crime. Bathroom, living room, mountain peak, alley. No particular scenic pattern.

Second, time of day. All the murders had occurred on Friday; logical, since that was the day of the meetings. Maybe the perp made a shopping list of foods to buy, then a list of members to kill. Ellie shuddered. Jeannie had been murdered Friday morning, Brian Friday afternoon, Esther and Darlene—Friday nights. Did Robbie have an alibi? Four alibis?

What about signs of a struggle? Peter had suggested that Jeannie was bound, and the neighbors hadn't heard any calls for help. In the case of Esther, the only screams had come from granddaughter Glory ("Tweety eats worms"). The convenience store counterman had not heard one peep from Darlene, but Darlene's throat had been sliced, effectively silencing her. There was no trace of blood, hair, or fibers under Darlene's fingernails. Or Esther's.

Documents. Nothing except the report cards and the Benedicts' appointment book. No clues there. Dead end.

Telephone calls. So far, only the one between Ellie and Darlene, although the police were still investigating.

Finally, background on the victims. All had either reached or were within ten pounds of goal weight. Which led to the motive: jealousy. Robbie was a W.W. Two rejoin. What had Peter said earlier? Something about wacko jealousy.

Could Robbie Janssen be jealous enough to kill?

Ellie didn't bother drying her hair as she rushed to the telephone.

Peter wasn't at the precinct. The sergeant asked if it was an emergency. "Yes. No. Maybe," Ellie admitted, and the sergeant promised to have Lieutenant Miller return her call as soon as possible.

She could be jumping to conclusions. Peter would play devil's advocate and automatically attack her theory, despite his desire for a lead. Or would he?

He had admitted to grasping at straws earlier. This theory wasn't straws; it was the whole kit and caboodle, the entire milkshake. If Robbie's watch had been destroyed because of bathwater, if Robbie's clothing had accumulated blood stains, if Robbie's home contained the *knife*.

Ex-husband Tony had made fun of Ellie's morbid interest in newspaper murder stories. His sarcasm had hurt. But Peter wasn't like that. Or was he?

Don't play decoy, honey.

Don't worry your pretty head, honey.

Lock the door, honey.

She entered the bedroom, then quickly donned black corduroy slacks and a lilac cable-knit sweater. Peter had accused her of lacking a sense of urgency. Wrong! She wanted to stop this murdering bastard. *ASAP. Today. How. How's that for urgency, Loot?*

Returning to the family room she checked Janssen's address on the index card. It was an apartment complex not far from her. An optional line on the card asked for occupation, and Robbie had filled in "postal clerk."

Ellie replayed the last Weight Winners meeting. Janssen had been there, standing in his usual spot against the wall. His shirt had been cleaner, or at least the plaid flannel hid spots. His blue suede shoes were still unraveling at the soles. She glanced down at Robbie's card. He had maintained his weight at the same amount as the week before, which, Ellie remembered, he'd accepted stoically. Anything that wasn't a gain was considered a win.

She fixed her mind like the telescopic lens of a camera, blocking out all but Robbie's slumping figure. Shirtsleeves sloppily rolled to the elbows. *No watch.* She was sure his arm and wrist had been bare. She was pretty sure. She was positive. Well, almost positive. *A definite maybe.*

"Robbie Janssen had a watch," she sang, knotting the laces on her sneakers, "eee-yi, eee-yi, oh."

A broken watch. Holy cow. Old McDonald had a cow, eee-yi, eee-yi...

Oh, it didn't really prove anything. Unless the malfunction was the result of water damage. A skilled repairman could tell. Why didn't the phone ring with Peter's call? Who lacked urgency now? Lieutenant Miller had probably received her message and filed it away for "later." Dammit, should she call again or wait?

Still undecided, Ellie curled up on her family-room couch with the latest Lee Karr novel, but she couldn't concentrate. After ten minutes, without turning a page, she slammed the book shut. A startled Jackie Robinson clawed the cushion and growled low in his furry throat: *What's the deal, Ellie-woman? First no sweets, now no sleep. Mee-ow.*

"I can't wait for Peter, I just can't," Ellie said to the cat. She wanted desperately to validate her broken-watch theory, and figured the piece of jewelry would be somewhere in Janssen's apartment. There was a good possibility that the watch hadn't been repaired yet, since, Ellie guessed, the man's personality included a predilection to avoid mundane chores. His untidy clothes and shredded shoes were an indication of that trait—and proved that shy Robbie didn't have a wife or mother in residence. Maybe. Another definite maybe.

Of course, if Robbie was the killer and believed his watch might be connected to Jeannie's murder, he would have destroyed the evidence. But Ellie had just thought of the clue, and Peter—with all his years of experience—hadn't. Well, that wasn't fair. She had never mentioned it to Peter in her description of Robbie. Even Robbie probably wouldn't connect the broken watch to evidence of a crime. Watches went on the blink every day. And didn't TV mystery shows conclude with the most unlikely, careless goof to condemn a murderer? ("Aha! You were supposed to be skiing, but there's not one trace of snow on your boots.")

Almost three o'clock. Past the lunch hour and well before quitting time. The post office didn't close until five. Robbie would be safe behind his postal cage. He had once mentioned that his only days off were Sundays and Fridays. Today was Tuesday.

Civil service jobs didn't leave much room for improvisation, except for multiple obscure holidays. Just to make certain, Ellie glanced at the card again, then touchtoned Janssen's home number and let the phone ring a dozen times before replacing the receiver.

Damn, her car was useless since she'd alert the cops across the street. They'd follow. That meant jogging the few miles to the apartment complex. It might have been a problem a couple years ago, but now she was used to jogging.

Ellie peered out through the windowpane, between the plants, and noted that the sky looked like an ugly gray sponge, bloated to bursting, waiting to be squeezed. In the distance, a few flashes of lightning split the haze.

Raiding her son Mick's closet for his outgrown Denver Bronco windbreaker, she pulled the hood over her damp hair and carried two fresh-brewed mugs of coffee across the street. Both policemen were politely grateful, and Ellie considered confessing her revelation to the sympathetic uniforms. She could dump the whole thing in their laps—her theory, not the coffee—risking their smirks or condescending laughter, or even (God forbid) indifference. Then she could return to her comfortable family room, light a fire, and wait for Peter.

It was tempting.

But that's what caused so much trouble in my marriage, she thought. Apathetically sitting around, reading, vegetating, stuffing my mouth with calories, letting my muscles atrophy. She could not regress to that kind of existence, nosir.

"As God is my witness," she swore, brandishing her fist toward the ceiling light fixture, "as God is my witness, I'll never be fat or lazy again."

If Robbie hadn't destroyed or repaired his watch, it would be available later, after Peter called. But what about other clues? The soiled blue shirt, a scrapbook of clippings spotlighting the murders, or even a bloodstained knife could be hidden inside Janssen's apartment. Ellie imagined the newspaper headlines applauding her intelligence and daring. Earlier, Peter had complimented her "fine mind" plus her ability to probe. And, most important, the sooner the perp was caught, the sooner the killings would cease.

Very good. Perp caught, killings would cease. That was a logical justification for sleuthing. What else had Peter said their first night together? *Self-preservation.*

Screw self-preservation when so many lives were at stake. Besides, Robbie was safe at work, wasn't he?

Ellie left her phone off the hook; when Peter returned her call, he'd get a busy signal and wouldn't worry.

Feeling ridiculously furtive, she left by the back door, skirted a neighbor's yard, and tentatively greeted their large golden retriever, Midas. The doggie bags of scraps and bones she'd brought home from various restaurants for Midas hadn't been wasted, thought Ellie, as the retriever gave her a barrage of tail wags and swallowed the rest of his warning bark.

Halfway to the apartment complex, the first new raindrops spattered the ground. Ellie took a moment to savor the odor of wet pavement before she increased her pace, arriving at the entrance to the complex in what she assumed was record time.

A gigantic FOR LEASE banner, mounted on a steep hill, marred the scenery. Instead of following a twisting road, Ellie climbed to the top of the hill and paused, panting. Dozens of identically shaped duplexes spread out in the rainy distance, each unit painted a different color. The square boxes resembled the houses on a Monopoly board. In fact, the complex was called Marvin Gardens, and Ellie had a vision of the yellow space on the game she, Mick, and Tony had often played together. Grinning, she recalled how furious Tony became if he lost, claiming real estate was his expertise. Ellie could never convince him that luck, not skill, was an important ingredient in the game. She hoped Lady Luck had followed her this afternoon.

She consulted a detailed map, mounted on a waist-high stand, protected by a Plexiglas covering. Janssen's home was on the extreme southwest corner, the top half of a duplex. It had recently been painted blue-gray, almost the same color as Peter Miller's eyes.

Uh-oh! Blue-gray-eyed duplex. Marvin Gardens.

"Jeopardy." An omen? Ellie had the feeling Peter wouldn't be overly thrilled even if her theory turned out to be correct. There was a degree of male chauvinism in her lieutenant, not unlike Tony or even Mick.

"It's okay to dabble in crime solving, as long as I don't place myself in danger," she murmured, jogging to the front of the structure. "But I'm in no danger. I'll just duck in and out of Robbie's apartment quick as a wink. And collect all the evidence."

Would Peter be angry enough to end their relationship?

She'd have to deal with that "later." Right now the problem was how to get into Janssen's apartment.

She had put her wallet and keys in the zippered pocket of the blue and orange windbreaker. Now Ellie reached for those two items as she climbed twelve wooden steps to the tiny porch, then stood in front of the door. One of her keys fit the lock, but wouldn't turn; she hadn't really believed she'd be *that* lucky. She'd never tried to open a latch with a credit card, but had seen the feat performed dozens of times on TV and read about it in her novels. She bent, wiggled, and almost chipped the edge of the Bernstein Visa, but the lock remained stubbornly bolted in place. So much for forced entry.

Shaking her head in disgust, Ellie felt rainwater penetrate the jacket hood, soak her hair, and trickle past the collar to her neck. Maybe this whole thing was a dumb idea. Retreating down the steps, she surveyed the building.

On her left, Janssen's balcony jutted out into space. Sliding glass doors revealed white drawn drapes. Was it a trick of the rapidly increasing rainfall or did Ellie really see an inch of space between the door handle and the outside wall? As though Robbie had slammed the glass shut and its latch hadn't caught.

The occupant of the first floor had decorated his patio with a rusty hibachi grill, a webbed chaise lounge and chair, plus large unused bags of charcoal. The equipment was scattered about the leaf-strewn surface. Ellie appropriated the lightweight chair, placing charcoal bags on its seat to steady it and give her a higher perch. Even so, it wobbled precariously as her slippery sneakers fought to give her body a balanced pose. The balcony was eight or nine feet above her wet head.

Ignoring the fact that she had always been afraid of heights, she stretched her hands toward the balcony.

The tips of her fingers touched wood that was butter-slick from rain. She pulled herself up quickly, like an Olympic gymnast. For a moment she believed she had failed as her fingers glided backwards.

I'm not afraid of dying, only falling, she thought. Holy cow, it's nine or ten feet. I won't die; I'll just break a few important bones...like the ones in my head.

Feeling a sudden, surging rush of adrenaline, she hoisted herself up until her knees were wedged between the balcony's slatted railing. Then, as splinters threatened the palms of her hands, she maneuvered her torso, rump, and legs over the wooden parapet.

Lady Luck had followed her up the chair and charcoal, onto the balcony. Robbie's door *wasn't* latched. Ellie slid it open.

NINE

THE WHITE DRAPES LOOKED and felt like Turkish taffy. Ellie pushed at the sticky, unlaundered fabric, until, parting the middle, she emerged into Robbie's living room.

A dog would immediately shake itself while a cat would tongue itself dry, thought Ellie. But she just stood there, dripping rainwater. And the only words that flitted through her were: *Final Jeopardy. Category: Unreal Estate. Questions: Grace Toof. Answer: "Who is the woman that Graceland is named after?"*

Dumb? Incoherent? Maybe, but Ellie had been prepared to find a few sticks of furniture lost in an expanse of cheap shag carpeting. Instead, the room overflowed with Elvis Presley memorabilia.

Not Elvis in his prime, either. No boyish curl corkscrewing downward toward a sneer. No slim, swiveling hips or thrust-forth pelvis. Where was the Elvis of Ellie's repressed youth?

Almost every poster and dozens of thumbtacked magazine photos showed Presley toward the end of his career. The rock 'n' roll idol looked heavy and bloated, his lock of hair a wiggly exclamation point above puffy cheeks, fan-shaped sideburns, and double chin. Sparkling sequined costumes struggled to contain his build.

Ellie's eyes were drawn to the one piece of artwork that deviated from that pattern. In its place of honor, above a dilapidated foam-rubber sofa, hung a rectangular painting on a black velvet background. It showed Elvis in a progression of poses, from young heartthrob with glitzy guitar to older nightclub entertainer complete with flowing scarf. In his last position, the singer stood on a fluffy cloud, a heavenly aureole surrounding his head.

Another framed picture, atop a floor-model television, included a preteen Robbie Janssen standing next to the performer. Robbie was overweight, but neatly attired in suit and tie. His face looked animated, his hair well groomed, combed in an imitation Elvis pompadour. Peering closer, Ellie saw that Janssen had cleverly blended himself into the publicity-release photograph, utilizing two pictures to create one.

Turning away from the pathetic montage, she tugged on the drapes' drawstring, hoping to filter in more light. As the curtains creaked sideways, a tall figure fell forward. Ellie's frightened scream caught in her throat.

Heart pounding, she instinctively put out her hand to ward off the intruder, and came in contact with stiff cardboard. Another Elvis, life-size, with his hand bent forward over a microphone. It had obviously been used as a promotion piece during one of Presley's last public performances, because, again, the singer's body was bloated. Ellie giggled nervously while righting the cardboard figure behind the drapes. Then she shook her head.

"Stop it," she said out loud. "Stop laughing, you idiot. This is sad."

She didn't know very much about psychopaths. Could Robbie's mind have snapped with the death of his idol? She'd read and seen mysteries with religious fanaticism as a motive. Could this be similar? But why kill Jeannie, Esther, and Darlene? Because they were getting thin while Elvis—and Robbie—were overweight? *Farfetched.*

Holy cow! Ellie had never realized it until this moment, but, although taller, Darlene had resembled Priscilla Presley. The same clear complexion, classic smile, and full, pattee lips. A haunted look had shaded Darlene's eyes, as if she'd put her shattered life back together...just like Priscilla Presley.

Maybe Robbie meant to murder Darlene and killed the others to throw investigators off the track. Hadn't Ellie seen a similar plot on a movie-of-the-week a few months ago?

"No way," murmured Ellie. "I'm not sure I'd believe it if I hadn't thought of it."

She pictured herself saying: Listen, Loot, let's surmise, for the sake of argument, that Robbie noted Darlene's resemblance to Priscilla Presley and tried to initiate a relationship. Darlene turned him down or, worse, laughed at him. He went bonkers and began killing nice ladies so that he could eventually slash and rape Darlene. Brian *was* an accident; Robbie planned to kill Kelly, so he wouldn't be suspected when he took care of Darlene-Priscilla.

Peter would pat Ellie's head or send her into the kitchen to brew coffee. Or pop popcorn.

Kitchen. The time has come (the walrus said) to search for a bloody knife.

Next to the living room the narrow kitchen's walls were also covered with Elvis. Pictures, Scotch-taped on the vent above the stove, were so spattered with cooking grease that the magazine or newspaper print from the other side showed through. Janssen's sink was filled with dirty glasses and a few crusted pots and pans. Serrated steak knives lay in the potpourri of unwashed utensils, but no long, sharp blades. A plastic trash receptacle held empty frozen dinner containers and sugar-free pop cans. Wrinkling her nose, holding her breath at the aroma of bloodstained, Styrofoam chicken-parts packages, Ellie carefully sifted through the garbage—no knife—then washed her hands under the sink faucets.

Robbie's refrigerator door displayed magnets shaped like food—pizza, beer cans, cookies, and a layer cake. A cute pink piggie held an octagonal sign that read: STOP! DON'T PIG OUT. Beneath its too-cute snout, its jaws clipped mimeographed calendar pages. Friday's squares were inked with the identical scripted words: *Weight Winners.*

W.W Two meetings?

Or did the message mean to choose a victim?

Friday, October 31, had HALLOWEEN PARTY block lettered and circled with ink from a red felt-tip pen. This coming Thursday: AMC—LOVE ME TENDER. AMC? Of course…American Movie channel. *Love me Tender.* Elvis's film debut. Elvis's film debut. (Love me tender or you'll die?) Ellie flipped to December. Only one space—December 3—was filled, again with block lettering: HBO—VIVA LAS VEGAS.

Otherwise the date boxes were empty, and Ellie felt a surge of pity.

Then fear. How long had she been here? Jogging to the complex. Climbing the balcony. Studying the decor. Ironically, *she* had forgotten to wear her own watch. The small clock stove was covered with dried grease, and the numbers behind the glass were impossible to decipher.

Rock 'n' roll, Ellie. Search 'n' scat.

A round, painted Elvis clock, mounted on the wall above the kitchen entrance, had a dangling cord too short to reach an outlet. Decoration? Or had Robbie stilled the hands at the moment of the singer's death? Ellie shivered.

Her soggy corduroy slacks clung uncomfortably to her legs. Her sneakers squished as she hurried down a hallway and peered into a small bathroom. Streamers of dental floss dripped down a sink containing the usual apparatus for cleansing and shaving. No wristwatch. A quick glance inside an under-the-sink cabinet revealed a bundle of dirty laundry, including the blue cotton shirt. Distastefully, Ellie separated it from the other clothes and folded it over her arm.

She walked into the bedroom, a shock after the crowded walls of the living room and kitchen. Except for an unvarnished wooden dresser and an unmade bed with a yellow blanket, the space was vacant. Closed cretonne curtains hung crookedly from a roped running track. It was so dim that Ellie's eyes were drawn to the dresser's surface where an electric candle sent up a battery-powered glow. She fumbled for a wall switch and watched the ceiling fixture flicker into life.

Robbie's candle stood before a dime-store frame whose nonglare glass protected a *People* magazine cover photo of Karen Carpenter. Had Robbie identified with the anorexic singer, or wished he could find peace-in-death from an overdose of thin?

Damn! There went the Darlene-Priscilla theory. Somehow the adoration of an overweight Elvis and a shrine to Karen Carpenter didn't seem the sinister traits of a vicious murderer. A new motive. Could Robbie have confused people nearing their goal weights with Karen?

There was no watch in sight, and Ellie reminded herself that she didn't know what time it was. The window was blurred by teary raindrops, and the sky outside looked slate gray. Swiftly she checked the dresser. Four drawers. Pennies, cuff links, underwear, several sweatshirts and sweatpants. No wristwatch. The closet revealed a few clothes on wire hangers and an old pair of cowboy boots that needed to be resoled. She ran her hands along the inside of the boots, although she believed that if Robbie was clever enough to hide the watch in the footwear, he'd be smart enough to dump it or get the damn thing repaired.

Dead end. Ellie felt grubby and stupid and...

Caught.

She froze as she heard the click of key in bolt, a door opening, the hum of a TV commercial, and theme music introducing the local five-thirty newscast.

Next, the rustle of grocery sack and the opening of the refrigerator. The hiss of a pop-top can, the *whoosh-thunk* of footsteps, and the unmistakable sound of a man urinating. The toilet flushed. Okay, would Robbie return to kitchen or living room?

Neither. The shower head squirted, bringing the sound of rain inside the apartment. With her detailed mind, Ellie couldn't visualize any robe gracing the bathroom's interior. In a few minutes Robbie might enter his bedroom... nude!

Jesus, I have to get out of here, and I don't have much time.

Time. The brilliant notion that had brought her to this predicament, and what had she achieved? The theft of a dirty blue shirt whose stains, Ellie now decided, were remnants of sweat and ketchup, and whose smell indicated the faint lingering odor of men's cologne.

She sidled along the wall of the hallways past the half-open bathroom door. Fortunately, the sound of Robbie's voice muffled any footsteps.

"Come gather 'round me boys," he sang, "and I'll tell you a tale, all about my troubles on the old Chisholm Trail. Comma ti yi yippi, yippi yay, yippi yay, comma ti yi yippi, yippi yay."

Cowboy boots in the closet, thought Ellie. If John

Wayne had been overweight or anorexic, would Robbie have created a shrine to the Duke?

Stifling the urge to giggle, she made it down the hallway and entered Janssen's tiny vestibule.

Thank you, God, she offered silently. Robbie hadn't latched the front entrance; she wouldn't have to fumble with bolts.

"Comma ti yi yippi, yippi yay, yippi yay…"

Why wasn't Robbie yodeling Elvis songs? wondered Ellie, reaching for the doorknob.

"On a ten dollar hoss and a forty dollar saddle, started up the trail just to punch some cattle. Comma ti yi yippi, yippi yay…"

Ellie sneezed.

The shower stopped splishing.

She opened the front door. "Please, God," she whispered, "let me make it safely outside and I'll be a good girl from now on. No more snooping."

"What are you doing here?"

Never mind, God, guess you want me to snoop.

Ellie turned, releasing the blue shirt behind her back, hoping it would land somewhere outside Robbie's vision.

"Hello," she said, grinning like an idiot. "I knocked but nobody answered, and the door was open a crack. With all the, well, trouble recently, I decided I'd step inside and make sure you were okay."

"Ellie Bernstein? Ellie, is that you?" Robbie's face turned beet red. "I was taking a shower."

Yes, I know. Comma ti yi yippi yay for me. Why didn't I wait at home for Peter?

Robbie had thrown on his grayish postal-uniform pants. Droplets from the shower mingled with brown chest hair, and his pectoral muscles sagged.

"I should be more, uh, careful 'bout locking my

door," he said, "but I live alone. I have nothing worth stealing and nobody'd murder me. Why bother? I ain't skinny."

"You will be someday." Ellie took a few steps backwards. "I was jogging, passing by, so I thought I'd see how you were coming along on the diet. I like to do that sometimes...check up on my members...and...and you live close, so...I decided..."

She couldn't go on. There were too many holes in her improvised excuse. Jogging? Just passing by? In a downpour? At almost six o'clock in the evening?

Robbie stood, a statue dripping water on the hallways shag, his arms pretzeled across his naked chest like a coy virgin. One arm had MOTHER tattooed inside a heart. Sparkling rings winked from the third finger of each hand.

And then Ellie saw it—the watch on Robbie's left wrist. It hadn't been removed from his shower. It not only existed and worked but was obviously waterproof.

"If you wait here a few minutes, I'll drive you home," Robbie finally said.

"Please don't bother."

"It's no bother. Or is your car parked nearby?"

"My car? It's at home. When I started out earlier it wasn't raining. You know how the Weight Winners handbook says to exercise rain or shine," finished Ellie lamely.

"Well, you can't walk back in that," said Robbie, pointing toward the open door where rain fell in a shimmering curtain. A strong wind whipped the beaded veil of drops back and forth. "I admire you, Ellie, jogging in the rain." Robbie paused, then added, "You don't seem awfully wet."

"I had an umbrella," she improvised, "but I slipped climbing your steps and the wind, well, I dropped it."

"I'll get it for you." Robbie took a few eager steps toward the doorway.

"*No!* I mean it's ruined; inside out."

"Okay, let me turn off the TV and put dry clothes on, then I'll drive you home."

"Yes, thank you, I'd appreciate a lift," said Ellie, suddenly bone-tired.

While Robbie disappeared into his bedroom, Ellie scooped up the blue shirt that lay in a dripping heap on the front porch. Not knowing what else to do, she stuffed it down the front of her windbreaker, where it immediately saturated her sweater. *Good.* An uncomfortable punishment for her breaking and entering.

Robbie, in black pants and an oversize sweatshirt whose blue letters advertised that POSTMEN DELIVER, handed Ellie his own umbrella.

"I like Elvis," he muttered as they descended the twelve steps.

"Do you? Me too."

"I have pictures and…uh…photographs."

"Oh?"

"Didn't you see them?"

"Well, I was standing in the entry," Ellie hedged.

Robbie's face brightened. "I almost met him once… uh…Elvis…uh…" Unable to think of anything else to say, he led the way to his car.

The car was another surprise—an early-model shiny red Corvette. Ellie had expected an old dented heap, and again she reminded herself not to prejudge. Still, she wished she could open the small compact trunk and search for an incriminating weapon. Dammit, why the hell did she insist on looking for nonexistent clues? Her abysmal foray into Robbie's apartment should have taught her a good lesson.

Janssen seemed embarrassed as he squeezed behind the steering wheel. "I've always wanted a sports car," he confessed. "I even named her Vetty Grable. Get it?" He patted the dash. "Almost called her Vet Midler, but I like Vetty Grable better."

Vetty Grable. Charming. Adorable. Ellie felt renewed shame at her suspicions.

To emphasize her miserable guilt, Robbie peered down at his watch. "It's late for you to be out walking alone."

A remnant of caution made Ellie reply, "That's okay. A friend of mind knows where I am…where I planned to go today. With all the, er, accidents recently, I leave an itinerary every time I step outside the house."

"Good idea. You're such a pretty lady," said Janssen in a low, husky voice. "I can't wait until I lose all my weight like you did. Although I think you're thin now… uh…just right…uh…"

With this personal revelation, uttered under the reflection of a street lamp, Ellie again saw Robbie turn beet red.

He drove the short distance, then maneuvered his Corvette toward the Bernstein curb. "Shucks," he said, "should have turned in at the drive."

Shucks? Another cowboy-ism. John Wayne rescuing the wayward schoolmarm. Shucks. The word sounded endearing, thought Ellie, especially when it came from the mouth of this shy, lonely man.

"Thank you very much, Robbie. I'll see you Friday at the meeting. You're doing so well on the diet, I'm sure you'll be successful, and—"

"There's a police car across the street, Ellie."

"Yes, I know. Thanks again, Robbie."

Running through the rain, she waved good-bye over her shoulder, and noted how the squad car's door opened, then closed while she scurried toward her house. The cops stayed inside their vehicle; maybe they were jotting down Vetty Grable's license number. Perhaps they wouldn't snitch, but if they did, Peter would get a full report.

After changing into a fluffy, floor-length yellow bathrobe, Ellie lit a fire in the fireplace and buried Robbie's shirt amid the kindling. Poor, sweet man. How could she have possibly suspected him? Vetty Grable! Robbie couldn't murder a moth. When the blue material became consumed by flames she felt better.

Then she plumped couch pillows, and...

Peter! Ellie raced toward the phone. While hanging up the receiver, she experienced a memory flash. *Robbie'd pulled up to her curb, and he hadn't asked for her address.*

The Corvette's interior had been dim, but hadn't Robbie seemed *nervous* at the sight of the squad car? Shucks, anybody would be fidgety at the sight of a police cruiser.

Shucks on a shingle! Why hadn't she asked Robbie for alibis, *four* alibis? Where was he during the murders?

As a sleuth, she sorta' stunk. What would Robbie's neighbor think when he discovered his chair heaped with bags of charcoal? Had she drawn Robbie's drapes closed? No. Dear God, she hadn't even turned off the bedroom light. Would Robbie believe he'd left the drapes agape and the light on? Or would he recall Ellie's idiotic grin as she stood by his front door? His open-a-crack front door.

Was she in any danger? Only if Robbie was the killer!

Ellie suddenly thought of another non-blasphemous cuss, one she hadn't used since her son Mick was perhaps six or seven years old. In order to nullify Tony's frequent shits and fuck-its, Ellie had devised a litany that, if delivered correctly, sounded wicked.

"Fauna, Flora, and Merryweather," she swore.

TEN

THE MOVIE THEATER SMELLED like popcorn. And Milk Duds. And dirty sneakers. And Peter.

"Kiss me. Kiss me as if it were the last time."

Ellie watched Ingrid and Bogie melt into a passionate embrace. She felt Peter tighten his arm about her shoulders. Then, leaning over, he kissed her somewhere between her ear and chin.

She and Peter were acting like kids. Here they sat, almost in each other's laps, watching the first film from a festival of Ingrid Bergman classics, and necking. Did they still call it necking? Making out? Turing her head slightly, Ellie met Peter's lips.

"We should have stayed home," she gasped. "I have a VCR. We could have rented—"

"It's not the same," Peter interrupted. "I adore Ingrid on the big screen, larger than life. Those eyes, that mouth, her sexy accent, those broad shoulders—"

"Shhhh," warned a man in the row behind them.

Play-it-again-Sam played "As Time Goes By" and Ellie cuddled against Peter's chest.

"Have you heard anything new about Kelly Benedict?" she whispered.

"Not now, sweetheart, enjoy the movie."

"Sorry, it just popped out. It's so hard to forget."

"Nothing new from the hospital. She's alive. You're lucky to be alive, Ellie. If you ever do another stupid thing like breaking and entering a possible suspect's apartment, I'll kill you myself."

"Shhhh!"

"I tried to call you, Peter."

"You should have waited until I called back."

"Are you serious? I suppose you wanted me to sit by the phone twiddling my thumbs."

"What happened to curling up with a good detective—"

"I did! But I couldn't concentrate."

"Shhhh!" "Shhhh!" "Shhhh!" The sound came from several nearby sources.

Ellie watched Bergman and Bogart talk about their days when they worked for the French underground. Shucks, brave Ingrid could roam all over the place, and spit in the faces of murdering Nazi perpetrators. Bogie didn't suggest she sit by the phone, twiddling her thumbs, waiting for his call.

Fauna, Flora, and Merryweather! Ellie leaned forward in the plush red seat, her back rigid.

"What is it now?" whispered Peter.

"If I had found incriminating evidence inside Robbie Janssen's apartment, you wouldn't yell at me."

"I'm not yelling. How can I yell in a movie theater? That's probably why you wanted to come here toni—"

"What? *Casablanca* was *your* idea. Besides, you did at least forty-five minutes worth of shouting before we even left the house."

"I don't want you sticking your nose into my murder case. That pretty nose could easily get sliced off."

"*Your* murder case? *My* members are being killed."

"That's what I mean. Dead is dead. If you're dismembered, you can't say, 'Ooops, sorry Lieutenant darling, didn't intend to become a corpse on you. I'll listen better next time.' Dammit—"

"If you two don't shut up, I'll find the manager," said the man behind them.

"Why don't you show him your badge and gun, Peter?" Ellie's voice dripped with sarcasm. "Doesn't a police detective have more clout than a theater manager?"

"What's that suppose to mean?"

"Your attitude. Your damn smart-ass, know-it-all attitude."

"I think you should examine your own motives, lady. You want to solve the mystery, collect the evidence, then toss it to me like a leftover bone. I'm suppose to stand here, grinning like an idiot, a dog wagging his tail."

"A dog doesn't grin, except in cartoons. However, your idiot remark was appropriate."

"Why am *I* the damn smart-ass know-it-all cartoonish idiot? Christ, Ellie, *I* didn't break and enter—"

"The balcony door was open!"

"*I* didn't search for a knife in the trash. And *I* didn't burn a possible piece of evidence."

"Shouldn't have told you about that."

"You'd never have confessed anything at all if my diligent police—"

"Officious officers! Kibitzing cops! How many times do I have to tell you? Robbie didn't do it. How could a person who names his car Vetty Grable stick knitting needles through an old lady's neck?"

"That's beside the point!"

"Are you making a pun, Peter? If you are, it's not funny."

"It wasn't intentional, dammit!"

For a few moments, Ellie seethed silently. Peter's wrong, she thought, or was there a grain of truth in his leftover-bone statement? Did she still ache from Tony's ridicule? Allow her ego to override judgement? With a sigh, she untended her muscles, then pressed her mouth close to Peter's ear.

"I adore it when you wag your tail; it's such a nice tail," she murmured. "You claim you fell in love when you saw my fanny swivel into Good Shepherd's hallway. I fell in love with your tailbone. It has such character."

"Christ, what am I going to do with you?"

"Shhhh!" "Shhhh!"

Ellie felt a barrage of Milk Duds pelt the nape of her neck. One invaded her sweater and nestled between her breasts.

Peter ran his hand under her sweater.

"Cut it out," she whispered.

"Hush Norrie, or the nice people will get angry again."

"Norrie?"

"That's what I'm going to call you from now on. It's short for Eleanor, and you seem to ig-*nore* my advice."

"I'm ig-noring your last remark, but I kind of like the nickname. Peter, what are you doing?"

"I think I've found a Milk Dud...ahhh, got it. Wow, here's another one."

"Stop it! That's not a Milk Dud; that's my nip—"

"I'll stop if you scurry up the aisle and buy us some buttered popcorn. I'm hungry."

"Why should *I* scurry?"

"Because *I* enjoy watching your fanny swivel. Please get the giant box, Norrie."

"Are you kidding? Small box, the smallest they have, or I'll eat it too. I can't resist that stuff."

"Norrie?"

"Yes, Peter."

"I love you. Buy us a couple of Cokes too, okay?"

Ellie rose and slithered down the row, stepping on toes.

She had never been so conscious of her tush before, and wished she hadn't worn her tightest jeans. Her blue sweater was okay—large, loose, almost floppy, hiding the nipple that still tingled from Peter's brief caress.

Strolling through double exit doors, Ellie momentarily felt blinded from bright lobby lights. Then she noted that the next Ingrid Bergman film on the schedule was *For Whom the Bell Tolls,* costarring Gary Aw-shucks Cooper.

Another vehicle for a brave heroine.

Another (dead) skinny hero in Robbie's repertoire?

But at the end, Elvis wasn't skinny. Well, he lost at least two hundred pounds after he died. The ultimate weight reduction program. And it came with a guarantee; you would never, repeat, *never* gain anything back. Ellie shuddered.

There were no other customers at the candy counter, so she quickly purchased a giant box of popcorn, remembered Peter's love-you Cokes remark, and added a couple of large Diet Pepsis to her order. *Phony butter and counterfeit sugar,* she thought, watching the girl behind the counter place all three items in a cardboard container. The paper cups fit snugly inside cut-out holes.

Glancing around the empty lobby, Ellie admired the dignified opulence of the old theater. Red and gold flocked wallpaper surrounded mirrors with gilded frames. The domed ceiling sported a hanging chandelier. On her left were carpeted steps leading to a balcony. Because it was a weeknight, the stairway had been blocked off by a red velvet rope.

They don't build theaters like this anymore, she thought, with both an inside and outside lobby. They've even posted movie stills behind glass windows.

She walked toward the wall next to the lobby entrance,

then gazed at photos of Ingrid Bergman and Cary Grant. *Notorious.*

"Don't turn around," said a hoarse voice. "I have a knife and I'll use it if you scream."

Ellie felt the sharp pointy blade pierce her sweater, then her bra.

"I won't scream I promise," she said calmly, although her heart pounded. "Who are you? Can't we discuss—"

"Walk slow, very slow to the balcony landing. Step over the rope. Climb the stairs and don't turn 'round. If you do what I say, I won't hurt you."

Like hell you won't!

"What'cha waitin' for? I'm gonna count to three. If you don't move your butt, I'll twist my knife in your back, understand? One...two..."

Ellie walked forward.

Why didn't somebody stop them? she wondered, balancing her container as she maneuvered her legs over the velvet rope. The balcony was closed, and she was positive nobody was allowed upstairs. Then she recalled the empty lobby. Okay, but what about the candy-counter girl? Ellie snuck a quick peek. No candy-counter girl, dammit! In fact, there were no candy-counter customers, which was probably the reason there was no candy-counter girl. Brilliant, Ellie! Move to the head of the class. Move to the top of the stairs. Do not pass go, do not collect two hundred...dollars to doughnuts, the perp had lurked, waiting until the counter girl disappeared. And Ellie had played right into his hands by admiring placards from Alfred Hitchcock's let's-scare-the-bejesus-out-of-you suspense film.

Admit it, Ellie, you're scared. *Okay, I'm scared.*

She could pretend to stumble. But if she fell backwards, she'd hit the knife—*sorry, Lieutenant*...and if she tripped forwards, she'd probably roll down the steps and break her neck...*didn't mean to become a corpse on you.*

Unchallenged, Ellie and her attacker climbed the staircase until they reached the balcony. Her eyes dilated from sudden darkness while ceiling stereo speakers emphasized the sound of Bogart's voice:

"Now, now. Here's looking at you, kid."

Now, now, here's looking at you, perp, thought Ellie.

Now! Turning abruptly, she flung the popcorn and Pepsi into her stalker's face, and heard a roar of rage as the man instinctively clawed at the salty puffs and sticky liquid flowing into his eyes.

Through the darkness, she registered stocking cap and pea jacket. Then, still half blind herself, Ellie scampered away, found another staircase, and leaped up the steps two at a time.

Entering a projectionist's booth, she glanced over her shoulder and felt a surge of vertigo.

The staircase was empty; the perp hadn't followed. At least not yet.

"You ain't allowed in here, miss," said an old, stubble-chinned gentleman sitting in a canvas director's chair and holding a copy of *Penthouse* magazine.

"Somebody was going to attack me, probably kill me," Ellie started to explain, but couldn't continue because her heart raced, duplicating the syncopated rhythm of the film's accelerated music.

"Attack?" The man licked his lips, looked down at his magazine, then back up at Ellie. "Attack?"

"Never mind. Could you call the manager? Ask him to walk me down to the lobby? Please hurry."

"The manager ain't here tonight."

Ellie stumbled toward the open square in the front wall and leaned way out. Her body blocked light beams and created a shadow, obliterating an airplane flying toward freedom—freedom or a nearby landing field. Cut and print.

Cut! She had almost been cut, sliced, notched, carved.

There was a distinct murmur from the audience. Heads bobbed. In another moment, feet would stomp.

"Peter!" she screamed at the top of her lungs. "Lieutenant Peter Miller! Help!"

She felt dozens of eyes gazing upward. Zombie eyes. Soft-boiled-egg eyes. Did one pair belong to the killer?

Dozens of mouths must be agape with stupefaction because she smelled fresh popcorn and Juicy Fruit gum.

Pants must be agape because she could swear she smelled the musty rubber of a condom.

Her vertigo returned.

The projectionist grabbed her sweater at the nape of her neck and hauled her backwards. His other hand circled her ribcage and tweaked a breast.

A freebee they used to call it in high school, a free feel. First base.

Would this nightmare never end?

"Peter! Help! *Hic.*"

SLOUCHED OVER HER KITCHEN table, Ellie sipped from a mug filled with equal portions of brandy and coffee. Her hands shook. No doubt she was pale, because all the blood had drained from her face. And she couldn't stop hiccuping. Peter had tried mouth-to-mouth resuscitation, a paper bag, even the Heimlich maneuver, but he couldn't stop the spasms. Furthermore, Ellie was positive that *Ingrid* had never hiccuped in the aftermath of danger.

"Feeling better?" asked Peter.

"Yes. Sorry about, *hic,* shouting during the climax, *hic…*"

"Lots of people shout during the climax, Norrie."

"...of the movie," she finished, then held her breath, counted to ten, and hiccuped. "Sorry," she repeated, "can't seem to stop."

"Please don't apologize, sweetheart," said Peter, his voice tender. "You're allowed to get scared. Come here and sit on my lap. That's a good girl. What's the matter, Norrie? Do you feel sick to your stomach? Truthfully, that's a more typical reaction than hiccups."

"No, I'm okay, honest. I'm just trying to get a picture in my head...*hic.* Anything to help...*hic.*"

"Relax. It's when you don't try so hard that things come to you."

"It was dark in the balcony, *hic,* and I could barely make out a thing, *hic,* just lumps of seat backs that looked like cemetery headstones, *hic.* Didn't anybody see him?"

"The ticket-taker was in the manager's office, talking on the phone. The manager wasn't there."

"Yes, I know, *hic.*"

"The woman behind the candy counter was..." Peter paused, his cheeks ruddy. "It was her time of the month and she, well, she said her tummy ached."

"Cramps! She had her damn period, Lieutenant. Jesus!"

"I think I like holy cow better," he mumbled.

"Damn, *hic,* damn, *hic,* damn, *hic.* I wish I could remember, *hic,* whatever it is I'm trying to remember."

"Okay, baby, calm down. If you don't stop hiccuping, I'm going to drive you straight to the emergency room. Finish your brandy. Good girl. Now put your head on my shoulder. Close your eyes."

"A smell," she said, so startled that the hiccups, at long last, evaporated.

"What smell?"

"Our killer has an odor, Peter. When he was close behind me, he smelled like…" Ellie raised her head and sniffed. Then she buried her face against Peter's shirt.

"I can't remember," she wailed. "All I can smell is popcorn."

And Juicy Fruit gum.

And a musty condom.

And dizzy.

Did dizzy have an odor?

Yes. It smelled like pure, unadulterated terror.

Like the piss in your jeans.

Like the pale, stale breath from hiccups.

Like the sweat that stained your body when you awoke from a nightmare, then realized that you hadn't been asleep after all.

ELEVEN

GEORGE BUBBLES SHOVED a handful of carrots into a bag while at the same time, he surveyed veggie shoppers. Most of the women pushed carts filled with little kids. George had nothing against children, but they tended to eliminate candidates for any successful Night Out.

Hold it…over there by the tomatoes stood a juicy tidbit with long blond hair. She turned, and George recognized the young co-ed. Sandra something. Sandra Connery, as in Sean? Or Connors, as in Chuck? George pictured a long rifle and a finger on the trigger. Yup, Connors, as in Chuck.

Music major he recalled. Would Sandra Connors as in Chuck agree to join him for a sing-along at the Dew Drop Inn? Heck, nothing ventured, nothing *gained,* ha-ha.

But before George could ask, Sandra ran down the aisle toward another young blond woman.

"Natalie, Natalie, I just noticed the time. I was due at Ellie's house five minutes ago. Will you, won't you, will you, won't you, will you please tote my groceries back to the dorm?"

George watched the other girl toss her head and laugh.

"Okay, Alice," she said. "How come you've never forgotten your dumb lines?"

"*Alice's Adventures in Wonderland* was my all-time favorite show."

"That's because you played the lead, Sandra. I was the queen of…" Natalie's voice diminished as the two girls turned a corner.

Double-damn, thought George. I'm due back at work. Lucky my store is right next to the supermarket.

He dropped his bag of carrots on top of clumped radishes, then headed toward the Safeway exit. And had almost exited safely when he bumped into Tubby Evergreen.

"Hey, watch where you're goin', asshole," Tubby said, racing toward the cookie aisle.

George immediately forgave the lack of recognition and the insult. Tubby weighed lots more than George. Tubby made George look almost skinny. But not too skinny. After all, skinny people were getting killed. They ventured, and lost, and died.

FATHER O'SULLIVAN RECOGNIZED the desperation in the unseen woman's voice, the melancholy despair in her forgive-me-Father-for-I-have-sinned.

He mouthed the standard reply, hoping his tone reflected sympathy, then heard agitated sobs. How terrible was this woman's transgression? Father O'Sullivan prayed it was a little sin, not a big one.

The crying sounds abruptly ceased, then changed to heavy footsteps running toward the back of the church.

Leaning against her rake, Sister Maria paused to watch the woman exit and rush past, scattering Sister Maria's neat pile of leaves.

Holy Singing Nun, she thought, that's Lulu Evergreen from my Weight Winners class.

ROBBIE JANSSEN RETURNED from his lunch break and positioned himself behind the window.

A shame they'd never made an Elvis movie set inside the post office. Too boring? Not really. Elvis could have sung through the bars of his postal cage and danced 'round the mail sacks. After all, there were plenty of songs about the postal service. "Please Mister Postman" or "Love Letters in the Sand" or "I'm Gonna Sit Right Down and Write Myself a Letter."

"Oh she wrote me a letter and said she couldn't live without me no more. Next please." Robbie waved toward a man with an armful of wrapped packages.

Who would play Elvis's girlfriend? The singer always had a pretty girlfriend in his movies.

Robbie weighed the first package.

Ellie Bernstein? No, she looked young, but she was, well, mature. Too bad Darlene was dead.

Robbie balanced the second package on his fingertips, then slid it onto the scale.

"How 'bout Ellie's little friend with the long blond hair? Sandra something."

Robbie weighed the third package.

Sandra *Connors,* yeah, perfect. She studied music at Colorado College, sometimes sang over at the Dew Drop Inn. Pretty Sandra Connors was the perfect choice.

ELLIE WATERED HER PLANTS. Outside, the distant mountains were silhouetted against a cloudless sky.

Today the sun shone, its rays bouncing off the glass dome of her police cruiser. Ridiculous—a total waste. Peter had once claimed he hated waste, yet the stalker would never approach with that vehicle parked across the street. If she had to be spied on, why not use an unmarked car? Because then she'd be a decoy. Peter wanted an ounce of protection rather than a pound of entrapment.

Ellie brought her attention back to Sandra, who noisily chewed bubble gum, cracking it between her teeth.

Removing her feet from a pair of Capezio ballet slippers, Sandra curled her legs under her curvy bottom and leaned against a couch cushion. With pursed lips she created a hug pink bubble that magically disappeared back into her mouth before it could stick to her freckled nose.

"So that was the end of Gary," she said. "I don't know why he thought I'd sleep with him just because he invited me to a hot-tub party. Anyway, I don't look that hot in a bathing suit. No, no, I really don't, Ellie, although I try to shave around my undies' crotch. Natalie doesn't. Ugh!"

Shifting positions, Sandra raised one leg toward the ceiling, flexed her shapely dancer's calf, then relaxed as she replaced the leg under her rump. She wore black tights under denim cutoffs. A Colorado College sweatshirt had been scissored to leave her midriff bare.

She'd just regaled Ellie with an involved recitation of her latest romantic interlude. Gary the hockey player—with whom she'd shared a meaningful, albeit platonic relationship—wasn't very smart or very tall, like Mick, for instance, but he was okay "personality-wise" and popular with students who counted. Sexual rejection had kept the athlete lusting after the young sophomore for three weeks, until he'd finally gone in search of easier prey.

Sandra's sleek blond hair plus her round eyes (the color of Limoges china, thought Ellie) created a reincarnation of Lewis Carroll's original *Alice's Adventures in Wonderland*. All Sandra needed was a pinafore and pantalettes. A smattering of freckles marred the angelic exterior and gave a hint of the intelligent humor within.

"Oh, I almost forgot," said Sandra. "How's Mick?"

"Almost forgot?" Ellie grinned and crossed one faded denim leg over the other. She, too, wore a sweatshirt, orange, unscissored. "Mick's fine. In fact, the last time I talked to him, he asked about you."

"Really? What did he say?"

"He said, 'How's that small, slender, beautiful actress who is going to sing with my band when she grows up? The one who's so insecure about how gorgeous she really is.'"

"He did not!"

"Well, it's close, anyway. Mick did ask about you and he said something about your singing with his band."

Like a magnet, Ellie's son had attracted a group of Boulder student musicians and formed an ensemble to entertain at dances, weddings, bar mitzvahs, whatever. They called themselves Rocky Mountain High, after John Dusseldorf's (Denver's) famous song.

"Mick said I was slender and beautiful?"

"He didn't have to. It was in his voice. You can't believe it, can you?"

"No. I was fat for such a long, long time."

She had met Sandra two years earlier when the girl was a senior in high school. Although a freshman at Colorado University, Mick still occasionally dated perfect Lisa, who seemed to surround herself with physically imperfect peers. Quiet, shy, and *starved* for affection, an overweight Sandy had worshipfully attached herself to Lisa, then developed a terminal crush on Mick.

Ellie had seen the girl at Mick's spring-break birthday party, an outdoor barbecue. Poor Sandy, standing apart, stuffing her mouth with hot dogs, potato salad, and chips. Recognizing the symptoms, which paralleled those of her own childhood, Ellie had cornered her, then talked persuasively—*bonded*, Mick would say—and the result was a membership in Ellie's first Weight Winners group.

Sandra shed thirty pounds, dropped her Sandy nickname to go along with a "new personality," then revealed a soaring soprano voice, shyly hidden before her metamorphosis. Jazzercise sessions awakened a dormant desire to dance again ("when I was a kid I had ballet lessons, Ellie, and actually learned to prance on my toes, but I was so chunky and graceless, I gave it up.") Thus, Sandra had dismissed her plans to become a nurse or teacher for a show business career.

Sandra still attended lectures at least once a month and Ellie hoped to call her daughter-in-law one day. Which was a distinct possibility, since Mick had not only noticed the physical beauty but had seen that she was beautiful inside, too.

"So what else is new and exciting?" asked Ellie, bringing her attention back to the present.

"Is Mick coming home this weekend?"

"No, Muffin, why?"

"Rats!" Momentarily, Sandra's eyelids drooped in disappointment. Then, raising her long lashes, she said, "Ellie, Ellie, listen to this. You won't believe it. The campus is holding a beauty pageant for Halloween. All the contestants will be dressed in Cinderella ball gowns, but we—I mean they—have to wear Lone Ranger masks. The mask is suppose to appease the feminists by keeping the entries anonymous. Give me a break! Anyway, there's a big party tomorrow night to select the ten finalists who'll compete at a Halloween ball on the thirty-first."

"You're one of the contestants."

"How did you know?"

"I'm an amateur detective. At least I'm able to solve the puzzles on printed pages..." Ellie paused, then added lightly, "Besides, Muffin, you goofed and said 'we.'"

"I love it when you call me Muffin. Do you know how long it's been since I actually ate a blueberry muffin?"

"You once insisted you could never give them up, remember? Tell me about your pageant."

"The drama department and choir both nominated me. Can you believe that?"

"Sure can."

"Well, the other girls are prettier, but there's a talent portion and I'm going to sing an aria from *The Barber of Seville*. Rosina's soliloquy. Anyway, even though I'm not all that beautiful, I can belt out a song the best."

Sandra might still have doubts about her appearance, thought Ellie, but she was secure in her talent.

"I thought about dancing," she continued, stretching her toes toward the ceiling again, "but since the choir is backing me, and two other girls, including Natalie, plan to do short ballet numbers, I decided I'd have a better chance singing. I wish Mick could be there tomorrow night."

"Tell you what, Muffin, I'll give him a call. I can't promise he'll be able to make it, but if he's free, I'll offer to finance him home for the weekend."

Sandra's expression alternated between delight and dismay. "Please don't pressure him; I mean, if he has other plans, I'll understand, I mean, it's *no big deal*."

"Mick would want to be with you. And there's somebody *I* want him to meet."

"Hey, you're blushing!"

"I am not!"

"You are too! C'mon, details."

"He…Lieutenant Peter Miller…he calls me Norrie," Ellie began, then revealed all the details. Well, almost all.

FRIDAY NIGHT.

Sandra surveyed herself in the mirror as she twined

flowers around the crown of her head, decorating the strands of her topknot ponytail. The remainder of her long hair cascaded down her bare back.

Ellie had sent over the fresh sprigged bouquet for luck and enclosed a note that read: "Knock 'em dead, kiddo."

Applying makeup, Sandra drew heavy black liner around her eyes, since she considered them her best feature. And because they had to shine through the damn feminist-inspired mask. Then she sprinkled glittery gold powder over blusher and eyeshadow, studied her face, decided it looked okay, and suddenly felt like Cinderella.

She wore a blue gown, her own design, stitched by a local seamstress in return for two months of housecleaning. The dress was a study in contrasts—high-necked and demure in front, dipping to the waist in back. The long skirt had side slits that, with movement, revealed her legs and two frilly garters around each thigh. High-heeled sandals helped minimize her bulky dancer's muscles.

"Okay, Muffin," she said to the mirror, "you're as ready as you'll ever be. Knock 'em dead, kiddo."

THE PARTY AND PRELIMINARY pageant took place in an old Victorian-style building a couple blocks from campus. The house was rented by a group of students who, although not fraternally organized, had nailed the Greek symbols for sigma, epsilon, and chi over the front door: *SEX*. The iron-spiked gate in the fence surrounding the lawn, house, and garage squealed out a musical greeting.

Selected as one of the finalists, Sandra didn't know if she had come in first, second, or tenth—and it didn't really matter. She was dancing on a cloud, especially when a voice whispered in her ear: "I wouldn't have picked a scrawny kid like you although the talent part sure pulled you over the edge. You sounded great.''

"Thank you, Mr. Bernstein, sir...I think. What do you mean scrawny?''

Mick surveyed her critically. "Well, you'll never keep Dolly Parton awake at night.''

"You think I'm too small on top?'' asked Sandra, wondering how she could possibly grow her breasts by the end of the evening.

"Hey, I was only teasing. Why are you newly hatched thin people so sensitive? You're just like Mom.''

"Because deep down we're still fat-ish people.'' On tiptoe, Sandra threw her arms about the boy's neck and gave him a hard hug. "Oh, Mick, you came to my pageant. Did...did Ellie pressure you?''

"Of course not. She *bribed* me. Travel expenses,'' he added quickly when he saw Sandra's expression. "Besides *I* had to bribe the judges. And when that didn't work, I threatened them.''

"Really? How did you threaten them?''

"I promised to invade the party with *my* band and play Lawrence Welk music all night. One anna two anna—''

"Jee-sus!''

"Why else do you think you were chosen as a finalist?''

Mick cupped her chin with one hand and gave her a kiss.

Sandra studied him admiringly from beneath her lowered lashes. Mick's coloring was a mix-and-match of his parents' genes. The thick hair was a Robert Redford blond, like his father's, but his blue-green eyes were all Ellie.

John Russell had been hired for the evening, and his fingers flew across the keys of an old piano like migrating birds. The crowd called for Sandra to join him. She was delighted, having sung with John before. The musician's wispy tailed braid swirled as he and Sandra collaborated on an original rock ballad. In the crush of well-wishers she lost sight of Mick.

Assuming he had stepped outside, away from the smoky interior, Sandra slipped through a side door and walked the length of a railed porch. No Mick. Turning to go back into the house, she collided with a man and almost fell.

"You okay?" he asked in a rather hoarse voice.

"Where on earth did you come from?"

"Ain't you the Connors kid?"

"Yes, I am. Who are you?" Sandra squinted toward the face that went with the voice, but the roof of the porch threw a dark shadow over everything. She couldn't see anything but a knit stocking cap, pulled down low, hiding hair.

Knit stocking cap. Hadn't Ellie said something about watching out for a man in a pea jacket and knit cap. The murders: Mrs. Dobson, Mrs. Abramowitz, Darlene...

Frightened, Sandra took a few steps back. The figure moved swiftly behind her, crushing her against his chest, covering her mouth when she opened it to scream.

Then she was lifted off her feet and carried around a corner, along a short path. Beneath her backless dress, her skin prickled with the touch of his scratchy wool jacket. Something hard—it felt like a knife—pressed against her leg.

They entered the dark garage, and she could smell paint, kerosene, and oil cans. An old rusty Volkswagen convertible, minus tires and top, dominated half the space. The man placed her facedown on the VW's front seat, where she breathed in the odor of mildewed seat covers.

"Ever done it this way before, little girl?" asked the man, ripping her skirt all the way down.

Sandra thought of the hours she would have to house-clean to pay for her ruined gown, and fear became anger.

Had he drawn the knife, if that's what it was? She wasn't certain.

Counting to ten (one anna two anna three anna ten) she vaulted over the car's side.

Surprised at her sudden move, the man reached out but grabbed only sky blue cloth.

"I have time," he said, chuckling, placing his bulk in front of the exit, then kicking the door shut before she could get a good look at his face.

"Waiting only makes it more fun, and I like you better without the dress, even tho' you're too skinny for my taste. Taste, get it? I heard you sing, little girl. Will you sing for me?"

"I...uh..."

"Sing the pony song."

"I don't...I can't..."

"You know, the song about a pony and food. Pasta."

What was this insane man talking about? Sandra's eyes blurred with tears. It didn't matter. She honestly didn't believe she could sing now if her life depended on it. And it probably did.

"The pony song, the pony song," shouted the man angrily. "Yankee Doodle went to town, riding on a *po*-nee. Stuck a feather in his cap and called it mac-a-*ro*-nee."

Oh. Pasta. Macaroni. Jee-sus!

The man advanced with mincing steps. "Yankee Doodle-cakes went to town, riding on the Pole's knee."

Sandra's eyes darted desperately around the garage, searching for an escape. A small square window to the left of the back wall was the only source of illumination, and moonlight dimly outlined crude wooden shelves. She spied a box of safety matches next to some candles and charcoal. There were also oily rags—*fire hazard*, she thought incoherently.

The man waved his hands and snapped his fingers.

"Stuck a banana in his cap...yes, we have no ban-an-as..."

In the muted glow from the small window, Sandra thought she saw the sparkle of a ring on the man's finger. Then absurdly, she remembered her lines from *Alice's Adventures in Wonderland*.

"They are waiting on the shingle," chanted Sandra, "will you come and join the dance?"

The man halted, his arms suspended in the air—away from his knife.

"Will you, won't you, will you, won't you, will you join the dance?"

The man chuckled, and moved his hands down to applaud—closer to the knife.

"Will you, won't you, will you, won't you..."

From the corner of her eye, Sandra saw an open kerosene can almost within reach.

"Will you, won't you," she chanted as she grabbed the box of matches, lit three together, and ignited the rags. Then she snatched up the kerosene can. "Will you, won't you, will you—"

"Shit, what the hell are ya' doin'?"

He stumbled forward, but paused when Sandra turned the can upside down and swung an arc of fuel. She threw the rags on top, and a flamed trail advanced toward the garage entrance. As he retreated, Sandra screamed several times at the very top of her soprano range.

The man opened the garage door and fled, but now Sandra was trapped by her own fire. Peering toward the window, she saw the blurry outline of a face. Sure that the monster had returned, she began to breathe in short gasps.

"No, please, no," she moaned, on the verge of fainting.

A calm voice said, "Muffin, come over to the window."

Muffin? Only two people called her that. Ellie. Occasionally Mick. Still dizzy, her eyes tearing from smoke, Sandra staggered toward the window. At the front of the garage, students hosed hissing flames, and she could hear sirens.

"Mick? Is that really you?"

"Put your arms through the window, Muffin, and I'll pull you out."

"It's too small."

"It's not too small. It's just the right size."

"I'll never fit."

"You'll fit. I promise."

"I'm Alice going down the rabbit hole, right?"

"Right. Okay, I've got you. A little more. That's my good girl," he murmured tenderly.

Mick had yanked the window frame off by its hinges, and Sandra felt splinters attach themselves to her bare skin. Finally, she stood upright.

"I feel funny," she said. "Sick. I think..." Over and over she kept hearing the words *will you, won't you, will you, won't you, will you join the dance.* She felt her legs turn to jelly and watched Mick step forward. "I think I'm going to throw up, Mick, sorry."

"That's okay. No big deal."

"No...big...deal." Sandra breathed the cool night air, staggered toward Mick's extended arms, leaned forward as though she planned to hug him, and fainted.

SHE OPENED HER EYES. She was on the ground and her slip had hiked up and Mick could see her undies and she was so embarrassed.

"Did I throw up?"

"No."

Mick looked scared to death. *Scared to death.* Sandra giggled.

"Jesus, Muffin, are you all right?"

"Sure." She giggled again, then began to cry.

"Okay, that settles it. We'll drive to the emergen—"

"No, not the hospital! Take me to your mom's." She closed her eyes.

When she opened them again she was riding in Mick's van, her head cradled on his lap, but everything looked blurry because her eyes were still crusted with tears.

Then she had the sensation of being carried and wondered if Mick could see her underpants and wondered if she'd shaved her legs close enough to the pink elastic bands. Yuck! Wouldn't it be awful if hair stuck out? Natalie was careless about shaving, and when she wore a bikini it was so repulsive and...

A woman's voice kept repeating:

"Muffin...*hic*...Muffin...*hic*...Muffin."

And a warm hand captured, then fingered, her wrist.

"There doesn't seem to be any damage," said a voice. "There was no penetration, Mrs. Bernstein. I'm..."

A doctor, thought Sandra, because a doctor's voice always dripped like syrup poured over pancakes.

I wasn't raped, Sandra tried to say, but her throat was too rusty, and her eyes were glued shut.

"Her pulse is normal," continued the syrupy voice, "but I'll give her a shot; a tranquilizer."

"No needle," Sandra managed to blurt. "Go 'way."

"I don't believe...*hic*...a shot's necessary," said Ellie. "Thank you very much...*hic.*"

Sandra heard another voice say: "Can you give Ms. Bernstein something for hiccups, Doctor? She seems to get them every time she's frightened."

"Alice wants to sleep," murmured Sandra.

And heard the syrup say: "Maybe that's best right now."

When Sandra opened her eyes for the third time, she lay on Ellie's poofy-cushioned couch. She wore a furry yellow bathrobe. A washcloth draped her forehead. Tweezers and assorted splinters decorated the nearby table. She sat up.

"Lie down!" shouted Ellie and Mick together.

She shook her head, and the washcloth flipped to the carpet. "I'm okay. Did I sleep long? Is today tomorrow?"

"Nope," said Mick. "After the doctor left, you snored like a buzz saw for twenty, maybe thirty minutes." He sat and placed one arm across her shoulders.

"Give me a break! I never snore."

"How do you know? You were asleep. Buzz-saw city, right, Mom?"

Sandra glanced around the room. She saw a worried Ellie, standing next to an attractive man with a mustache. It had to be Lieutenant Peter Miller because he looked exactly the way Ellie had described him.

Miller wore a white shirt and jeans. He eased his body onto the couch and pressed close to Sandra's other side. Holding her hand, he said, "My name's Peter."

"Yes, I know. I mean I figured…I know about you…I mean, Ellie said…she told me…oh, rats!"

"Do you feel okay enough to answer some questions?"

"Sure." Sandra auditioned a smile.

"Why don't you start by telling me exactly what happened, everything you can remember."

"Well, I went outside the house looking for Mick," she began, and related the tale of the awful man, her capture, and the episode inside the garage. "Mick said I would fit and I did," she concluded breathlessly.

"Now I'm going to ask you a really important question."

"You want to know if I can describe what the man looks like. I can't. I'm sorry. It was so dark on the porch and in the garage, and he never got close enough to the window so I could see his face. Everything was real blurry, except I think he might have worn a diamond ring. When he dragged me through the yard, my back was against his chest."

"I understand. Let's take it from step one, okay? Was the man tall?"

"Not really. Medium height, I think. Average."

"Was the man fat? Thin?"

"*Gargantuan.* Well, I guess that's not really fair—I mean, well, he seemed big because I was scared."

"Did you notice his clothes, honey?" asked Miller.

"He wore this bulky wool jacket, brown or green. Black pants I think, but I'm not sure. They could have been dark blue. Maybe jeans, washed over and over, because they weren't stiff. Oh, but that would have made them light instead of dark. Kill, uh, strike the jeans bit.''

Miller grinned. "What did you do, Norrie? Train this young lady in your method of total recall?'' Turning toward Sandra again, he added, "That's very good, honey. Most people wouldn't remember half as much. Anything else?''

"I don't know about his shoes. I guess I never really saw them. You see, I kept thinking about the *knife*," said Sandra dramatically. She allowed herself a small quiver, and drew closer to Mick, inviting him to tighten his arm about her shoulders, which he did. "Wait! He had a hat—"

"Peter," interrupted Ellie, kneeling by the couch.

"Hold it a minute, Norrie."

"But Peter—"

"What did the knife look like, Sandra? Do you recall him dropping it after you started the fire?''

"I never saw the knife. I felt it when he dragged me toward the garage. It was in his pants. A long blade and handle. He never pulled it out.''

"Thank god," breathed Ellie. "Peter, ask her if the hat was a stocking cap.''

"Did you feel anything else?''

"No.''

Miller patted Sandra's hand, leaned forward, and turned toward Mick. "Earlier you said you didn't see anybody leave the garage. Did you happen to notice a man wearing a bulky jacket during the party? Anytime at all?''

"No, sir.''

"It's Peter. Some of my close buddies call me Pete.''

He was *bonding*, thought Ellie, smiling for the first time since Sandra had arrived.

"Mick, did you see my undies," whispered Sandra.

"Jesus, did you lose your undies?"

"Never mind."

"Anything unusual about his cap?" Peter asked Sandra.

"No. You can buy them in all the stores. Target. Walmart. Sears. The cap was knitted, like a sweater. Black or brown. Ellie said to watch out for a man in a stocking cap, but I didn't think he'd show up at my party."

"Okay honey, look beneath the hat and what do you see?"

"Nothing."

"Just let your mind zero in on the stocking cap. Now the face."

"Nothing. Honest. I never realized how hard it is to picture a face without hair. It's like those paper dolls I had when I was a kid. They all looked alike until I put clothes and hair on them."

"Ask her about a smell."

Peter frowned. "Please, Norrie, let me do my job, okay? Did the man have any kind of smell, honey?"

"I don't know. When he carried me through the yard, he held his hand over my nose and mouth. Inside the garage, I smelled seat covers and kerosene. I'm sorry."

"Do you feel up to looking through some photographs?"

"Sure. You bet. I'd love a drink or something."

"I'll fix some hot chocolate," said Ellie, "and add a few drops of brandy. I think I have some brandy left from our last catastrophe."

Mick scooped Sandra up and carried her to a chair at the butcher-block kitchen table. She cuddled against his chest, this time thoroughly enjoying the ride. Then, shifting through the Polaroid snapshots, she finally pulled three from the pile and handed them to Peter.

"I can't swear any of these are the killer," she said. "I mean I wouldn't swear on a stack of Bibles. But they all look a little like him, especially the bodies and their, uh, chin shapes. They all had, well, double chins. I know that doesn't sound very nice…"

"Fauna, Flora, and Merryweather," swore Ellie. "Don't worry about insulting that maniac, Muffin."

"Fauna, Flora, and who?" asked Peter.

"Merryweather," Mick grinned. "Mom had me believing it was a curse, like 'go to hell' or something. Later I found out that Fauna, Flora, and Merryweather were the three good fairies in Disney's *Sleeping Beauty*. Fauna's the fairy of song, Flora…um…beauty, yeah beauty, and Merry…" Mick raised his eyebrows and glanced toward his mother.

"Happiness," she replied sadly, having half hoped that Sandra wouldn't recognize a club member. "Peter, may I see the photos? Please?"

"Just a minute, Norrie." After studying Sandra's selections, he handed them over to Ellie.

She gasped. The photographs Sandra had chosen included Robbie Janssen, Tubby Evergreen, and George Bubbles.

"I could be wrong, Ellie. Maybe I picked those three pictures because they're familiar. I mean, I've met Tubby, Robbie, and George at the meetings, right?" Turning toward Peter, she added, "I don't want to get anybody in trouble."

"Take it easy, honey. This isn't proof, but it is a lead. The only one we've got."

"Except for the smell," stated Ellie. "And the ring. Muffin said she saw a ring. Holy cow, Peter!"

"What is it?"

"Robbie Janssen wears a ring. Two, actually. One on each hand. Did you see one ring or two Muffin?"

"I don't remember." Sandra turned toward Peter. "But I do remember something else. The man said he heard me sing. Do you think he meant the party? His voice didn't sound all that young. Maybe somebody saw an older man, kind of heavy, lurking. He'd stick out like a sore thumb."

"My detectives are questioning the students right now."

"John Russell played the piano. Maybe he saw… *rats!*"

"Maybe he saw rats?" asked Peter, puzzled.

"The man said he heard me sing but didn't say where or when," explained Sandra. "I sing at the Dew Drop Inn…with John. Do you suppose the killer could have heard me there?"

TWELVE

"WHY NOT, PETER?"

Ellie settled back against a cushion and sipped from a snifter that contained the last of her brandy. Sandra slept in a guest bedroom where Jackie Robinson shared her blanket. Mick had been sent to an open-all-night supermarket.

"Why can't you grill Robbie, George, and Tubby?" Ellie asked again.

"Because they're not cheese sandwiches. We don't *grill* suspects. Unless they volunteer, we can't even take your club members in for questioning without proof." Peter plopped down beside her on the couch. "What facts do we have? Hat, coat, sparkling ring, and three snapshots that Sandra's not even positive about. You can't grill, or even slightly singe, a suspect with that evidence."

"Okay. Sorry. In the movies—"

"Movies have a scriptwriter; everything fits. Remember that film with Glenn Close and what's-his-name, Lloyd Nolan's kid. Jeff—"

"Bridges. Lloyd Bridges's kid. *The Jagged Edge*. I figured out the ending halfway through. What about it?"

"They went to trial on circumstantial evidence. And a real perp would have dumped the typewriter after he was acquitted."

"Yes. I know."

"Stop it, Norrie."

"Stop what?"

"Your face has a snoop-on-my-own expression."

"Don't worry, Peter, my Visa card doesn't work, so I can't break and enter."

"I'm serious."

"I know."

"Stop saying that!" He turned sideways and shook her shoulders very gently. "Promise you won't sleuth."

"Okay, I promise. Really, Peter, I learned my lesson at the movie theater."

"I certainly hope so."

"I can't believe I was so stupid."

"For once we agree. Typewriters don't magically appear on closet shelves. Knives, either. It was stupid to search Janssen's apartment. What if he's our murd—"

"Oh, I'm not talking about *that*. I meant Sandra. When I mentioned members at their goal weights, I never thought about Sandra. She attends meetings at least once a month. Tonight was all my fault."

"You can't blame yourself."

"Yes I can. W-What if she had been k-k-killed?"

"Are you crying, Norrie? Aw, don't cry." Peter pried her fingers apart, removed the empty snifter, placed it on the coffee table, and patted his jeans. "C'm'ere, darlin'."

My Loot is going to have a perpetual dent in his lap, thought Ellie, shifting positions. However, he's right about one thing. It isn't positive to blame or snivel. The idea is not to get mad, but to get even. Pulling a tissue from her pocket, she blotted her tears and blew her nose.

"Do any other graduates attend with Sandra's regularity?" asked Peter.

"Uh-uh. Not at Good Shepherd."

"How about John Russell?"

"John's ten pounds *below* weight; he doesn't attend meetings. Peter, stop nibbling my earlobe. Mick'll be home any minute, and I'm trying to remember a clue I've missed. Cut it out. Please. I can't think.''

''I can't help it. Before, when you blew your nose into that soggy tissue, it was so damn sexy. Hey, that's a joke, Norrie. Smile.''

''Oh my God, I know what I'm trying to remember.''

''Sexy nose-blowing?''

''Sandra said the man sounded raspy, like he had to clear his throat from phlegm. My attacker's voice sounded the same way. Maybe our killer has a perpetual cold.''

Peter sat up so quickly, he almost dumped Ellie onto the carpet. Tightening his arms, he said, ''Colds aren't perpetual. Could be he smokes.''

''No, the smoking theory eliminates Robbie, George, and Tubby. In fact, Tubby once said he and Lulu gained more weight after they gave up smoking. But if our killer has a cold or...or allergy...the first day...the morning Jeannie was killed...there's something...I can't focus on a clear image.''

''Close your eyes, sweetheart. Relax.''

''Okay. Good. I'm getting a picture in my head now. At the meeting...that morning...George had a cold. I heard him complaining about it to Hannah when he justified eating doughnuts. But lots of members do that, justify their cheats because of a real or imaginary illness. I do it myself. Robbie...''

''What about Janssen, sweetheart?''

''When he came into the room, he sneezed and pulled a handkerchief from his pocket. That's the memory image I caught when you said that bit about blowing my nose.''

''And Evergreen? Please don't tell me he sneezed, too.''

"Tubby didn't show up on the morning of Jeannie's death. He and his wife, Lulu, were eating goodies from a smorgasbord." She opened her eyes. "Dammit! What's the use, Peter? Robbie sounded normal when he discovered me in his apartment; maybe he only sounds guttural when he plans to murder somebody. George is skipping meetings. Tubby has an abrasive edge to his voice, as if he wants to share a nasty secret. Even Lulu…if she's a suspect…you once suggested two people working together…even Lulu sounds hoarse…on the verge of tears." Ellie closed her eyes again. "Did I think of something helpful? We've got to stop this killer. God, I'm suddenly so exhausted…the hiccups and the brandy did me in."

Peter stroked Ellie's tangled hair until her breathing deepened. Her mouth quivered, and she gave several small, troubled sighs.

Please God, he prayed silently, *don't let Norrie end up like Cathy.*

WELCOME TO WEIGHT WINNERS—
A SLIP OF THE LIPS IS A POUND ON THE HIPS.

Dumb message, thought Ellie. First of all, a slip of the lips usually resulted in a kiss from Peter. Secondly, what she really wanted to say was, lock your doors until this monster is caught. And eat as if your lives depended on it.

She gazed with dismay at the long table in front of her. Eleven people sat, waiting for her lecture. Sometimes thirty or forty members attended the Friday morning class. Occasionally Ellie had dragged chairs from other rooms, stacking them in rows behind the table. No need for that today. Empty seats appeared like gaps in a smiling mouth where teeth should be.

Tubby and Lulu Evergreen sauntered in, more subdued than Ellie had ever seen them. Tubby glanced around the room, an actor counting his audience. Where was Dumbo? Nokeo? Baldy? *The others gave me that name, instead of Slim, and when they did, I really belonged to the gang, you know?*

Yes, Ellie knew, although when she was a kid her classmates hadn't dubbed her Olive Oyl or any other skinny name. They had called her Ellie-Belly.

Lulu and Tubby made the total thirteen bodies—fifteen if she counted Peter and William McCoy. McCoy was sticking like glue to Wanda Henry. The young detective still felt his carelessness had been responsible for Darlene's murder.

Me, too, thought Ellie. She wasn't blameless. She should have been more *urgent* with Darlene, and she'd goofed royally by not remembering Sandra.

News about Sandra had spread along the proverbial grapevine—juicy grapes filled with shivery sugar and seeds of terror. Thus, members who had been successfully losing weight stayed away. Some had even packed up and left for safer pastures. Like California, where ordinary folk selected random victims to shoot on freeways. In California you could be killed if you were young, old, fat, thin, famous, infamous. In California it was all a game of Russian roulette. Or "Wheel of Fortune." Or good ol' "Jeopardy." (If you're planning to be in the vicinity, send us a postcard.)

Ellie didn't know what effect the recent murders would have on her proposed Halloween celebration. She had negotiated with the church to change the usual time of her meeting to late evening, planning to hold a festive party. Her members had been looking forward to the diversion, determined to bring individual snacks, spouses or lovers, creative costumes. Ellie and Wanda had promised to provide the beverages and decorations. Wanda had even sent hand-printed invitations to each member.

Wanda Henry was such a treasure. What would the group do without her?

Wearing her pleated skirt, crocheted sweater, and Scarlett O'Hara cinch belt, Wanda glanced toward Will McCoy. Will had made it clear how much he admired his charge.

Henry had been annoyed, had grumbled something about how he could damn well protect his own property, or Wanda could quit Weight Winners.

On the other hand, the twins thought Will was neater than all the Mutant Ninja Turtles put together. They loved the way Will showed them his car radio (and siren—yikes!), shared his Indiana Jones hat, and sternly warned them about the gun at his waist. Guns are dangerous, he insisted, guns can kill.

"People kill, not guns," Henry had told the twins.

The twins. Wanda heaved a deep sigh.

She wanted to divorce Henry so badly, but he'd fight for custody of Joseph Jr. and Rebecca, her roly-poly double exposures. Henry said he'd take Wanda to court and get the kids. He could prove adultery, claimed he'd followed her and seen her with men from the class. What men? Robbie Janssen? George Bubbles? The elderly gent whom Ellie called Beau? Truthfully, there weren't that many male members. Henry had to be bluffing. Wanda knew he was bluffing, even though she *had* strayed once.

Once she'd accepted a motel invitation from an attractive Weight Winners graduate. The businessman lived in Tulsa and had visited Ellie's church group for his monthly maintenance check. He had taken Wanda to lunch after the meeting, and they'd spent a couple of hours on his bouncy motel mattress. *Once.* Once upon a mattress. *Jeez.* A big mistake, but at least Wanda had found out what she'd been missing all these years.

Her parents would side with Henry. They thought him a virtual God—after all, he had taken their obese daughter off their hands following high school graduation. Henry provided a steady income, children—what else did she require? They made it very clear that all this losing weight nonsense was jeopardizing her marital relationship.

Jeez, Henry seemed to have gained all the weight she had lost, adding to his considerable bulk; a football hero's body gone slack. Her husband's job required him to sit in the cab of a truck and push buttons, or lounge inside an office. He owned half the construction company.

Henry repulsed her in bed, and Wanda had been rejecting his advances, asserting herself for the first time in her life. Well, actually the second time, since she'd stubbornly continued to work for Weight Winners despite Henry's disapproval. Well, actually the third time, if you counted the man from Oklahoma.

Again she glanced at Will McCoy, who had thick brown hair, a cute face with a pug nose, freckles, and a dimpled Don Johnson smile.

Wanda shifted her gaze to Ellie—her idol. Ellie had been divorced and grown stronger from the experience. Ellie was so nice, so sweet, so understanding. If Wanda told Ellie about the man from Tulsa, she'd understand.

Turning abruptly, Wanda knocked her file to the floor. Damn! Will bent down to help her collect the index cards, and they bumped foreheads. Momentarily, Wanda thought the handsome detective would kiss her right there in front of everyone.

"My boss is beginning the lecture," she murmured, pointing toward Ellie with a shaky finger that ached to trace Will's dimpled cheeks. Wanda's *fingers* had lost weight, too. Her wedding band didn't fit anymore.

Ellie stood with her back to the chalkboard. She looked fondly at Hannah, who was bursting with pride at the loss of another four pounds. Hannah munched carrot sticks from her plastic bag. The navy blue pants were beginning to sag, but she had confided how she had no intention of indulging in a new wardrobe until at least fifteen more pounds became weight pollution. She seemed to be watching the entrance for somebody to appear—George Bubbles? Hannah had confessed that she'd visited the Dew Drop Inn with George, then cheated with tacos.

Robbie Janssen pressed against the wall in his usual pose, wearing a plaid shirt and black pants. Ellie wondered if he had noted the disappearance of his oiled shirt. Poor lonely Robbie. Windowpane sunshine highlighted silver links from the watchband on his left wrist. And the rings that decorated his fingers. Peter seemed fixated on Robbie, but despite the jewelry, Ellie had virtually eliminated him as a suspect. Quite simply, she didn't think he'd have the guts to stalk and slash people.

Tubby cracked his knuckles, and Ellie shuddered; the sound reminded her of Esther's knitting needles.

The ebullient Tubby and his cartoon-appendage wife rubbed Ellie the wrong way sometimes, but she couldn't imagine the two as killers out to avenge the weight loss of others. The Evergreens made fun of themselves and their peers verbally—everything out in the open. They didn't fit Ellie's image of mentally deficient, sexually deprived crazies, seething on the inside. Of course, she didn't know how Tubby behaved when he left the class. Or Lulu. They could have violent tempers.

What about Bubbles? He didn't take the diet seriously, but he could be jealous of weight losses, and he *justified* everything. Wasn't that the MO of a wacko psychopath? George would be her first choice among the three suspects. She could imagine him killing Jeannie or Esther. But the World's Greatest Lover had hovered around Darlene like a bee drawn to honey, and he could have stalked Sandra.

Ellie supposed Peter and his staff were watching the three suspects closely, checking them out, investigating every possibility. Did George wear a sparkling ring?

Bringing her attention back to the small group waiting for words of encouragement, Ellie reminded them about the Halloween party, then instructed everybody to stock sugarless gum, not candy, for trick-or-treaters. That way, leftovers wouldn't be tempting.

Hannah nodded her head, and confessed that last year she'd felt ill after munching her way through an entire bag of miniature Three Musketeers bars.

"This year," she said, "I want to look like Jane Fonda more than I want to eat—I mean, *swallow*—Three Musketeers."

That statement relieved tension and provoked laughter. *Bless Hannah!*

One brand new member, a beautiful woman who resembled Nell Carter, had joined the class—obviously ignorant about the recent murders.

Lulu whispered in the new member's ear and she bolted for the exit.

Bless Lulu, thought Ellie.

Sister Maria glanced from Lulu to the woman rushing

out, then directed her gaze toward Ellie. Mumbling under her breath, Sister Maria fingered her rosary.

She wasn't afraid to die and preferred to enter Heaven skinny, but she was worried about her lovely leader.

"Please, Lord, protect Ellie Bernstein," prayed Sister Maria, "for she knows what she does, and does it anyway. God bless Ellie."

FRIDAY NIGHT.

The poster on Hannah Taylor's wall depicted Garfield standing on a scale. Bubbled above the fat cat were the printed words: I'M NOT OVERWEIGHT. I'M UNDERTALL.

Bubbled. George Bubbles. Hannah missed him, had been tempted to call him, but, picturing their first (and only) date, she'd kept her hand away from the phone.

Hannah thought about how she and Jeannie had bought their posters together. Jeannie had selected one that stated: TODAY IS THE FIRST DAY OF THE REST OF YOUR LIFE.

Shuddering, Hannah vacuumed her spotless carpet.

Well, almost spotless. She glanced at her elderly, black, no-breed dog and remembered how Jack and Earline had rescued Hershey from the animal shelter fourteen years ago.

"The man at the pound promised he'll be a medium-size dog when he grows up, Mom," Earline had announced.

Hannah had stared at the puppy's enormous paws, then shared a smile with her husband; big feet meant big dog.

Yet Hershey *had* grown into a medium-size Heinz. He still had extralarge paws, and during the last six months, he had become deaf, arthritic, and lost partial control of bladder functions, but Hannah loved him dearly. Some "killer."

The phone's ring pierced the hum of her vacuum cleaner.

Sarah Wilcox's voice sounded panicky. "Hannah, I'm so scared."

"Why?"

"Why? Cheese and crackers, Hannah, I'm within two pounds of goal weight."

"But you're not in our group anymore."

"I was before I got the daytime nursing job and switched to nights. My records haven't even been transferred from Wanda's file yet. Maybe the terminator thinks I'm skipping meetings or something."

A widow, Sarah Wilcox lived in the same residential neighborhood as Hannah, and she constantly whined about an overweight, lazy son. A pain in the rear end at Weight Winners meetings, Sarah lost weight easily. ("I don't know why you have a problem, Hannah, it's not that hard.") The well-organized woman was the type who would portion-pack her food amounts as carefully as she portion-packed her life.

"Did you call the police?" asked Hannah.

"I did, but they were very uncooperative. They said somebody named Lieutenant...something...a beer... Budlight, I think. Anyway, he'll get back to me later."

"Well then..."

"Hannah, would you stay here with me tonight? Until Lieutenant Budlight calls and tells me what to do."

"Really Sarah..."

"Please?"

"Why don't you stay with family?"

"I can't stay with Frank Junior. That second wife of his hates me and her kids run around the place naked and she never dusts. Besides, Junior makes fun of Weight Winners."

"He does?"

"Junior was a member once. When Ellie first took over the church group. He lost a lot, then fiddled with the diet and put it all back on. Junior…well, I hate to say this about my own flesh and blood, but he cussed when I told him I was two pounds away from goal. He used the F-word."

"Do you want to sleep at my house, Sarah?"

"Cheese and crackers, I can't do that. Tomorrow I'm expecting a call from the sweepstakes people verifying that I'm a winner, but I don't know the exact time."

Sarah Wilcox was a coupon clipper and contest addict—as Jeannie had once been. "I don't know what I've won," she continued. "It could be a CD player, but if it's cash, I'll split it with you."

She must really be frightened, thought Hannah. Sarah was notorious for pinching a penny until Lincoln screamed.

"I don't want your money. I'll be there in about twenty minutes," said Hannah, capitulating.

"The key is under the mat."

"What? Aren't you home?"

"This is a pay phone. I'm playing bingo and the big game is coming up. A thousand-dollar jackpot. I bought ten cards. There's food in my refrigerator, legal Weight Winners portions. Do you know what I did after I heard about Esther and that Darlene person? I tried to eat the wrong food. I wanted to put the weight back on, but I couldn't do it." Sarah laughed bitterly. "I've been brainwashed by Ellie. Then I thought about getting a dog for protection, a Doberman or German shepherd, but you know how dirty animals are."

Hannah looked lovingly toward Hershey. He snored, his head resting on both front paws, and she noted that his chin whiskers were graying like a piece of stale chocolate.

"Sarah, why don't you give me a call when you get back home. By then your Lieutenant Budlight—"

"It could be very late, Hannah, and…"

"And what?"

"Well, I ended up getting a dog…a shepherd. I thought it was an omen since I used to attend meetings at the Good Shepherd Church. But I couldn't bring myself to buy one of those big ones, Hannah, so I got a puppy and the breeder said if it didn't work out I could bring him back. Then I bought some of those 'beware of dog' signs, but I forgot to put them in the yard. The puppy's not trained yet and I left him locked inside the kitchen. It must *smell*. I'll pay you to walk him—"

"What's his name?"

"I didn't give him one because I'm not sure I'm going to keep him. I call him Dog. I forgot to feed him, too, and he might yip or cry. Cheese and crackers!"

GEORGE BUBBLES AWOKE and forced great gulps of air into his constricted chest.

The dream. Buried alive in mashed potatoes.

His clothes were soaked with sweat. Discarding the wet garments, George stepped into a tepid shower and laved his body with a bar of deodorant soap.

Then, knotting a towel about his waist, he reached for the phone. In the middle of dialing Hannah's number, he slammed the receiver down, walked slowly to his dresser, and looked into the mirror above.

"She doesn't want to talk to me," he said to his image. "She probably never wants to see me again."

George had once offered coupons to his fellow dieters; the furniture store where he worked had been holding a promotional contest with a new VCR as first prize. Nearly every member had filled in names, addresses, and phone numbers. Then George forgot to bring the coupons to the store. Now he separated Hannah's coupon from the others.

Instead of calling he'd knock on her door, fall to his knees, and apologize in person, he thought, checking Hannah's address. Though he had been there once before, he wasn't at all sure he could find it again.

This morning's weather report had predicted the season's first freeze. Bring all the potted plants and veggies inside, folks, it might even snow. *Snow!* Maybe that was why he'd just dreamed about mashed potatoes.

After shrugging his shoulders into a thick jacket, George blew a kiss toward Christal's portrait.

"YOU GOT BEER," screamed Tubby Evergreen, slamming the refrigerator door. "Jesus, you got ice cream. You got all kinds of bakery cookies. What's the matter with you?"

"You said to buy that stuff," replied Lulu, backing up through the entrance from the kitchen into their living room. "You said you wanted it here so you could show how strong you were by not eating it."

"You dumb bitch, I told you *not* to buy fattening stuff."

"That was before. Then you got mad because it wasn't here. Don't you remember?"

"There's nothing wrong with my memory. How can I stick to my diet when you keep buying the wrong food?" Tubby fisted his knuckles and swung at his wife.

Lulu didn't have time to duck. She felt her head explode, then she spit out a broken tooth as she whirled around and crashed into the piano.

When she opened her eyes, Tubby had left the room—no, the house. His jacket and hat were gone, too. Lulu thought about locking the door, but she was afraid. Tubby might be even more pissed if she did that. Maybe she should call Sister Maria. The sweet nun had handed over her motherhouse number this morning at the meeting.

Reaching for the phone, ignoring her throbbing, bruised mouth, she sang, "I've got a mule and her name is Lulu, fifteen miles on the road to absolution."

ROBBIE JANSSEN WATCHED Elvis put the guitar down on the porch and embrace the pretty girl.

He's not such a hot kisser. Guess when you can sing like that, you don't have to kiss good.

Robbie checked his watch, then the TV listings in the newspaper. Except for the Elvis movie he had just seen, there was nothing exciting on television tonight. Shrugging his body into a jacket, sliding his fingers into a pair of driving gloves, Robbie decided to cruise for a while in Vetty Grable.

"Cruising 'round the corner, watching pretty girls go byyyy."

Okay, thought Robbie, he didn't sound like The King. He'd never sound like Him. God, it was cold outside. His ears were freezing. Better wear a hat. There was a hat in Vetty Grable's glove compartment.

HANNAH SHIFTED on the sofa. She had found a foam-stuffed pillow in the linen closet, and a blanket as well, but Sarah kept her sofa covered with smooth plastic. No dirt would invade the early-American plaid material, but it was uncomfortable.

The small living room had two armchairs covered in plastic, a standing lamp, and an etagere bursting with clutter. Miniature glass animals, dime-store statues, imitation Waterford crystal, and a Norman Rockwell Mother's Day plate filled every space. There was also a polished urn containing the ashes from Sarah's dead husband, Frank. Three red and white BEWARE OF DOG signs leaned against the etagere's bottom shelf. Sarah's sofa completed the room arrangement, facing the TV and stereo. The turntable was ancient; no wonder Sarah hoped to win a CD player.

"Dog" dozed in the kitchen after a Puppy Chow meal and a long walk. At least Sarah hadn't forgotten to purchase a cushioned wicker basket and squeak toys for her new pet. The shaggy animal had been so unabashedly grateful that Hannah had felt less resentful about giving in and coming to spend the night.

Sarah hadn't returned yet from her bingo game, and there was absolutely nothing of interest on the TV after "Jeopardy" unless Hannah watched David Letterman, who was sometimes funny and sometimes dopey. Maybe tonight his show would include animal tricks, which Hannah loved to watch, although she had a feeling the animals didn't always love to perform. Sarah's musical taste ran to and ended at Liberace.

Her bedroom bookcase included every bodice-ripper ever published. So Hannah had no choice. Letterman—with or without the animal tricks. Maybe she should leave a note, take Dog home with her, and wait for Sarah's call. Undecided, Hannah removed her glasses and rubbed her eyes.

"Jeopardy" ended and a local commercial began—a frenzied, screaming spokesman tossing discount clothes every which way. Hannah's eyes (which had started to blink shut during "Jeopardy's" announcement about how everybody would receive a year's supply of Lean Cuisine) blinked open at the strident pitch. Despite the lack of glasses, Hannah saw a shadowy figure looming above the sofa, and the blurry blade of a long knife.

Instinctively, she slipped off her cushion as the knife traveled down, slashing through the plastic and stuffing. The intruder swiftly circled the sofa. Hannah's feet lashed out and made contact with a small penis dangling from an open fly. The intruder let out an *oomph* but didn't drop the knife.

Hannah rolled over and over, finally bumping into the etagere. She heard the crunch and tinkle of breaking glass and reached for her specs, but they were too far away. Maneuvering to her knees, she began to throw etagere items, hoping her aim was true. Her hands closed around the funeral urn, unbroken, and she hurled that as well. There was a *thunk*. The intruder took a few steps backwards, then advanced again. The doorbell rang. Hannah screamed. Ellie Bernstein's voice shouted: "Open it, Peter, hurry!"

The killer hesitated, then took off toward the rear of the house—a locomotive chugging Frank's ashes. While Peter ran after him, Ellie helped Hannah to her feet, steered her around the broken glass, and seated her in a plastic-coated armchair.

"We were at the hospital all evening," said Ellie. "One of the nurses thought Kelly Benedict had come out of her coma. They wouldn't let me see Kelly and she didn't wake again, if she ever *did,* but she's still alive. Lieutenant Miller called his precinct and they relayed Sarah's urgent message, so we decided to stop here on the way home to reassure her. Oh, Hannah, it's lucky we did."

"Lieutenant *Miller?* Sarah thought they said Budlight. Miller. Bud. That's funny, Ellie, but I can't laugh. Would you turn off the TV please? David Letterman laughs too much. Did you ever notice that? He chortles every other sentence. Do you know where the word *chortle* comes from? Jeannie once looked it up. Lewis Carroll combined chuckle with snort."

"Easy, Hannah, take a deep breath. You're safe now, sweetie." Ellie punched the TV knob, then watched Peter enter. He was covered with leaves and twigs.

"Got clear away; don't know how; left a trail of ashes, but they stopped at a tree. He wasn't up in it," finished Peter lamely, reaching for the phone. After talking low, then hanging up, he knelt by Hannah's chair and carefully went through the now-familiar questions.

Hannah pointed toward her glasses on the floor near the couch. "I'm half blind without my specs," she admitted. "Everything was fuzzy. All I can remember is that he wore a heavy jacket and some sort of hat."

"A stocking cap," exclaimed Ellie.

"No, it was a ski mask. Wait a minute, I just thought of something else. I can't see without my specs, but I can still smell…"

"Go on," prompted Peter.

"I could be wrong."

"Hannah, tell us," urged Ellie. "It might be helpful."

"All right, he used lots of cologne or after-shave. I know because Earl, my late husband, wore it too. Earl was in the navy and he used to make jokes about nautical perfume. Old Spice. Oh dear, I suppose hundreds of men choose that brand." Hannah hesitated, then said "George Bubbles wears Old Spice."

Holy cow, the movie theater, thought Ellie. The smell

of cologne had challenged the aroma of buttered popcorn. That's what she couldn't remember.

"Anything else?" Peter asked Hannah.

"It was a man. I kicked his, uh, penis."

Peter glanced through the open front door. Flashing squad lights dotted the street. Police would search the neighborhood, but Peter doubted they'd find anyone.

"One other thing, although it might not be important," continued Hannah. "Tonight, on the phone, Sarah Wilcox told me that her son Frank Junior hates Weight Winners. He was a member but never reached goal and gained back everything he lost. Oh, that's ridiculous. I can't imagine a son trying to stab his own mother, can you?"

"Thanks, Ms. Taylor," Peter said, rising. "I'll arrange protection for Ms. Wilcox. Do you want to stay here a few days? Share the protec—"

"No, thank you," interrupted Hannah. "With me, it was a mistake. I'm not even close to goal weight. But I will be," she added confidently, "and by that time you'll have caught your killer. Lieutenant Miller, did I forget to lock the door? Is that how the man got in?"

Peter held up a tiny shard of plastic. "No ma'am, you locked it. He used a Safeway check-guarantee card to slip the bolt. Unfortunately, he didn't chip enough off to show an initial or partial number."

Dammit, thought Ellie, credit cards work for everybody except me.

Hannah said good-bye and went to calm the frightened watchdog.

LATER, SLUMPED ON the front seat of Peter's Scamp, Ellie closed her eyes, emotionally exhausted. The car radio played golden oldies by the Carpenters, and she remembered Robbie's shrine to Karen.

Then her tired mind focused on her trip through Robbie's apartment. The bathroom. A dirty sink with toothpaste, razors, streamers of dental floss...plus a three-masted sailing ship imprinted on an off-white container whose red scripted letters spelled out the words Old Spice.

THIRTEEN

ELLIE SAT AT HER kitchen table. In front of her was a cup of cold coffee, a US West directory, plus a computer printout, single-spaced, enumerating diet-club members and their phone numbers. On the bottom of the page was SARAH WILCOX, followed by her number and the word UNLISTED.

The directory, however, did list one Frank Wilcox, Attny., and one Wilcox, Frank P. Although Ellie could barely recall the heavy man whose face had worn both a gray stubble and gray scowl, she didn't think Sarah's son was the lawyer type. That left Frank P.

Unless Frank Junior, like his mother, wasn't listed.

"Dammit, Peter!" Rising, Ellie opened a packet of Tender Vittles Gourmet Dinner. "*You* could tell me if Wilcox, Frank P., is Sarah's son."

Friday night, after Ellie's revelation about the Old Spice bottle, Peter had again warned her about unauthorized investigations on her part.

"Will you take me with you when you check out Frank Wilcox?" she had asked, ignoring his grumpy mood, which she assumed was caused by his frustrating inability to catch Hannah's intruder. "Please?"

"No."

"But I can decide if Frank's the one who spied on me during my morning jogs, or stalked me at the theater."

"No, you've done enough—"

"Damage?"

"I was going to say help."

"Really, Peter? I've done enough help? You need a course in grammar."

"And you need a course in keeping your nose out of my business."

"Here we go again. It seems to me that the police need all the *help* they can get. In a movie, the killer would have been arrested and the mystery solved by now. On TV, they figure it out in one or two hours, minus commercial breaks. Unless it's a miniseries."

"Low blow, lady. Those comments don't even deserve an answer. In fact, I'm tired of this whole discussion."

"Where are you going?"

"To the precinct. Since there's a time limit on solving cases, I don't need your sarcasm making my job more difficult. *My job!* If you want any information, check with one of the inept policemen parked across the street, guarding, I might add, your lovely fanny."

"I thought you fell in love with my fanny," began Ellie, but Peter had already slammed the door.

Their discussion (argument) had led to three nights of disturbed sleep with only Jackie Robinson for company.

Damn all men! Lieutenant Miller had dropped from the tree like a piece of ripe, juicy fruit, then hightailed it out the door after one teensy-weensy argument (discussion).

Now Ellie watched her cat munch soybean meal, ground yellow corn, and phosphoric acid as she reached for the kitchen extension.

"Hi, Sarah, this is Ellie Bernstein. How are—"

"Cheese and crackers! Have to make this short, Ellie. I'm sure he bugged my telephone."

"He who?"

"The terminator."

"Who?" Ellie conjured up Arnold Schwarzenegger.

"You know, the diet-club killer."

"I don't believe he had time to fiddle with your phone, Sarah. It all happened very quickly. Are you okay?"

"No, I'm not. How would *you* feel if a bloodthirsty fiend tried to murder *you?*"

"He tried to murder Hannah."

"He thought it was me; that's the same thing. *No, Dog!* Stupid animal wants to chew my slippers. I changed the locks, and Lieutenant Budlight said he probably won't come back, but a killer—*down, Dog!*— always returns to the scene of the crime."

"Look, I don't want to keep you, Sarah. I was going through some old club records, uh, reorganizing. A long time ago your son was a member, and I wondered if he still lived at the same address."

"Junior used to have a nice house. Now he lives in a slum. It's his wife's fault. She never dusts. *Down, Dog!*"

Sarah recited the new address; it matched the one in Ellie's up-to-date directory; Frank P-for-perp. After hanging up the receiver, she muttered, "Hah, Peter, there's more than one way to skin a cat. No, not you, Jackie Robinson. Finish your chicken by-products."

Her present dilemma was how to get across the city without being followed. Despite Peter's comment about inept police, her cops were vigilant. She wasn't planning to enter the Wilcox house. *No way.* She just wanted to spy from a distance and see if Frank resembled the figure lurking behind a gnarly tree trunk. Perhaps he'd be wearing a pea jacket, knit stocking cap, or ski mask. Maybe he'd reveal a sparkling ring and reek of Old Spice.

Donning Mick's Bronco windbreaker over a heavy white ski sweater and black cords, Ellie strolled across the street toward the squad car. "Grocery shopping," she stated, then slid behind the wheel of her Honda Civic.

Driving slowly up and down a crowded parking lot, she finally found a small spot surrounded by other vehicles. Her police cruiser maneuvered around the lanes of autos, trucks, and motorcycles, under the nervous gaze of motorists.

The small shopping center included a dress boutique, a clothes-cleaning establishment, and the new pizza restaurant that Henry had bragged about. Then came the Safeway supermarket, flanked by a discount furniture store. A figure stood within the recesses of the furniture store's doorway, surveying passers-by.

Holy cow! George Bubbles!

"Ellie Bernstein, is that you?" He spread his arms wide. "Step into my establishment."

Said the spider to the fly.

Aloud Ellie replied, "I have some grocery shopping—"

"Five minutes," pleaded George. "Let me show you where I work. If you see anything you like, I can buy it for you at a special discount."

Trapped, Ellie followed George through a heavy wooden door. He looked different, and she realized he wasn't wearing his usual World's Greatest Lover T-shirt. A garish green-plaid suit jacket partially covered a yellow dress shirt with frayed collar. Knotted under George's chin was a wide flowered tie.

Spindly end tables and gilt-framed mirrors cluttered the entranceway. Several hand-printed signs proclaimed that these items were FREE with the purchase of a living room suite. A Dalmatian with black lacquered spots and chipped muzzle was ON SALE AS IS—$25, and the empty store reminded Ellie of a tomb crowded with unlooted artifacts.

Their footsteps reverberated across the rectangular foyer. A face peeked around the corner.

Halting, Bubbles beckoned. "Carl, this is my lady friend, Eleanor Bernstein," he said possessively. Crooking her arm in his elbow, he led Ellie toward the back of the store to a display of bedroom suites.

She glanced down at the hand resting on her orange and blue windbreaker's sleeve. Two rings sparkled. An initialed circlet and a high school graduation crest.

"See anything you like? Test this mattress, Ellie. It's on sale, and I can probably get ten percent off the discount price." Dropping Ellie's arm, George sank onto a kingsize bed and patted the saggy place next to him.

"I have a water bed, George, so I don't need a matt—"

"Water bed? I get seasick. That's a joke, Ellie. Still, I'm always open to new experiences." He wiggled one eyebrow invitingly.

"I haven't seen you at meetings," she said, ignoring his eyebrow. In fact, she thought, the last time George had attended was on the morning of the Benedicts' van accident.

"Are you kidding, Ellie? People are getting knocked off when they lose weight. Double-damn, Ellie, I'm sorry. That was tactless, you being our leader and all."

"It's harder to follow the program when you don't come to meetings, George."

"Guess I'm meant to be fat." He paused, then burst out, "It ain't fair. Some people eat and never gain an ounce. We went for pizza and I swear Carl ate ten slices and looked thinner when he left than when he went in. I gained smelling the cheese."

"Yes, I understand," soothed Ellie, "but—"

"How's Hannah?" he interrupted. "How's she doing?"

"Fine. She'll reach her goal weight, George, because she's really trying."

"The cops questioned me."

Ellie couldn't decide if he sounded frightened or pleased. Pleased. As punch. "They did?"

"Yeah. Ain't that a pisser?"

"The police are grill—uh, questioning all Weight Winners members. They interviewed me, too. What did you tell them?"

"I said the only person I wanted to kill was that guy who opened his pizza joint in this center?"

Should she probe further? Ellie glanced toward the back exit door; probably led to an alley. Carl was nowhere in sight. George could slit her throat, wrap her in that striped green-and-peach-colored display sheet, drag her outside to the Dumpster...

"Did the police ask where you were during the murders?"

"Yeah. Well, I guess you're busy, Ellie, and I've kept you from grocery shopping."

"What did you tell them?"

"The double-damn truth. Hey, if you need furniture, just give me a call, okay?"

She nodded and turned to leave.

George remained seated on the mattress. He seemed to have forgotten Ellie's presence as he sang, "Ev-ry-body loves a lov-er, so no-body loved meeee...."

Liza Minnelli he wasn't!

On her way out, Ellie passed several patterned couches encased in plastic, and she recalled the horrible scene in Sarah's living room—foam rubber escaping from the open wound of a slashed sofa. George had just asked about Hannah. *How's she doing?* Had he been talking about her success at losing weight or her attack?

Come to think of it, why did the killer choose Sarah Wilcox? The bossy woman had recently left Good Shepherd for another group, and she hadn't been very popular. Of course, popularity wasn't a prerequisite. Or was it? The murdered victims had all been popular. Sandra and Hannah, too. Had the stalker followed Hannah to Sarah's house? Could peer adoration rather than jealousy be the motive?

If that was true, Tubby Evergreen would advance to the head of the class. He had kept the name Tubby because his childhood gang bestowed it upon him. Even when he went from skinny to overweight, he hadn't relinquished the derogatory nickname. At meetings, Tubby provoked uncomfortable, self-conscious laughter, but he would never be deemed a role model.

Did George Bubbles consider himself popular? No way. He tried too hard, and, at the moment, his self-esteem was lower than a saggy discount mattress.

Ellie pictured Robbie Janssen standing against the wall, trying to make his considerable bulk invisible. Could he harbor fantasies about standing in front of an audience, amassing applause—like his idol Elvis?

And now a new suspect. Frank Wilcox. Sarah's scowly, *unpopular* son had even quit the support group.

Thoughtfully, Ellie left the furniture store, passed through mechanized Safeway doors, grabbed a squeaky shopping cart, and threw items at random into the top basket.

Walking past shelves filled with bath products, she envisioned TV ads where men joyously soaped their armpits beneath pelting shower heads. Aren't you glad you use soap? Don't you wish...

Ellie halted abruptly. Robbie in the shower, warbling his comma-ti-yi-yippi-yays. And George had just sung that line from *Cabaret.*

What had Sandra said last Friday night? Something about the stalker wanting her to sing "Yankee Doodle."

"He wanted me to sing the pony-macaroni song, Ellie. What a loony-tune."

Was that an important clue? Did the killer deliver his deathblows along with a singing telegram? She had to tell Pete when she saw him again.

If she saw him again.

Abandoning her cart, Ellie zigzagged through the supermarket and parking lot.

Her Honda revved up quickly and she soon found herself on the Interstate, heading south. No blue and white police cruiser was visible in her rear- or sideview mirrors.

Holy cow! George Bubbles worked next door to Safeway. The card used to jimmy Sarah's lock had been a Safeway Check Guarantee Card. But anybody could apply for one of those. Ellie had one herself. It wasn't what Peter would call proof. Should she mention it when/if she saw him again?

Exiting the interstate, Ellie thought that, if memory served, Tubby and Lulu lived only a few blocks away. Why not kill two birds with one stone?

A sign above the mailbox had welded silhouettes of several fir trees and *THE EVERGREENS* paints in red letters. Then a gravel path led toward a brick house with extended chimney. There were no cars in the driveway.

Well, it was Monday. Tubby worked for the Motor Vehicles Department and Lulu was…a sporting-goods clerk? Hardware cashier? Something like that.

"No, Peter, I'm not planning to break and enter."

With a bold stride, Ellie approached the front door and

rang the bell. No answer; she hadn't expected one. Walking around the side of the bricked facade, she spied a hot tub prominently placed in the backyard.

The hot water kept the body from decomposing quickly.

Was Tubby familiar with the composition of scalding water? Did he know that the exact time of Jeannie's death would be hard to pinpoint? After all, the murderer *had* tried to make Jeannie's death look like an accident.

The house windows were curtained except for two narrow vertical rectangles on each side of the front door. Ellie peered through the glass, but all she could see was a small portion of the entrance hall, dominated by a coatrack. Clothing was piled haphazardly over the rack. Ellie thought she saw a gray-green wool jacket, but it could have been a bathrobe, or even a blanket. If there was a stocking cap, it lay hidden beneath sweaters.

She turned the front doorknob. Locked.

Unsnapping the clasp on her purse, reaching inside, Ellie fingered her Bernstein Visa.

I promised Peter.

Regretfully, Ellie walked toward her car. Gravel shifted under the soles of her sneakers. Tiny pebbles scattered, startling a tassel-eared squirrel.

The family that preys together stays together?

ONE O'CLOCK.

Parking three blocks away from the Wilcox address, Ellie jogged up the street, then halted to study her surroundings. A few tract houses had tricycles listing in their yards. Some lawns were watered and mowed, but several appeared defeated by fungus, mulched by falling leaves.

The weather had turned overcast and chilly, inviting people to inch up their thermostats and stay inside. And with school in session the streets were virtually deserted.

Unless Frank Wilcox was unemployed, thought Ellie, he wouldn't be home now. Damn! If only Peter had invited her along on his investigation. She was the diet-club group leader, so her presence wouldn't be suspect....

Suspects. Cops had already questioned George. How about Robbie Janssen? Did Tubby and Lulu have alibis? Investigating every possibility was a pain in the ass, especially if you weren't part of the investigation. *The couple who detect together respect together.*

If Robbie's apartment complex reminded Ellie of buildings on a Monopoly board, Frank Wilcox's house was a boxed Christmas present minus its bow. Peeling green paint surrounded scabbing red trim. One tree in the front yard grew a giant rubber truck tire that hung from a frayed rope. A dented station wagon, parked in the driveway, sported a red and white bumper sticker that read WHEN GUNS ARE OUTLAWED, ONLY OUTLAWS WILL HAVE GUNS, and somebody had fingered WASH ME in the dirt on the tailgate.

Ellie shivered. She could hear Peter. "Police work isn't all shoot-outs and car chases, Norrie. There's lots of boring paperwork and simple surveillance."

Well, she couldn't stand here and *surveil* all day. She had to have a plan. She couldn't think of a plan. She only knew she had to be careful, because she didn't want to end her life bleeding on the curb of a low-income housing development or stuffed inside a dusty wash-me tailgate. Taking a deep breath, Ellie climbed the four steps of a rotting wooden porch, then knocked on the front door.

The woman who answered wore pointy-toed heels, skin-tight, fuzzy, leopard-spotted pants, and a man's white shirt. Beneath fat green caterpillar-curlers, her spiky-lashed eyes were slitted suspiciously.

"You don't look like a bill collector," she said, blocking the doorway. "But if you are, he ain't here."

Ellie mumbled the first thing that came into her head, something about a product survey and free samples.

"Free? Did you say free?" The woman's face brightened. "Hell's bells, come in out of the cold. My name's Carol Wilcox, but everybody calls me Cher. My friends say I look like a character she played on her old TV show. What's your handle?"

"El...Eleanor Rigby, from the Opinion Institute of Nutrition Control," replied Ellie, then realized that she had just improvised initials for a misspelled OINK.

She entered the main living area, and the difference between this room and Sarah's almost took her breath away. First, there were pillows, each embroidered with one of the Ten Commandments. Threads from THOU SHALT NOT KILL unraveled like thin spaghetti. The pillows tried to hide fading slipcovers on a long, sloping couch. Piles of confessional magazines vied for dominance with outdated issues of *Soap Opera Digest.* A playpen held a chubby, sleeping infant with a dirty face and runny nose. On the wall hung a gold plaster-of-Paris Crucifix. The eyes of Jesus stared down on a television broadcasting the second half of "All My Children."

Cher lowered the TV's volume, but left the picture. Then she swept pillows to the floor and patted the couch.

"Rest your keister," she boomed.

From the back of the house came the sound of a stereo blaring forth a rap song whose lyrics were indecipherable.

"Tone down that dang music," shouted Cher, blasting Ellie's eardrums but not waking the baby in his pen. "My son Frankie always listens to that stuff. Guess he's going through a phase. Frank the third's almost ten. He's home from school, suspended for smoking. Say, if you have any questions about cigarettes, I'll fetch Frankie.''

''No, that's not necessary. I won't take up much of your time, Ms. Wilcox. I just want to ask a few ques—''

''I don't have to sign nothing?'' Cher plopped her keister down on the couch next to Ellie's.

''Uh-uh, this is for *advertising* purposes, so we know what the public likes to buy,'' Ellie improvised.

''I buy what's on sale. Except toilet paper. I think toilet paper should be soft, don't you? The no-name brands are too scratchy. What d'ya call 'em? Geriatric?''

''Generic,'' mumbled Ellie, extracting an appointment book and a ballpoint pen from her purse. On a page dated October thirteenth, she jotted down the words ''No generic toilet tissue,'' then tried to recall all the solicitations and questionnaires she had ever received.

''Ms. Wilcox, how old are you?''

''How old?''

''Twenty-five to thirty-five; thirty-five to forty-five; over fifty?''

''Oh, I see. Thirty-five to whatever you said. I used to look younger. Had long black hair like the real Cher, but it started falling out and I cut it. I was using that shampoo, what's it called? That stuff that comes in a green bottle. Every time I combed my hair, big chunks stuck to my comb. Put that down on your list, Miss Rigby.''

Ellie printed ''Green shampoo, ugh!''

''What about your husband?'' she asked.

''Frank? How old? Forty, although you'd think he was a kid sometimes if you know what I mean.'' Cher winked and a spidery row of false eyelashes stuck to one cheek. ''These dang things never work right,'' she said, removing the lashes and dropping them behind the couch. ''Fingernails, too.''

"What?"

"Those long fingernails you buy in the drugstore. It's a waste of money. They break when you clean house."

Clean house? Ellie glanced surreptitiously around the messy living room. "How long have you been married?"

"Nine years. No, better make that ten." Cher nodded toward Frankie's room.

"What does your husband do for a living?"

"Frank's a whatchamacallit." Cher crinkled her brow. "A restaurant ent...enterp...entrepreneur," she finally spit out, mispronouncing the word.

"He owns a restaurant?"

"Right now he's a bartender. But he's owned three. One his partner stole from him and two went out of business. Bad locations and the bastards that sold him the food and supplies cheated him. He even beat up on one of the meat men; Frank has a bad temper. The meat man sued and we had to get a lawyer. His name was Frank Wilcox, too. We picked him out of the phone book. He got my Frank off without jail, but it took every cent we had in the world."

Ellie printed "Bad temper."

"Do you and your husband drink regular or decaffeinated coffee?" she asked, thinking she'd lead the questioning to food and Weight Winners.

"Regular. Frank calls it leaded. Ain't he a card? I buy what's on sale. No, write down Taster's Choice. If I mention a brand name, do I get that one free?"

"I don't know," replied Ellie truthfully, then printed "Choice." "Have you ever bought diet products?"

"Diet products?" Her brow crinkled again.

"Skim milk, low-cal dressing or margarine. Frozen dinners like Lean Cuisine or the Weight Winners brand."

"Weight Winners...I've heard of that. My husband even joined their club once, but it didn't work."

"It didn't?"

"Frank was so mad. He said it cost money for nothing. Like fingernails. Frank put all he lost back on. His mother lost, tho'. She can afford fish and stuff. She inherited lots of money when Frank's daddy died, but she wouldn't give us a penny. Frank bought her a fancy plate for Mother's Day. Very expensive, and all she said was 'Thanks,' cold as you please. Frank wanted to borrow money for a new restaurant, but she said no." Cher laughed. "Well, you didn't come here to listen to my bitching. Frank's mother buys all that skinny food, but we can't afford it. Macaroni's cheaper."

Trying hard not to stare at the one eye that still boasted a spiky fringe of fake lashes, Ellie asked Cher a few more questions about specific foods, then shifted gears.

"What kind of clothing does your family wear?"

"Do I get clothes free, too?"

"My company's interested in *laundry* products."

"Oh," said Cher, disappointed. "Well, the kids wear mostly jeans and T-shirts. I guess I wear mostly Frank's old stuff," she stated, thumbing the white shirt whose ends were tied in a knot at the waist of her leopard spots. "I don't use no bleach," she added unnecessarily.

"What about winter jackets?"

"We get them at K Mart on sale, or the Army and Navy store. The kids are into the camouflage stuff."

Ellie printed "army-navy jacket" under "choice."

"What about hats?" she asked, holding her breath.

"The kids wear baseball caps with John Deere on 'em." Cher paused, then said accusingly, "We got 'em free for the *advertising*."

"And your husband?"

"He's got one of them knit things. Keeps his ears warm. I had a fur coat once. Real rabbit. I don't give a dang what those fancy-shmancy animal...uh...uh..."

"Activists?"

"Yeah. I don't care what them actorvists say. The rabbit was already dead, right? Maybe it died of old age. Anyhoo, a customer left her jacket in the bar and she never came back, so Frank gave it to me. I washed it with that detergent the TV says washes anything in cold water...all-temperature Cheer it's called, but the fur fell out. Guess if you wanted a *bald* rabbit, you could wash him in Cheer."

"Okay, I guess that takes care of my questions, Ms. Wilcox, although I have a few for your husband. When will he be home?"

"I don't know. I mean, he's out of town right now looking for a job."

"I thought you said he was employed...a bartender."

"He is. Sometimes Charley over at the Dew Drop Inn calls him if it's gonna be real busy, like when the piana guy plays for a big party."

"How long has Fr—Mr. Wilcox been gone?"

"Seems like a year, but it's probably a week or two."

Ellie wrote "Not home on Fridays," then asked, "When do you expect him back?"

"Do you have to question him for free samples? That ain't fair, Miss Rigby, it's chauv...chauvin...sexy-ist."

BEHIND THE WHEEL of her Honda again, Ellie decided her visit had been successful despite Frank's absence. She had found out that he was away from home at will and could stalk anytime, day or night. He hated Weight Winners. He wore one of "them knit things" for a hat. Cher bought military jackets. Frank had a bad temper.

And even though he hadn't attended meetings recently, he'd recognize Ellie, might easily menace her in the park or movie theater. Wait a minute. How would he know which members had reached goal? Sarah? Sarah had a big mouth and could have bragged about successful members, suggesting that her son was a loser...a failure.

Grasping at straws, Miss Rigby?

Dammit, she'd meant to ask questions about after-shave and men's cologne. Peter Falk would have turned at the door, paused, then said, "Oh yes...by the way... does Frank splash his stubbled jaw and smelly armpits with Old Spice?"

Peter *Miller* would have...how the hell *would* Peter phrase the question?

He wouldn't. Cher'd never talk to a sexy-ist cop.

On the other hand, Peter could charm the spots off Cher's pants. He'd merely share that lopsided grin and say, "My girlfriend wants to buy me some after-shave for my birthday. What do you suggest?"

Cher would bat her fringe of false lashes. "Frank likes that one with a boat, Lieutenant, 'specially when he plans to murder skinny people."

Ellie wondered if she should deliver some free samples. Although OINC didn't exist, she felt sorry for Cher Wilcox.

One other thing came to mind: Frank hated his mother. Sarah had lost weight on the diet. She had refused to loan him money. Could a son stalk his own mom?

Ellie put her car in gear and pulled away from the curb. Then she remembered. Cher said Frank tended bar when John Russell played piano for big parties. And it was during those events that Sandra sang at the Dew Drop Inn. She'd have to tell Peter when/if she saw him again.

Driving toward the interstate, Ellie thought she caught

a glimpse of a blue and white squad car. But there were always plenty of police around, particularly toward the end of the month when they had to make their ticket quotas.

Fortunately, she wasn't speeding. Just sleuthing.

A woman who can sleuth will keep her youth.

Especially if she's killed before old age sets in!

FOURTEEN

FIVE O'CLOCK.

The police car once again squatted like a blue and white vulture. Perhaps that was a stupid analogy, thought Ellie, because a vulture subsisted on carrion, and no dead, putrefying flesh decorated her lovely neighborhood where lawns were manicured, leaves raked, and skateboards leaned against undented Broncos.

Ellie's shower-damp hair curled about her face while Mickey's two rotund ears covered her breasts. Tucking the thermal undershirt into her jeans, she stepped back from the window and glanced around. She had always considered the family room disorganized, filled with a hodgepodge of authentic reproductions. But after Robbie's Elvis mausoleum, Tubby and Lulu's foyer, George's furniture store, and Cher's blowsy cave, her room seemed…well, dignified.

Except, of course, for undignified Roger Rabbit. From his framed poster, Roger grinned his lopsided grin (Peter's grin) and seemed to say: *Low blow, lady.*

No communication from Peter, not even a phone call. Should she call him and apologize?

Ellie sighed. She had honestly hoped to eventually, somehow, some way convince Peter to *wire* her, let her confront the suspects and ask questions, but now she realized he'd never agree. In fact, during this morning's jog, the damn squad car cruised alongside. Her stalker wouldn't show with her blue and white shadow there. Maybe *he* was the vulture, squatting from a distance, equipped with a high-power rifle. But carrion, my dear, is not on the Weight Winners diet.

Neither was crow! And she'd be damned if she'd apologize for wanting to help.

Why wouldn't Peter let her help? Playing decoy in the daylight wouldn't place her in much danger. After all, she'd successfully negotiated forays into homes of suspects and was proud of her improvisations. If Peter would only wire her. Was that asking too much?

"I don't want the woman I'm falling in love with to expose herself to danger," he'd said. Love, hah! He had angrily stamped out after one teensy quarrel (conversation).

Low blow, lady.

Blow, winds, and crack your cheeks! rage! blow!

Laurie, her friend from the library, quoted Shakespeare. "Shakespeare has a pertinent passage for every occasion," Laurie used to say.

Yup. True. A few years ago, Ellie had painted scenery for Mick's high school production of *The Merchant of Venice.* And watched rehearsals. And memorized a few lines. The quality of mercy bit. Plus: "If I can catch him once upon the hip, I will feed fat the ancient grudge I bear him." *Feed fat.* That's what had caught her attention.

She really shouldn't have made that nasty crack about cops needing help.

Low Blow.

Blow winds.

Crack your cheeks.

Feed fat.

Wire your midriff.

A Shakespearean refrain, forsooth.

"If I can catch her once upon the breast," muttered Ellie, "I will wire her midriff."

Curious, she looked up the word *wire* in the dictionary: a pliable thread, slender rod of metal; a snare.

Thread. Just like the unraveling embroidery on Cher's pillow, there were so many threads running in all directions.

Ellie walked to the fireplace, lit a fire, then collected a yellow foolscap pad and Magic Marker. Sitting cross-legged on the carpet, she made a list:

FRANK WILCOX
TUBBY EVERGREEN
GEORGE BUBBLES
ROBBIE JANSSEN

They all seemed to have the same motive. Envy of successful, popular Weight Winners members. Discontent with their own physical appearances. Sexual repression: Darlene's rape and the attempted assault of Sandra, plus the uncovered penis during Hannah's attack. The last image would tend to eliminate Frank Wilcox. He might kill his own mother, but he'd never sexually assault her. Too sick! Yet a sick mind had punctured Esther's neck with knitting needles after choking the sweet woman to death.

Under the five main suspects, Ellie wrote:

COUPLES WORKING TOGETHER
TUBBY & LULU
DAISY & BEAU
HENRY & WANDA

Why the last four? Those darling senior citizens because they were a couple; no other reason.

Wanda? Ridiculous. Why would Wanda murder successful members? Yet she had never been menaced. Ellie had been stalked during her morning jog and almost killed at the movie theater, but not Wanda. Why not?

What would be Wanda's motive? There *was* no motive.

Some murders have no obvious motives, Ms. Bernstein.

Ellie didn't agree. There had to be a reason—obvious or not—and, dammit, she was going to find it.

Wanda's husband? What would be *his* motive? Henry wasn't jealous of thin people, had no problem with his excess weight. Henry wasn't even a Weight Winners member. He had probably noticed Darlene—everybody had noticed Darlene—but Jeannie? Brian and Kelly? Esther? Sandra? Sarah? It didn't compute.

Back to the drawing board. Back to the photos Muffin had chosen.

George Bubbles—definitely an enigma. Today he had paraded her around the furniture store as his "lady friend" trying to impress his co-worker, Carl. George covered up his lack of self-esteem with a cheerful, cocky facade. Sad. So why had he joined Weight Winners? A place to meet women? Kill women?

And why did George ask about Hannah?

Everybody loves a lover, so nobody loves me. Motive: George killed from lack of love. He murdered popular members. He raped Darlene. It was possible.

Tubby Evergreen. No enigma there. Yet that comedic exterior could hide evil. The hot tub in Tubby's backyard bothered Ellie. And there was something else she couldn't quite put her finger on. What clue was she missing now?

Tubby's motive? Same as George, but less obvious. Everybody loves a lover, but nobody…nonsense. Tubby had Lulu. Lulu's motive? Again, the little green monster. Or maybe Lulu just followed her husband's orders.

Robbie Janssen. Poor, shy Robbie. He was too timid to stalk and kill. Yet his Corvette had surprised her. It didn't fit. Nothing fit.

Ellie scribbled furiously, filling the lines with names and theories.

Then, on the next page, she put Tubby Evergreen and George Bubbles at the top of a new suspect list, adding Frank, Lulu, and finally Robbie.

Dammit, this is getting me nowhere fast.

She heard a noise and glanced up, startled, to meet Peter's angry eyes.

"You didn't lock the front door!" he shouted.

"I'm sorry."

"You left the damn door open!"

"I forgot."

"After I've told you over and over to lock everything up tight. And trying to shake your police tail today, like some novice heroine in some garbage TV show. Well, it didn't work, lady. They watched you enter the Wilcox house. Jesus, Norrie, what if Frank had been the murderer? Do you have a damn death wish? They can make a movie and call it *Death Wish Three*."

"I think they already have one…Charles Bronson… wait a minute. Why three?"

"Janssen's apartment. Wilcox's house, and the theater."

"The theatre was *your* idea, remember? Ingrid's sexy accent and broad shoulders—"

"Don't change the subject."

Ellie rose to her feet. "Calm down, Peter."

"What the hell is the matter with you?"

"Look, this is my house, and you have no right—"

"No right? How do you think I'd feel if the killer carved—how much weight did you lose?—into your belly?"

"I'd feel worse. And don't call me Ellie-Belly."

"What? I didn't call—Jesus, you wouldn't feel worse. You'd be dead. You wouldn't feel anything at all. It's always the one left behind—the one who has to go on living—*shit!*"

Peter shed his suit jacket, throwing it across the room, knocking aside a window philodendron. He jerked at the knot in his tie, finally pulling it over his head, tossing the cloth lasso toward Jackie Robinson. He prodded the fire and sparks flew at the screen. Then, grasping Ellie's shoulders, he shook her, hugged her hard, and began to cry.

"Oh my God, what?" she asked, stepping backwards and staring into Peter's face.

"It's too much," he sobbed.

She noted the deep circles under his wet eyes. He's been working too hard, *too much,* she thought, and I haven't helped by complacently sneaking around behind his back.

"I'm sorry, so very sorry," she crooned, leading him to a chair and sinking down onto the carpet by his feet.

"It's too much, Cathy—I mean, Norrie."

Cathy? Ellie had a sudden intuition as things fell into place. When had he mentioned Cathy before? The afternoon she'd volunteered to play decoy.

"Peter, tell me about Cathy," she said softly.

"Not now."

"Yes, now."

He hesitated, then whispered, "Cathy was an artist..."

"Yes?"

"She was five feet nothing, a little slip of a girl. We had known each other since third grade. Everybody assumed...well, they didn't have to assume. It was always Peter and Cathy. There was never any doubt. We would get married and live happily ever after."

"She left you for another man?" Ellie mentally kicked herself; it had to be much more serious.

"God no, I wish that were true. I was on the police force in Denver. Just a uniform, not a hotshot lieutenant. Cathy and I decided to wait to get married until we had a substantial amount of money in our savings account. But she became pregnant and we set the date.

"There was an illegal ring of adoption agencies. Actually they were drug dealers, but covered up that activity with the adoption business. One illegal action laundering another. We had no proof. We wanted to use a decoy, but no one on the force was preg—"

"Cathy!"

"She was tiny. She had this pooched-out belly, like a kangaroo, even at four months. She looked so innocent, so believable. Nobody would ever suspect Cathy was connected with the police department. She loved the excitement, gathering the evidence. In all the years I knew her, I never realized that about her. The turn-on from danger." Peter shook his head. "She contacted the adoption ring, admitted she was Catholic and a starving artist who couldn't afford to keep her child. That's how they operated. They'd pay all expenses, then sell the baby for an exorbitant profit. Real sleaze operation."

Ellie waited silently for Peter to continue. Tears streamed down his face.

"It was a good old-fashioned raid," he finally said. "Precision timing. Everything worked...."

"Except?" Ellie prompted, wanting Peter to finish, knowing it was therapeutic for him to verbalize the tragedy.

"Except this spaced-out junkie came to buy some crack. He tried to escape, didn't care about uniforms and guns...just bolted. Then all hell broke loose."

"Cathy was shot?"

"She was trampled. Lost the baby, of course, but then she started hemorrhaging, and, well, she died."

"Oh, Peter, poor Peter."

"So you can see, can understand how I feel about all your...your extracurricular activities."

"But Peter, it's different."

"How is it different?"

"I'm not just an innocent bystander."

"Neither was Cathy—"

"Wait, let me finish. These are my people, my friends getting murdered. I'm not in it for the excitement or the danger."

Even as Ellie said the words, she knew she didn't mean them. In spite of her scare at the theater and Janssen's apartment, plus the initial fright outside the Wilcox home, she had enjoyed her sleuthing. The quick decisions, the escape from a possible life-threatening situation was heady, exhilarating. Except for the movie balcony, she'd never been in any obvious danger, unless Janssen had truly been the killer, or Frank had lurked in back of the house with his son's stereo....

Damn! Peter knew about her latest adventure. Is that why he was here—to start another donnybrook? To tell her to stay out of police business? He hadn't come just to check on whether or not her door was locked.

"Peter, what are you doing here?"

Adding a log to the fire, he stoked embers. His tears had dried and his face looked younger.

"I'm sorry, Norrie," he said. "I didn't mean to break down like that, but the unlocked door triggered…just one thing on top of another."

"I don't consider a man's tears a sign of weakness, Peter. I'd hate someone to pretend to be strong all the time to impress me, and I'm glad you have real emotions. What do you mean by one thing on top of another? You didn't come to see if my door was locked, did you? Or to apologize for our stupid argument. Why are you here?"

"Norrie, sit down."

"I *am* sitting. What's wrong?"

"I wanted to tell you before you heard or read—"

"Kelly Benedict."

"Died two hours ago."

"No, please God, *no*."

"Kelly woke once. She was coherent enough to confirm that the van going off the cliff wasn't an accident. It was definitely murder."

"That *bastard!* That bastard who's killing my friends. Kelly never did anything in her life to hurt another person. It's not fair, it's just not fair."

"I know." Peter sat, gathered her into his arms, and pulled her across his lap. "I'm sorry, sweetheart."

"You never met them," she sobbed. "To you they're just d-dead bodies. Sta-statistics."

"That's not true. Dead bodies are never statistics to me. I want to find this killer as much as you do."

"Oh, God, it isn't fair."

Peter held her while she wept against his chest. Finally she raised her face, eyelids swollen, her blue-green eyes slitted with anger.

"I never thought I could kill somebody...human or animal. I didn't realize I had it in me. If...if I knew it would stop the murders, I'd kill them *all*. Frank. Tubby. Robbie. George."

"You don't mean that."

"Didn't you want to kill after Cathy died? The innocent and the guilty?"

"Yes."

"Peter, we have to find this monster."

"I agree. We'll stop crying and concentrate. What happened inside the Wilcox house?"

"I pretended to take a survey so I could ask his wife questions," Ellie began, then related the details of her visit, adding every single thing she could recall about George Bubbles, the Evergreens' hot tub, Janssen's apartment, the ride home with Robbie in Vetty Grable, and the fact that Frank worked at the Dew Drop Inn during big parties.

"I don't know about Frank, but all the others wear rings. I think you're the only man left in the world who doesn't," concluded Ellie, smiling tremulously.

Showing Peter her doodled notes, she added, "There's one big question mark. I can't figure out how the killer knew where to find the victims. He could have followed Darlene and Sandra, but he'd have to know where to start. I assume he trailed the Benedicts after the meeting, yet he went straight to the homes of Jeannie, Esther, maybe even Sarah, unless he followed Hannah, but that doesn't fit because Hannah's not close to goal weight. Anyway, there are three Dobson's in the telephone directory, none of them listed as Jeannie. Only one Abramowitz—"

"How many Bernsteins?"

Ellie returned to her position on the beige carpet,

kissed Peter's knees, then replied, "Five, but my number's listed under Tony's name. I never bothered to change it. You were thinking about Robbie Janssen, weren't you? The fact that he knew my address without my telling him—"

"Oh my God, Janssen!" Peter grabbed Ellie's black marker and drew a circle around Robbie's name.

"What are you doing?"

"I can answer your big question mark, Norrie. I know who's been murdering—"

"Who? Who?" interrupted Ellie, thinking how she sounded like a confused owl.

Peter leaned forward to give her a quick kiss. "It fits, just like the missing piece in a jigsaw puzzle. Robbie Janssen works in the post office, Norrie. He would have access to all the victims' addresses. Don't you see? Frank Wilcox was an elaborate waste of time and effort. Wilcox hasn't attended meetings for two years and could never know who had reached their goal weights."

"Wait a minute. What about Sarah spilling the beans? She's been a member of Friday's Good Shepherd group until very recently, and she never shuts up."

"I suppose," said Peter grudgingly, "but Janssen knows everybody and he'd remember their full names, too. Sarah didn't. When I questioned her, she said she became frightened after the death of 'Esther what's-her-name' and 'that Darlene person.' And she calls *me* Lieutenant Budlight. On the other hand, Janssen could easily find the addresses through the post office. That morning at the restaurant, when you said all the file information was confidential, it threw me."

"Why are you so positive that Robbie would remember full names?"

"Janssen hasn't missed a meeting. I once watched you

read first and last names aloud, announcing losses. And don't you hand out graduation trinkets when members reach goal weight?''

''Not trinkets, Peter, certificates. I never thought about that address thing until today...before, when I was writing my suspect list. Some smart sleuth, huh?''

''All the deaths occurred on Fridays—''

''I did think of that, Peter.''

''—Janssen's day off.''

''Friday is George's day off, too. He once said it was the reason he could attend my lectures.''

''George Bubbles was safe at his furniture store when the Benedicts were murdered. Carl had the flu, and Bubbles came in to cover for him.''

''No, no.''

''No, no?''

''The furniture store probably stays open late on Fridays—don't they all? George met Hannah Taylor for happy hour at the Dew Drop Inn around five o'clock. She mentioned it when we were chatting by the scale. Holy cow! George had my members' addresses, too. We all filled out coupons for a VCR drawing. Jeannie, Esther, the Benedicts, Darlene, even Sarah Wilcox. Sandra might have attended that particular meeting. George could have copied—''

''Norrie, he went directly to work after the meeting. Don't you think we verified his story? Maybe business was slow and he left early.''

''How about after?''

''What do you mean?''

''He met Hannah at five. Esther was killed around eleven. Does he have an alibi for that?''

''Yes. Bubbles, er, spent the night with Hannah.''

"Oh. Did she say…never mind; it's none of my business. What about the other alleged perps' alibis?"

"Alleged perps?"

"Don't play dumb, Peter. The people Sandra picked from the Polaroids."

"Why are *you* playing devil's advocate, Norrie?"

Ellie pulled Jackie Robinson onto her lap and stroked the cat behind his furry ears. "A long time ago, I had a puss named Devil's Advocate," she murmured, and heard Jackie Robinson's loud purr. Background music—like Esther's knitting needles or Tubby cracking his knuckles.

Tubby!

"Dear Lord, Peter, Tubby Evergreen. Tubby works at the Department of Motor Vehicles. He'd have access to addresses. With computers, it would be easy—"

"While the Benedicts were being murdered, Evergreen was at that new pizza restaurant, raiding the buffet table. Wanda Henry saw him there while waiting for her husband to join her for lunch." Peter studied Ellie's pages. "This is terrific. I'm impressed."

"No, it's not terrific," she replied. "Robbie was my last choice among the suspects. I didn't want it to be any of them, but I especially didn't want Robbie to be our monster. On the other hand, Sandra did say the killer asked her to sing. Robbie could picture life and death as scenes in a musical. His Elvis fetish."

"Norrie sweetheart, you've just helped me solve my case with your question mark comment," said Peter. "Unless he has an airtight alibi for the Benedicts, I'm positive Janssen is our murderer."

"Does he have an airtight alibi for the other murders?"

"We haven't checked out every alibi, Norrie. We're guarding fannies, and we're kind of short on manpower."

"You could…"

Have additional woman power, she thought, swallowing the rest of her words because she didn't want to start another argument.

"…be grasping at straws," she finished, but Peter was already across the room, reaching for the phone.

What about Robbie's blue suede shoes? Ellie hadn't noticed shoes in Acacia Park when the stalker half hid behind a tree. The restaurant's window had cut him off at the waist. The theater balcony had been too dark and she'd been frightened. Scared or not, wouldn't she remember blue suede shoes?

Why the hell did she insist on playing devil's advocate? Dammit, they had finally found their killer, and diet-club members could once more follow the Weight Winners program without fear or reprisal.

But Robbie Janssen wasn't a murderer. He wasn't! Poor, lonely, shy Robbie, stuck behind his post office window, day in, day out. Old postmen never die, they just lose their zip.

"For twenty-four cents, Americans deserve a postage stamp that tastes better," murmured Ellie, then discovered that tears blurred her eyes again. Kelly. Dead.

Sobbing, she crossed the room, ducked under the phone cord, and buried her face between Peter's chin and shoulder.

Because, along with chocolate and sex, death was reality, too.

FIFTEEN

BAD HABITS ARE LIKE A WATER BED—EASY TO GET INTO BUT HARD TO GET OUT OF.

WANDA HENRY LEANED AGAINST the chalkboard, smudging the words "hard to get out of."

The meeting room looked very Halloween-y she thought. An evil, grinning pumpkin perched on the podium. Its eyes shined from the inside out with candlelight. Even the long table where Weight Winners members usually sat had been arranged near the front of the room, disguised by a stenciled paper tablecloth. Its centerpiece—a fish with a toothy death smirk and cucumber slices arranged in layered scales—was surrounded by Tupperware containers and serving dishes filled with legal snacks. A glass punch bowl held sugar-free ginger ale.

Wanda had raided a local discount store; broomed witches, black cats, and jack-o'-lantern cutouts hung from the orange crepe-papered light fixture. She had shopped for herself, too, and wore a short fringed skirt, vest, cowboy hat, and boots. All she needed was a horse named Buttermilk. Except she'd change the name to Skim Milk.

"Dale Evans Henry," she had told the twins.

"Dale *who?*" Becky had asked, and for a moment Wanda felt old, then young again. Especially when she pictured Will McCoy. She'd get a divorce after Christmas. To hell with Henry. He was bluffing. He wouldn't fight for custody of the twins, not in this best of all possible worlds.

Humming, Wanda stationed herself behind the punch bowl, happy that her husband, soon to be ex-husband, had declined to attend the celebration. She had tentatively asked but he had sneered: "Me party with a bunch of fat perverts? You gotta be kidding. I'd rather drink over at the Dew Drop."

Now Wanda ladled ginger ale into paper cups while glancing every now and then toward the window. The evening news had forecast rain, but it hadn't begun yet. Maybe it would snow. Wanda loved snow. Her food *nemesis* (Ellie's word) was whipped cream.

Jeannie Dobson had favored Twix candy bars. Esther, bagels and lox. Darlene, pretzels. Brian and Kelly... what? They'd never confessed.

But Robbie Janssen had confessed, thank God.

"Rise and shine and give God your glory-glory," Wanda sang under her breath. "Rise and shine and give God your glory-glory... Children of the Lord. Noah, he built him, he built him an ark-y, ark-y, dum dum de dum dum, he built him an ark-y, ark-y..."

HOORAY, THOUGHT ELLIE. Her party had attracted a crowd. People arrived early, with weigh-ins scheduled for 6:00 to 7:00 p.m. Despite the special occasion, Wanda's neat index file would be kept up to date with losses or gains duly recorded.

Robbie Janssen had been arrested. At first he had professed innocence, admitted Peter. But he lacked an alibi for the Benedicts, actually *any* of the murders, insisting he had been home alone watching television. Inside the trunk of his red Corvette, the police found a variety of winter garments and coats—including a dark gray-green pea jacket—which Robbie claimed he had been planning to tote to the dry-cleaning store in the Safeway shopping center, "that center with the new pizza place." The jacket had blood on it. Robbie said he'd cut his finger. Yeah, and Peter had a famous bridge for sale. Forensics was testing the blood to see if it matched Esther's or Darlene's.

No knit stocking cap. Peter said Janssen would have to be really stupid to keep a stocking cap after his unsuccessful encounter with Sandra. He had switched to a ski mask, and probably dumped *that* following Hannah's attack.

"Why did he keep the jacket?" Ellie had asked over a breakfast of French toast and low-cal syrup.

"I don't know," Peter had replied, munching Danish and bacon. "A jacket's more expensive and dozens of people wear them. Want a piece of bacon?"

"Dozens of people wear knit caps. Frank Wilcox wears one to 'keeps his ears warm.'"

"Norrie, leave it alone. Janssen had motive and opportunity."

"What motive?"

"You know the motive; we've discussed it since the beginning. Janssen was jealous. He was—what do you always call it?—a W.W. Two member. He had joined your diet club, quit, gained weight, then rejoined."

"But this time he did real well."

"Did he? Wasn't it a repeat of the first time? He had so much to lose, Norrie."

"And so much to win, Peter."

"Even if we eliminate jealousy, Janssen was lonely and sexually repressed. You scribbled that motive on your pad."

"I'll buy it for the attacks on Darlene, Sandra, even Kelly Benedict. But Jeannie? Esther? Sarah? Nope."

"Look Ms. Devil's Advocate, Janssen was obviously lying when we originally questioned him. Watching television, my ass. He had bought airplane tickets to leave Colorado Springs; said he was going to an Elvis memorial thing in Nashville. Several people at Sandra's party described a replica of Janssen lurking—"

"That's ridiculous, Peter. Muffin couldn't even identify him for sure."

"Look, the second time we questioned Janssen, he practically confessed."

"*Practically* confessed? I thought he confessed confessed."

"Robbie acknowledged he might have done it. Claimed he had 'blackouts.' Wanted to know if he was going to appear on TV."

"Give me a break, as Sandra would say. The poor man wanted recognition. He was probably picturing himself as Elvis in *Jailhouse Rock*. And you didn't discover the knife, did you?"

"Drop it, sweetheart. Look, if Janssen's innocent, we'll find out soon enough."

Ellie couldn't understand why she didn't feel more elated. Probably because she kept thinking about Robbie's apartment, especially the refrigerator door calendar. Bare except for meetings and Elvis movies. Peter had surmised that the words *WEIGHT WINNERS* meant selecting a victim, but now Ellie wasn't certain. Robbie claimed he watched TV during the murders. He *had* automatically played his television immediately upon arriving home *that day*.

The day she invaded his sanctuary. Could Robbie really be their killer? What evidence had the police collected? A half-baked confession, pea jacket with blood on it, Old Spice container, diamond rings, no alibi, access to addresses. Tubby Evergreen had access to addresses. So did George Bubbles.

Had Robbie been casting an Elvis musical when he told Sandra to sing "Yankee Doodle?"

Ti yi yippi yay for the police. Robbie yodeled in his shower. *Big deal! So do I!* At this very moment, Wanda stood by the punch bowl, humming like a bird. George sang in his furniture store. Did Tubby, Lulu, or Frank Wilcox sing?

Had Peter told her anything? Or were the police so damn anxious for a solution that they believed pathetic Robbie Janssen could murder in cold blood?

Norrie, leave it alone.

She shuddered when she remembered her ride back home in the rain. She could easily have been Robbie's next victim. Why hadn't he tried to kill her? POSTMEN DELIVER, his sweatshirt had advertised. Deliver what? A deathblow? But she'd mentioned something about leaving an itinerary, which might have made him think twice. He'd never asked her address. How did he know where she lived?

Holy cow, that was easy to figure out. Ellie stacked business cards near the scale for members who needed to contact her in an emergency. The cards listed her address and phone number. Why hadn't she remembered that before?

Yet Robbie *had* seemed nervous at the sight of her fanny-guarding policemen. Hell's bells (as Cher would say), almost everybody quaked at the sight of a cop cruiser.

The theater. Robbie could have trailed her and Peter. Maybe he was one of the unseen voices shushing them.

He could have followed her to the lobby…and he might have spied on her during early-morning jogs. Acacia Park was less than six blocks away from the Pike's Peak Post Office.

Poor Robbie. He wouldn't be able to follow his Weight Winners diet program inside a jail cell.

Or was he out on bond? No, they wouldn't release a murderer, would they? Why hadn't she asked Peter? Why hadn't she asked if Robbie knew about the hot water in Jeannie's bathtub? Or if he'd described any other evidence that had been kept under wraps?

And why did she still believe the killer was Tubby Evergreen? All the circumstantial evidence pointed to him, too. Hadn't Wanda insisted that Tubby slapped his wife around? If that was true, Ellie had no sympathy for Tubby, none at all. Her ex, Tony, used to hurt her with nasty, cutting comments. Wanda's husband did the same thing. Physical abuse was different, worse, much worse.

But Tubby was at the pizza parlor when the Benedicts were murdered. Wanda saw him.

Wait a minute! Wanda saw *Tubby*. What did Peter say? "Tubby Evergreen was at that new pizza restaurant, raiding the buffet table."

Had *Lulu* been there? A man attacked Darlene, stalked Sandra and Hannah, but couldn't Lulu have killed Jeannie? Brian and Kelly?

Were Tubby and Lulu working together? A pair of killers? The family that *preys* together.

Lulu worked at a sporting-goods or hardware store. She had access to knives and ski caps.

Leave it alone, Norrie.

Dammit, that was like telling a person to sit in the corner and *not* think about a white bear. It couldn't be done, and she couldn't stop mulling over poor Robbie.

People were arriving in droves. The news about Janssen's arrest had elicited a feeling of relief and safety, but reasons for the successful attendance went much deeper. A party where an overweight person didn't stand out or have to be funny was an event that couldn't be ignored. The group seemed comfortable and definitely festive. Even the brand-new member who resembled Nell Carter had returned, dressed as a chocolate clown. Ellie greeted her warmly.

Peter and William McCoy had been invited—special guests. Clothed as the Lone Ranger, McCoy had cowboy guns in tooled holsters. His black mask and white Stetson hovered above Wanda Henry's punch bowl.

Peter was consumed as a white rabbit, the bulky, furry material hiding his slim body. Thinking about Roger Rabbit's lopsided grin, Ellie had insisted he come as Peter Cottontail, agreeing to accompany him as Playboy Bunny. She was secretly proud of her scanty leotard over mesh stockings and high heels. Puffy tail and wired ears completed the costume. Her blue-green eyes were outlined with thick black kohl, and she had penciled whiskers over the blusher that enhanced her cheekbones.

"A tasty morsel," Peter had said, smacking his lips. "Is rabbit legal fare on your diet program?"

"Eight ounces before broiling." Grinning wickedly, she had added, "Remember what I told you when we first met? Taste and spit without swallowing."

"I don't want to sample, sweetheart, I want to eat the whole bunny."

"That's okay, Peter, *you're* not on a diet."

Then, hugging her detective, Ellie had felt a gun nestled in a shoulder holster beneath his costume.

Was he required to carry his weapon at all times?

Or did he have identical doubts about Robbie's guilt?

Were McCoy's Lone Ranger accessories real pistols?

Ellie kept meaning to ask, but she soon became overwhelmed by the crush of exuberant celebrants, and she lost sight of Peter.

Colorful costumes filled the room. Some had been rented (like Peter's) or purchased (like Wanda's) and several appeared to be homemade, stitched on a sewing-room Singer. Ellie saw Hannah, draped in a sheet, looking like a Grecian statue. White material was belted around her middle, showing off a newly discovered waist. Her hair curled on top of her head, and bright brown eyes shone through shadow mixed with glitter. She had discarded her old spectacles for square-framed glasses that made her face appear pixieish. Standing near the window, she chatted with George Bubbles, who wore his every week black trousers and World's Greatest Lover T-shirt.

There were orange pumpkins, white ghosts, and black-cloaked witches. Ellie smiled at one member, disguised as an ice-cream cone. A round face peeked out from a pistachio papier-mâché headdress, while layers of crinkly brown material wrapped the body in a swirling sugar cone.

Daisy and Beau were clothed as geriatric Superman and Wonder Woman. *Generic* heroes, thought Ellie with a smile, remembering Cher Wilcox's semantic mix-up.

One guest wore a Sesame Street Cookie Monster head and body, obviously rented. He had discarded the costume's paw to cover his feet with a pair of comfortable high-top basketball sneakers. *Damn!* As she watched, he inhaled a cigarette through the hole in his furry blue-faced hood.

Walking forward, coughing from the clouds of smoke, Ellie said, "Please put that out. They don't allow smoking inside the church."

"Sorry." The voice was muffled by the blue fur. "Didn't mean to break no rules." Dipping his cigarette's glowing tip into a paper cup of ginger ale, he held out the black and orange cup for Ellie's inspection.

"You can smoke in the parking lot," she said to the Cookie Monster, then paled under her blusher and whiskers as she spied a sparkly satin jumpsuit. There, over there by the door. Belly and thighs strained the garment's seams. The face was hooded, with crude openings for eyes and nose, and the cloth cover ended at a neck circled by a bright scarf. *Elvis!* Holy cow, could Robbie Janssen be out of jail? Attending the party he had so carefully emphasized with red ink on his sparse calendar page?

"What's the matter?" asked the Cookie Monster.

"I thought I saw Elvis Presley."

"Don't you read the papers? Everybody sees Elvis."

"WHAT ARE YOU supposed to be?" Hannah asked.

"It seemed like a good idea at the time," muttered George. "I couldn't think of anything else and it was sort of a joke. A joke on me. A fat Don Juan."

"Aw, don't be so hard on yourself. You've got some very nice qualities."

"Name two."

"Well, you have a nice sense of humor. You're a wonderful salesman. Remember how we all filled out those VCR coupons? You're kind. Yes, you are," she insisted when George shook his head. "You were ever so comforting at the meeting the day I was upset over Jeannie's death."

"Are you kidding, Hannah? I made you break your diet and come out drinking and…and…and everything," he finished lamely, looking, thought Hannah, like a small boy caught with his fingers inside the cookie jar.

"I couldn't face you after that," George continued. "I even went to your house and waited outside. Didn't have the nerve to knock on your door. Hannah, I have these dreams."

"Everybody has dreams, George."

"Not like mine. I have to tell somebody about them, somebody who won't laugh."

"I won't laugh."

"I know. You look great tonight, babe."

"I've lost seventeen pounds total," Hannah said proudly. "I stepped on the scale earlier."

"Would it be okay if I took you home after the party?"

"Well, I have my car, and I don't want to leave it in the church's parking—"

"Couldn't I follow? Just to talk, nothing else, I promise. I haven't done too good on Ellie's diet and maybe you can help. You're nice, Hannah, and beautiful. You've lost lots of weight and you don't look a bit like *her*, and I'm so glad you don't. Maybe I can tell you about my dream and we can drink coffee. This time I have Equal packets in my back pocket, not doughnut sacks." His lips quivered in a tremulous smile. "Tonight's Halloween. I can protect you from ghosts and goblins. Please."

George Bubbles wasn't Snoopy, thought Hannah. In fact, he reminded her of dear, sweet Hershey. George's brown hair was even graying like a piece of stale chocolate.

"We can leave right now," she said. "I've been afraid of ghosts, too, but I'm getting over it, and I'd much rather drink coffee with you than party, honest."

Hand in hand, they left, just as Tubby and Lulu made their noisy entrance, greeting members.

Tubby looked awful, thought Ellie, with a white tablecloth safety-pinned around his lower body. Above the oversized diaper, an undershirt was covered with a large bib stitched: MARY HAD A LITTLE LAMB, A LITTLE SPA-GHETTI, AND CHEESECAKE.

Lulu had come clothed as her cartoon namesake and wore a ruffled organdy tent dress. Her ringlets were held back from her face by two enormous red bows, and she'd created circles on her cheeks with lipstick. Below the bright crimson circles, Ellie could discern a fading bruise.

The couple carried a square box with a Pizza Hut logo. Grinning, Tubby opened the box to display a lime gelatin mold. People applauded.

"Peet-zah," shouted the Cookie Monster in a bad imitation of the real Sesame Street character. "Kook-key. Peet-zah."

Maybe Tubby and Lulu weren't working together, thought Ellie, maybe Lulu murdered alone. *No way.* Darlene was raped. Hannah's foot made contact with a dangling penis. Stop thinking about a white bear.

Following in the Evergreen's wake was Sarah Wilcox, a reluctant Frank…and *Cher.*

Dressed in fatigues, Cher walked straight toward Ellie. "Miss Rigby? Hell's bells, what're you doin' here? I know. You're taking another survey."

"I'm incognito, Ms. Wilcox."

"In-cog-what?"

"Disguised," replied Ellie, feeling an urge to giggle; everybody except Sarah, Frank, and George had appeared in-cog-what.

"Dang, I won't give you away," Cher shouted. "I didn't get my free samples yet," she added accusingly.

"Soon. I'm sure they'll arrive soon."

"You said you had to question Frank. He's here."

"Yes, uh, maybe later," said Ellie, retreating backward toward the punch bowl.

What was Cher doing at the party? Then Ellie remembered that Sarah's address was still indexed inside Wanda's file, so Sarah would automatically receive an invitation. She had brought along the whole family, except for her grandchildren, and Dog.

Sarah was one of the few diet-club members whose weight loss had left her looking pinched and wan. The excess poundage had given her a bit of rounded, padded personality. Now her edges were sharp, her body angled like a slingshot.

Ellie overheard Sarah confiding to the ice-cream cone about how she planned to invest in a new restaurant. It would serve a diet menu, with meals culled from Weight Winners recipes. Junior could manage the place *after* he reached his goal weight.

TUBBY EVERGREEN GULPED punch from his paper cup, and for a brief moment, Lulu thought he might consume the cup's stenciled black cat as well.

"Hard to tell a woman's shape when she's hidden inside her costume," he said. "Guess I'll have to walk around the room and feel 'em out for myself."

"Don't you dare," replied Lulu. "If you do, I'll drive home and lock the doors. I have our keys inside my purse."

"Are you threatening me?"

"Yes. Are you gonna hit me, Tubby? Right in front of everybody?"

"You stupid bitch. Wait 'til later."

"You stupid bastard. If you touch me again, I'll leave you. There's an organization for women like me. Father O'Sullivan said so."

"You saw the *priest?*"

"I sure did, and all because of Weight Winners. Sister Maria insisted I talk to Father O'Sullivan. It was awfully hard to sell him about you and me, especially you, but I did."

"Dammit, Lu, that was dumb. If the priest blabs, everybody'll think I'm a real shithead."

"The priest won't blab, but I will. I'll tell everyone. They won't like you very much, and that'll kill you, won't it? You'll lose your new gang. They'll change your name from Tubby to Shithead."

"Aw, Lulu…"

"Call me Lydia. This is the last time I plan to be Little Lulu. Starting tonight, I'm following Ellie's diet. Father wrote down the phone number of a group that protests abused wives, and he recommended a psychiatrist for you. If you won't see the doctor, I'm blabbing."

"Lulu—"

"Lydia. Funny, I was scared about confessing to Father because I felt like such a failure. Lulu can't lose weight. Lulu can't have babies. Well, guess what? *Lydia* will do all those things, with or without you. Do you understand, Tub—hey, what was your real name before you changed it."

"Steve."

"Do you understand, Steve?"

He nodded. "I have to see a shrink, right? Look, I can't promise it'll work."

"Just try, that's all I ask. Just try, Steve."

"Do you want me to get you a cup of punch, Lydia?"

ELLIE WATCHED AS eight or nine people formed a circle, holding hands, their voices rising above the recorded tapes Ellie had brought along. Half the group sang:

"She'll be drivin' six white horses when she comes, when she comes." The other half yodelled: "We'll all eat chicken an' dumplings when she comes." Laughing, they finished the chorus together: "She'll be comin' round the mountain when she comes, when she comes."

At the conclusion of the performance, Frank Wilcox suggested they record a videotape. "We could show it on MTV," he shouted, "sell copies, split the profits. I could buy a goddamn Baskin-Robbins franchise."

"Yogurt's more profitable," said the chocolate clown.

"We'll all eat frozen yogurt when she comes," warbled Frank. "Oboy, I've got another idea. We can change the song's lyrics to skinny food."

Aha, thought Ellie, so Frank *did* sing. Could he be the killer? *White bear. White bear. White bear.*

Ellie had promised the church minister that everybody would be gone and the area cleared and cleaned by eleven o'clock. Small groups waved good-bye. Individual ghosts floated from the room. Many people had left earlier, wanted to be home for the neighborhood trick-or-treaters.

"I bought tiny boxes of Sunmaid raisins," bragged Wonder Woman, clasping Superman's hand. "Candy was on sale and it sure was tempting, but I knew we'd eat it."

When the last clown, pumpkin, and son-of-a-witch had exited, Ellie began to take down decorations. Wanda had bought green plastic trash bags. Peter and Will pitched in, carefully removing the ceiling crepe paper. Rock music blared from Ellie's cassette recorder.

Even though her mother had volunteered to babysit, Wanda was worried about the twins. Grandmama (who was very heavy) didn't like to walk, so Joseph Jr. and Becky might still be trick-or-treating without any supervision. Ellie said that she'd finish cleaning and lock up the building. Peter, who had removed his hot, stuffy rabbit head, nodded toward McCoy.

After filling a carton with the punch bowl, leftover decorations and the carved pumpkin, Wanda glanced around the room.

"What are you looking for?" asked Ellie.

"Keys to the church door. The minister gave me an extra set, just in case. Could have sworn I left them by the scale."

"Don't worry about it. They'll turn up. I have my set of keys. Get out of here."

"Wait, the file. I have to take the file home and work on my Christmas present."

McCoy added the metal box, then hoisted the carton to his shoulder as the pair went through the door. Tonight the side exits were closed and locked, so Will and Wanda wandered through corridors, passing classrooms and restrooms, heading for the entrance that led to a huge worshiping nave and the front door.

"Ellie's tapes are so loud," said Wanda.

"What? Can't hear you with all that music in my ears." McCoy's dimples deepened and his freckles merged. "Remember that old joke about the banana?"

"Sure. Why do you have a banana in your ear? Can't hear you, I have a banana in my ear." Wanda giggled. "Ellie's music sounds so...I don't know...so sacrilegious."

Attempting a few impromptu dance steps, she almost whirled into McCoy.

He put the carton down and captured her in an embrace, while maneuvering their bodies against a wall.

"No, William, no."

"Yes, oh yes." McCoy ran his hands lightly over

Wanda's vest, then kissed the cleavage above her shirt buttons.

"Please, stop," she gasped. "This is a *church*. What if Ellie and Peter come along?"

"We'll drive to my apartment."

"I have to go home."

"Have you ever made love on the front seat of a detective's car, Wanda?"

"No, of course not, but—"

"Let's leave. Hurry."

They made a sharp turn around the hallway corridor.

A large figure stepped from a recessed pay-phone alcove and buried a knife in McCoy's chest.

The carton fell to the floor; the punch bowl shattered; McCoy whispered, "Screwed up again."

In slow motion, he reached for one of the guns encased inside his holster, then slumped to the floor. Just before total blackness descended, McCoy saw a blue furry figure in basketball sneakers.

Wanda cringed—paralyzed with fright—against the wall as the Cookie Monster pulled the knife from Will's chest. She knew she'd be next; she knew she should run.

But she couldn't move.

"Whore."

Wanda stood frozen in fear and silence.

"Nibble, nibble, little mouse. Let's eat each other instead of food. Kook-key. Peet-zah."

Then Wanda knew. "Oh my god," she cried, taking a few steps forward. "Dear God!"

A blue furry paw reached out and slammed her body against the wall.

Bleeding from a head wound, Wanda crumpled to the floor. *Sweet Jesus,* she thought before dizziness overwhelmed her.

"I done it once with a dead lady already," muttered the Cookie Monster. "Don't have time right now, but you should be out cold for a spell. Wanda Henry went to town, riding on a *po*-nee. Stuck a feather in her cap and called it mac-a-*ro*-nee. Good night, ladies. Baaa, baaa, baaa. Yes we have no bananas, we have no bannannas to-day."

Behind the mask, his eyes glittered, like candlelight shining from the inside out. Wanda moaned. "I can't hear you," said the Cookie Monster. "I have a banana in my ear."

SIXTEEN

SNOW BEGAN TO FALL.

Millions of tiny frosted flakes, thought Ellie, removing a wart-chinned witch that Wanda had taped to the window. *And I feel grrr-eat.*

"Did you hear that, Peter?" she asked, watching him dance with a broom, sweeping debris to the accompaniment of Bruce Springsteen's "Born in the USA."

"What did you say, sweetheart?" Peter smiled at Ellie. Fatigue had smudged the black stuff around her eyes, and the whiskers on her cheekbones had almost disappeared. She looked like a mischievous raccoon with bunny ears. "What did you say?" he asked again.

"I thought I heard something. Oh, well, maybe it was the music."

"Ahhh, Springsteen. I'm glad we have the same taste in music. We seem to have the same taste for everything."

"Oh, sure. Seafood versus barbecue ribs. Your war movies versus any romance films."

"Wait a minute. I took you to *Casablanca.* It's romantic."

"Except it doesn't end happily ever after. Ingrid boards a plane and flies away."

For a few moments they were both silent.

"And I'll kill if I don't get the left side of my bed back," Ellie finally said.

"I prefer to have you crawling all over my body in your sleep."

"I'll switch to opera tapes," she threatened, glancing toward her cassette recorder.

"I love opera."

"You do? Speaking of opera, I wonder how Sandra's faring at the Halloween Ball. Mick came home from Boulder to escort her, and I sprung for a new dress to replace the one that the killer...Robbie Janssen...Peter?"

"Oh, no, we're not going to talk about the murders or Janssen tonight."

"But Peter—"

"No, Norrie. Tonight it's just you and me, and the water bed. And once we hit the bed, I intend to wear earplugs since you always seem to noodge with questions when my defenses are down."

"This is important. Did you happen to catch the guest costumed as Elvis?"

"Of course. It wasn't Robbie Janssen, sweetheart. Hey, do you remember Kiss?"

"My first kiss?" she asked, puzzled. "Or do you want to kiss me?"

"Yes, but I meant the singing group."

"What made you think of *them?*"

"Elvis. We were talking about singers."

"This reminds me of our first dinner date; you're purposely changing the subject." Ellie sighed. "Mick had a poster of Kiss when he was seven. All the kids did. I remember the weird makeup and that stupid *tongue.*"

"Christ, how I used to envy that tongue."

"Mick loved the poster, but it scared *me* to death."

"Aha, so you *do* get frightened."

"Low blow, Lieutenant. You scare me. I never thought I could feel this way about anybody. All squishy inside."

"I feel squishy, too. Let's finish and hurry home. We can make love to your opera tapes."

"I have a recording of *Peter and the Wolf.*"

"You'll play the wolf?"

"Sure." Ellie licked her lips. "Did the wolf eat Peter? Or was it Red Riding Hood?"

"C'mere, Red." Leaning forward, he kissed the tip of her nose. "I'm getting turned on. Did Wanda slip an aphrodisiac into the diet ginger ale?"

Ellie studied his bulky white trousers. "Is your...are your defenses up or down?"

"Down." Glancing down, he said, "Up. Definitely up."

Laughing, she stowed the broom and green plastic bags inside a small closet, then studied the room. "It's clean. I'll come back tomorrow and dump our trash." Turning off the cassette recorder and tossing it into her purse, she reached for the light switch.

"Hold it, sweetheart, I've got to use the restroom." Peter patted her cotton-tail. "What secret ingredient did the Evergreens add to their gelatin mold? Or did Wanda's punch also include a diuretic?"

"The Evergreens...did you see their Pizza Hut bit?"

"Yup."

"What else."

"What else did I eat?"

"What did you see?"

He hesitated a moment, then said, "George Bubbles left early with Hannah Taylor. Frank Wilcox plans to film a videotape for MTV; the guy's a dreamer. Lulu Evergreen seemed to have her husband eating out of her hand. Literally."

"Do you think Hannah's in any danger?"

"No, but a policeperson followed her."

"Holy cow, Peter, did you plant cops?"

"Cops aren't trees or flowers, Norrie."

"I'm serious."

"So am I. Okay, okay, remember the ice-cream cone?" When she nodded, he said, "Detective Mary Ellen Johnson."

"So you *do* believe Robbie's innocent!"

"Where's the restroom?"

"Down the hall."

"I'm planning to shed this ridiculous costume, then you'll be in real danger. Wait for me, okay?"

"Always."

Later, she thought, when his defenses are down, we can play "Jeopardy." I'll ask the answers and Peter can give the questions. Later. Soon. Sooner or later.

Ellie watched him leave, then glanced around the room again. Damn, she'd missed a small pile of debris near the chalkboard. Should she retrieve the broom? No. Merely a scrap of orange streamer and a cigarette filter.

Flora, Fauna, and Merryweather! Had the Cookie Monster smoked another cigarette?

Wrinkling her nose, Ellie picked up the butt, dropped it into the wastepaper basket, then had an overwhelming sensation of déjà vu.

Once before somebody had scrunched out a cigarette. Once before she had tossed a butt into the trash.

"They don't allow smoking in the church."

"Right. Don't want to break no rules."

"Could be he smokes or has a deep voice."

"No, the smoking theory eliminates Robbie, George, and Tubby."

Ellie staggered backward and reached for the podium to steady herself.

It's the Cookie Monster!

Ohmigod, I have to tell Wanda!

Grabbing her purse, Ellie ran down the corridor past

the men's restroom, turned a corner, and saw Detective William McCoy's body on the floor. Wanda lay sprawled against the wall.

Ellie knelt next to Wanda and grabbed a wrist. *Thank God.* Wanda was out cold, but her pulse throbbed.

McCoy's cowboy shirt was covered with a spreading bloodstain. Ellie crawled toward him. His pulse was weak, yet the Lone Ranger might live if an ambulance arrived in time.

Dial nine-one-one! Hurry!

"Peter!" she screamed, rising, turning toward the pay phones, fumbling inside her purse for coins. The cassette recorder fell, its play button hitting the floor as it landed. Sounds of Springsteen's "No Surrender" whirred into life and filled the corridor.

Peter's voice was muffled, but audible. "Norrie, I'm coming. Don't move! Shit, it's locked!"

There were two phones. The first had an OUT OF ORDER sign. Ellie rushed inside the second alcove. She reached for the receiver, then stared uncomprehendingly at her hand. The instrument had been snipped and there were bloodstains on the coiled black wire.

"Peter!" she shouted again, scrambling further down the hallway until she reached the minister's office; there'd be a phone inside. She grasped the handle but the door was bolted. She rattled the knob. Frustrated, she pounded on the beveled glass insert. The door opened, and a fuzzy blue figure filled the entrance.

"Well, well, if it ain't the head whore," he said pleasantly. "Bingo. I finally struck the jackpot." In his Cookie Monster voice, he shouted, "Bing-go. Jack-pot. Kook-key."

Chuckling and snorting, the blue monster jangled a set of keys attached to a round metal holder, keys Ellie had seen the friendly minister carry on their conversational tours through the building.

Keys that Wanda had left by the scale.

Ellie had forgotten all about them.

Where the hell was Peter?

As if she'd spoken aloud, the Cookie Monster said, "I locked the men's bathroom from the outside when you was in the room. Your cop'll have to break the door down."

Dropping the keys, the monster removed his smiling headpiece, and a furious face stared at Ellie.

"Henry," she whispered.

"Why did you have to interfere? When Wanda was fat, I had her under control. It's all your fault."

He gave an angry roar and flung the headpiece toward Ellie. With a scream, she fled down the hall.

The monster followed, holding his blood-stained knife.

Running fast, Ellie turned another corner and ducked into a restroom marked *GIRLS*. Her legs spasmed from her sprint. Breathing hard, she secured an inside bolt at the top of the door. Good Shepherd, like many old buildings, had inside and outside locks on every door. Ellie grabbed a sink for support. There were two sinks, three toilet stalls, one bracketed mirror, and a paper-towel dispenser. Nothing could be used as a weapon. No window.

Henry. Dammit, she had briefly considered him a suspect, had even written his name on her yellow pad, then thought *no motive.* Once she'd snapped a photo, but Jackie Robinson had clawed it to death, so Sandra couldn't pull it from the pile and...

Dear Lord, she should have guessed when Peter said Wanda had seen Tubby at the pizza parlor while *waiting for her husband to join her.* Henry had walked through the church parking lot that day, the day the Benedicts were murdered. Ellie had seen him. Wanda hadn't. She'd been inside, fielding questions from members. Henry had changed his mind about collecting Wanda and followed the Benedicts instead. *Why?* Why kill Brian and Kelly?

Choking back a sob, Ellie tiptoed toward the restroom door and leaned against the wood, listening. She heard a faintly audible Springsteen singing about dancing in the dark, then the sound of splintering wood and running footsteps. An anxious voice called her name.

"Watch out, Peter! It's the Cookie Monster! He has a knife!"

She heard nothing more; no sound at all. Had Henry stabbed Peter?

Desperate, she pressed close to the door. She had given away her hiding place by shouting, yet she had to find out what was happening. Slowly she released the bolt, inched the door slightly ajar.

The plunging knife barely missed.

Henry pushed as Ellie pressed her shoulder against the wood, trying to close the door enough to secure the bolt. But her strength was no match for Henry's. Counting to three, she released her hold on the door, and the fuzzy figure stumbled inside with his momentum. Swiftly Ellie edged past again and fled down the hallway.

Dear God, what had Henry done to Peter? Was he injured? Dead?

She finally reached the church's front entrance hall, tripped over a basket of flowers, and felt an excruciating pain in her right knee as she hit the floor. A banner was strung across the basket's straw handles. White letters on a black background read: REQUIESCAT IN PACE. Flowers delivered for a funeral, she thought, as the colorful blooms swirled into a kaleidoscope of petals.

"Don't faint," Ellie warned herself, rising to her feet.

"Hiccup, but don't faint." Then, turning toward the wide double-door entrance, she screamed.

Henry stood there, blocking her way out.

She turned to the left and entered the sanctuary with its rows of pews. Then she ran, wincing as pain shot along her injured leg, racing toward the pulpit. Shots rang out behind her, and she increased her pace despite the pain.

Shots! Peter's gun?

She remembered McCoy's holster with the cowboy pistols. Had they been real guns? Why hadn't she stripped one from Will's unconscious body?

Ingrid Bergman would have done it.

Any heroine on a poorly written cop show would have grabbed Will's gun. Both guns.

Her journey down the aisle seemed endless. Finally, she climbed a platform and ducked behind the wooden lectern as two bullets pinged off a brass-coated, life-size statue of Jesus.

"I coulda' hit you," yelled Henry, "but I want to have some fun first. I want you to make up for all the times Wanda said no."

"Is that why you killed the others?" Ellie called, stalling for time, praying for a miracle. "Because Wanda refused—"

"I thought Wanda would get scared and quit," Henry interrupted, "or you'd have to close down your meetings. Don't you understand?"

No, I don't, thought Ellie. "Yes, I do," she said, keeping her voice level although inside she was quaking like Jell-O. "But Henry, how did you know where to find them? The, uh, victims."

"I went through Wanda's file. She took it home to make her stupid Christmas presents."

"Why did you kill Jeannie Dobson?"

"I met her when she visited Wanda at our house. She was the first because she listened to Wanda about leaving me. I heard them. She was talking about helping and all, letting Wanda stay in her second bedroom with our kids. I didn't mean to kill anybody else, but the Dobson lady was so easy. Then I got my idea about scaring everybody and closing you down."

"Did you follow me, Henry? Did you wear an army jacket and wool stocking cap?"

"Yeah, wanted to scare you, maybe even kill you if I got the chance. Kept the coat and hat at my construction site so Wanda couldn't find 'em."

"Why did you murder Esther?"

"Who?"

"Esther Abramowitz."

"Oh, yeah. I met her at one of your meetings when I picked Wanda up for lunch. She was gonna knit a muffler for Wanda. I went to her house, and she answered the door when I rang. 'Good shopping,' she said in Jewish."

"Good Shabbas," murmured Ellie. The traditional Friday night greeting. Poor Esther.

"It didn't matter," said Henry. "She was old."

Didn't matter? Ellie shuddered.

Enjoying his confession, Henry continued in a conversational tone. "The couple in the van I just, well, followed. I was supposed to meet Wanda at the pizza joint, but I decided to pick her up at the church instead. Those two were in the parking lot, hugging and kissing and practically *doing it* in front of God and everybody. It ain't fair. Wanda never does that no more. She used to when I brought her candy, but not no more. The side of the van said Benedict Interior Decorating and I remembered the name from Wanda's file. They were both close enough to…whatchamacallit…goal weight.''

"Why did you choose people close to goal weight?''

"'Cause I wanted others to stay away; eat again. Without no members, you'd have to call off the meetings.''

"Darlene—''

"The hooker? I went to your house first, but you was busy in the bedroom with your cop. Then I seen Darlene by accident. She was on my list but I didn't want to kill her. She was so beautiful, and Darlene didn't give it away like you and Wanda. She sold it, but not to me. She wouldn't take money from me. *Bitch!*'' He paused, panting with fury. He had removed the other paw, and his gun hand shook.

Henry's left-handed, Ellie thought irrelevantly as she noted his diamond-studded wedding band

Should she make another run for it. She moved her leg, testing, and a sharp pain coursed all the way up her thigh to her crotch.

Henry had calmed down. "I went to the Wilcox house. Found her address in my wife's file. She was the only skinny one left, 'cept for you, Wanda, and the little college brat.'' He paused, then added, "The lady in front of the TV was a mistake.''

Ellie shook her head. Her white bunny ears wobbled, but remained in place. *"I was a mistake,"* Hannah had announced in Sarah's antiseptic living room.

Sick to her stomach, Ellie had no desire to question Henry about Sandra. She didn't want to hear another of his justifications, didn't think she could take it without springing at the furry body and raking her nails across his perspiring, smiling face.

But she had to say something, keep him talking.

"Why did you hurt Wanda?'' she asked, curbing her

panic. "You said you killed the others because Wanda wanted to leave you, but *you* couldn't have her if she's dead."

"Neither could nobody else. You wouldn't stop the meetings, Ellie, not even after I almost knifed you at the movies."

"I'll stop, Henry, honest."

"Your cop arrested the wrong person," he shouted. "I could tell Wanda was going to leave me soon. Flaunting her skinny body at every man...twelve years of marriage down the drain. I was a football player in school, could'a had any girl. But I married Wanda and she was so grateful. We was so happy. She sang all the time. Everything was okay until she joined your diet club. It's Wanda's fault that I killed all those people."

"You can get help, talk to a doctor," cried Ellie, "and I won't tell a soul about—"

"Hey, you think I'm stupid?"

No, crazy. A wacko psychopath.

Henry's expression changed from self-pity to a crude leer. "Treat me good and I might let you live."

"I don't believe you."

"Cross my heart and hope to die," he chanted. "Look, I'm throwing my gun away. That proves it."

Ellie heard a clatter as the revolver skidded under pews. But Henry still had his knife. Did he think *she* was stupid? She stood straight, her body partially hidden by the minister's stand.

"All right, come up here and I'll make you feel good," she said, then held out her arms in a gesture of supplication, duplicating the posture of the statue of Christ behind and to the left of her.

"Whore! You'll make me feel good? You're nothin'

but a bag of bones.'' He eyed her bunny figure from heels to ears. "Sing me a song."

"What?"

"Wanda used to sing when we was happy together," said Henry sadly. "My favorite was the one about Noah's ark-y. The animals, they came on, they came on by two-sie, two-sies. El-e-phants and kanga-roo-sie, roo-sies, Children of the Lord. I like songs about animals."

"Why do you like songs about animals, Henry?"

Stall! Keep him talking!

"When I was a football player, they yelled a special cheer just for me. I was the only one on the defense they did that for. 'One, two, three, fumble. Henry is the whole darn jungle. Growl, Henry, grrr-owl.' Didn't rhyme good, but it was *my* cheer. Every person in the stands growled. The whole stadium growled."

Grrr-eat! I was sure out in left field with my Robbie-Elvis theory.

"The old lady wouldn't sing nothin' at all," continued Henry, "prayed in Jewish instead, so I killed her right away, then stuck needles in her neck 'cause she wouldn't sing. Darlene sang the sheep song. Baaa, baaa, baaa. The Connors kid was supposed to sing the pony-macaroni song. At the party tonight they sang about six white horses. You can sing the cow song, Ellie, the one about that old guy and his farm animals. Wanda sings it to the twins."

"I know which song you mean, Henry. Old MacDonald had a farm—"

"Eee, ei, eee, ei, *oh.*"

"And on this farm he had some cows—"

"Eee, ei, eee, ei, *oh.*"

"With a moo moo here and a moo moo there. Here a moo, there a moo—"

"Okay, that's enough moo moos."

The blue body lumbered toward the platform. Henry's eyes looked insane and saliva dribbled from the corners of his mouth. He climbed the steps of the pulpit, his hands behind his back...clutching his *knife,* thought Ellie.

She waited until he was close enough for her to smell an odor of sweat and spicy cologne—Old Spice, dammit! She'd sniffed it when Henry flexed his muscles after the meeting on the morning Jeannie had been killed. *Christ.*

Stepping behind Jesus, Ellie pushed with all her strength. The statue fell forward, landing on top of Henry. Surprised, off balance, he crumpled to the floor.

Swiftly Ellie pried the knife from his hand and stabbed once, twice, three times.

One, two, three, don't fumble, everybody growl.

She dropped the weapon and staggered to the edge of the platform.

Peter was laboriously making his way through the doorway, holding his blood-soaked side. So Henry had managed to knife him. Her warning had come too late.

Maneuvering from the pulpit, Ellie limped toward the doorway, toward Peter.

"Watch out Norrie! Behind you!"

She turned and gazed, mesmerized, at the figure lurching down the aisle. Above his blue ruff, Henry's face was contorted with anger. She had stabbed his back. So how come blood poured from his mouth and covered the hand that again clutched the knife.

"Norrie, move," shouted Peter. "Dammit, move!"

She started to run, but Henry dove, tackling her by the left ankle. As Ellie pitched forward, she spied the gun under a pew. On her stomach, she writhed, wiggled, crawled, and reached for the pistol, so tantalizingly close to her stretched-out fingers.

Henry's slippery hands slid from Ellie's ankle, and he grabbed her ass, then roared in agonized frustration when he merely captured her puffy cotton-tail.

She inched toward the gun and finally grasped it.

I don't know how to shoot this damn thing, she thought, even as she swung the heavy metal grip in a wide arc and made contact with Henry's skull.

He screeched, his hands going to his head.

"Oh!" screamed Ellie, all the rage from the murders exploding in that one sound. She swung again, and this time Henry lay motionless.

"My God, Norrie, are you all right?" asked Peter, leading her away from the mound of blue and red fur.

"I guess so. I hurt my knee a little," she said, then burst into tears.

Peter extended his arms, and she hid her face against his shirt. The blood seeped from his side, but he insisted that the injury was only a surface wound and Henry's knife had not slashed anything vital.

McCoy was badly wounded but still alive. Wanda—regaining consciousness—had desperately prodded a semi-conscious Peter into full awareness. He'd rushed toward the nave, sending Wanda to the minister's office to phone for squad cars and an ambulance. Even as Peter explained and soothed Ellie, they could hear sirens.

They stood together, wrapped in each other's arms, comforted by their mutual warmth and knowledge that they had both survived.

Three policemen appeared in the nave, guns drawn. Peter pointed toward Henry.

"You never, *hic,* really believed it was Robbie, *hic,* did you?" Tears steamed down Ellie's face, erasing the last vestiges of bunny whiskers.

"Yes and no," Peter replied. "There were four murders, five counting Kelly Benedict. Two failed attempts, thank God. Stop hiccuping, honey. It's over. You're safe.''

"That's why I'm hic—*hic*."

"Except for Janssen," continued Peter, "the alibis checked out. George, Tub…if you can't stop hiccuping, Norrie, please stop crying. Okay, movie theater. The ticket guy didn't remember a heavy man in a pea jacket and cap, but he was on the phone talking to his girlfriend most of the night, and our perp sneaked inside."

"My God, Peter," she sobbed, "you really have been busy, *hic*."

"Janssen couldn't or wouldn't confess the details we'd kept secret. Jeannie Dobson's bathwater. The number seven-oh carved around Darlene's belly button."

"Why didn't you, *hic*, tell me?"

"Because I didn't want you starting up that decoy nonsense again, even though that's exactly what happened, dammit!"

"Then it's over? It's really over?"

"Yes, sweetheart," replied Peter. "No more meddling in murder mysteries, okay? Okay, Norrie?"

Before she could answer, two children ran through the nave's entrance and skidded to an abrupt halt.

Holy cow! Wanda's kids! Becky was costumed as Belle from Disney's "Beauty and the Beast." Joseph Jr. was, of course, the ugly, fanged Beast. Snow dripped from their costumes.

The Beast dropped his sack. Candy corn, sugarless gum, colorful lollipops, Three Musketeers, Hershey kisses, and a box of Sunmaid raisins skittered across the aisle.

Awkwardly, Peter bent down and retrieved a kiss wrapped in silver foil.

"Put this trophy on your fireplace mantel," he said.

"If it doesn't melt," murmured Ellie, melting against Peter's chest again. "I'll consume it in three seconds flat. Don't forget, my darling Lieutenant, that I'm a chocoholic."

Fortunately, police hid the blood-soaked Cookie Monster.

The children scrambled for their goodies.

"Shoo, get out of here!" shouted one policeman.

"Trick or treat?" chanted the chubby Beast.

Behind the mask his eyes blazed with mischief, and he smacked his lips, creating little sucking sounds of enjoyment.

"Trick or treat!" repeated Joseph Jr. (who, Ellie surmised, would one day be nicknamed *Henry* Henry). "Trick or treat, trick or treat, give me something good to eat!"

WILDCRAFTERS

A VENUS DIAMOND MYSTERY

SKYE KATHLEEN MOODY

A Hawaiian honeymoon and a new husband must wait while Seattle Fish and Wildlife agent Venus Diamond heads a massive search into the disappearance of a baby in the Bogachiel wildlife preserve. Natives believe the baby was snatched by "the Unknown," a half-man, half-elk creature of Native American lore. Venus suspects the incident may involve recent elk poachings in the area, and carcasses found with sawed-off hooves.

But what she discovers is a fanatical quest for eternal youth that drives human desires to hideous proportions where no one is safe...not even the most innocent.

WORLDWIDE LIBRARY ®

Visit us at www.worldwidemystery.com   WSKM332

Take 2 books and a surprise gift FREE!

SPECIAL LIMITED-TIME OFFER

Mail to: The Mystery Library™
3010 Walden Ave.
P.O. Box 1867
Buffalo, N.Y. 14240-1867

YES! Please send me **2 free books** from the Mystery Library™ and my free surprise gift. Then send me 3 mystery books, first time in paperback, every month. Bill me only $4.19 per book plus 25¢ delivery and applicable sales tax, if any*. There is no minimum number of books I must purchase. I can always return a shipment at your expense and cancel my subscription. Even if I never buy another book from the Mystery Library™, **the 2 free books and surprise gift are mine to keep forever.**

415 WEN CJQN

Name	(PLEASE PRINT)	

Address		Apt. No.

City	State	Zip

* Terms and prices subject to change without notice. N.Y. residents add applicable sales tax. This offer is limited to one order per household and not valid to present subscribers.
© 1990 Worldwide Library.

MYS98

DEATH OF AN EVANGELISTA

ALLANA MARTIN

A TEXANA JONES MYSTERY

When trading post owner Texana Jones discovers
the body of a man in a Mexican taxi, she barely
escapes becoming a scapegoat for corrupt *federales*.
Unfortunately, the innocent cab driver is left
to take the fall.

Then another body is found, leading Texana deeper
into the kinds of secrets that life in the desert hides
well—and the dark places of the human heart
where the borderline between good and evil is
easy to cross....

Available January 2000 at your favorite retail outlet.

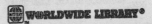

WORLDWIDE LIBRARY®

Visit us at www.worldwidemystery.com   WAM335